ALL THE
LONELY PEOPLE

Martin Edwards

Andrews UK Limited

Copyright © 1991, 2012 Martin Edwards.

This edition published in 2012 by
Andrews UK Limited
The Hat Factory
Luton, LU1 2EY
www.andrewsuk.com

This book is sold subject to the condition that it shall not, by
way of trade or otherwise, be lent, resold, hired out or otherwise
circulated without the publisher's prior written consent in any
form of binding or cover other than that in which it is published,
and without a similar condition being imposed on the subsequent
purchaser.

The characters and situations in this book are entirely imaginary
and bear no relation to any real person or actual happening.

The right of Martin Edwards to be identified as author of this
book has been asserted in accordance with section 77 and 78 of
the Copyrights Designs and Patents Act 1988.

Introduction © 2012 Frances Fyfield
Appreciation © 2012 Michael Jecks
Excerpt from Suspicious Minds © 2012 Martin Edwards.

Contents

Dedicated to my parents.

Man, when perfected, is the best of animals, but, when separated from law and justice, he is the worst of all

Aristotle: *Politics*, trans. Jowett, bk. I ch. 2

Introduction

Harry Devlin is a real lawyer, operating at the blunt, sharp end of the law that features the smell of the cells, the scent of desperation, the small time crooks, desperadoes and drunken losers who are the stock in trade of his native city, once known as the Venice of the North. However, his Liverpool of the early nineties is not glamorous; nor is Devlin's trade. He deals in litter and detritus; his judgement is not always sound and he knows the symptoms of loneliness like the noise of his own breath. He can hum the song, too.

Martin Edwards breaks boundaries with his hero, creating not the slick, American advocate beloved of the times when this book was written. Nor a self sufficient loner who listens to jaz, nor a cynic, but a flawed man who has never learned to ration compassion or realise that not everything is his fault. It's a brave move to make a hero out of a loyal and jilted man whose wife has betrayed him big time. El machismo Devlin isn't: brave in the real sense, he certainly is.

What distinguishes this book and those that follow and what makes them classics of a kind is this marvellous quality of compassion and the celebration of all that is heroic in the corrupted ordinary. Devlin and his author love and forgive their clients and their friends even when they hate them, and that is the lot of the humane man. You don't stop loving people because aren't nice and you can't stop loyalty if it happens to be in your blood.

She said you weren't a fat cat, more like Robin Hood in an old suit. So says Liz, Devlin's wife, but bravery is not sartorial, anyone more than loyalty is founded on reason.

Another distinguishing feature of this book is the descriptive prose. Martin Edwards excels in his evocation of a place he refuses to romanticise, and as a fellow lawyer, I have never read better descriptions of the criminal circus down in the cells below the Magistrates Courts on a Monday morning, where pity, brute force, ambition and pragmatism juggle for space against a background smell of bleach. If you're lucky, that is. Edwards wins on smells alone.

Influenced as he is by the best of English lawyer writers, such as Michael Gilbert and Cyril Hare, Martin Edwards has produced a character of which Raymond Chandler would approve, i.e, a man who goes down mean streets and is not himself made mean.

And who, in true English style, gets it wrong before he gets it right.

Smashing, honest to God, right up to the mark stuff.

Frances Fyfield

Chapter One

Your mind's playing tricks, Harry Devlin said to himself.

As he reached for the front door key, he could hear a woman laughing inside his flat. Yet when the police had called him out on duty four hours earlier, he had left the place in darkness, empty and locked. For a moment he paused, as if frozen by the February chill. Had she come home again at last?

The laughter stopped. In the silence that followed he glanced up and down the third floor corridor, sure he must have been mistaken. But a long evening in Liverpool's Bridewell, trying to persuade grizzled detectives that two and two did not make four and that his latest client was innocent, had drained his imagination. It was midnight and he was too cold and weary for make-believe.

She laughed again and this time he knew he was not dreaming. He would have recognised that sound of careless pleasure after an eternity, let alone a lapse of two years. A wave of delight swept over him, succeeded after a moment by puzzlement. He realised that the door was ajar and, taking breath in a deep draught, strode through to the living room.

"So what kept you?"

She spoke as though resuming a conversation and the lazy tone was as familiar as if he had last heard it yesterday. Curled up in his armchair, she was watching television: Woody Allen's *Love and Death*.

He drank in the sight of her. The black hair - in the past never less than shoulder-length - was now cut fashionably short. Nothing else about her had changed: not the lavish use of mascara, nor the mischief lurking in her dark green eyes. All she wore was a pair of Levis and a tee shirt of his that she must have found in the bedroom. She had tossed her jersey and boots on to the floor. On the table by her side stood a tumbler and a half-empty bottle of Johnnie Walker. She scarcely glanced at him as she murmured her greeting; she was captivated by Diane Keaton, turning Woody down.

"Liz." The croakiness of his voice was embarrassing.

In response she favoured him with the gently mocking smile that he remembered so well from their time together. She said, "Your reactions may be slow, darling, but there's nothing wrong with your memory."

"How did you get in here?"

"The duty porter. I told him I was an old friend. The truth, if not the whole truth, you'll agree. I explained it was your birthday and that I wanted to give you a surprise. He seemed to think you'd be pleased to see me. Showed me up himself." She pulled a face of comic disapproval. "You ought to complain about the lousy security. I might have been your worst enemy."

With a rueful grin, he said, "Aren't you?"

"Careful, that's almost grounds for divorce."

The heating in the room was oppressive. She had switched it up to furnace level. Already he felt a moistening of sweat on his brow. Shrugging off his raincoat and jacket, he dropped into an armchair, scarcely able to take his eyes off her.

"Nice place you have here."

A wave of her slim hand encompassed the lounge. It was furnished in the same home-assembly teak they had bought during their engagement. In one corner, a top-heavy cheese plant leaned precariously towards the curtained windows. The walls were lined with book-crammed shelves: *Catch-22, Uncle Silas* and *Presumed Innocent* sandwiched a clutch of old movie magazines and an ink-stained guide to the Police and Criminal Evidence Act. Sheaves of paper spilled from every available surface, covering half the carpet. Legal aid claim forms awaited completion amid scrawled notes about his cases and a jumble of junk mail.

"Splitting up must have suited you," Liz said breezily. "No one to nag about tidiness."

Crazy, he thought. He'd rehearsed this moment a thousand times, when she came begging for a second chance. The right words should come easily. So why did he feel a schoolboy's tongue-tied inadequacy?

He contemplated an elegant tracery of cobwebs, hanging from the ceiling above her head. "Life's certainly different these days."

"I'll bet. So where have you been, you old stop-out? I was here before nine. Good job you don't lock the drinks cupboard."

"The police lifted a client of mine. A petty burglar, trying to finance his taste for smack. I've been down in the interview room all evening."

"Harry, why do you bother?"

"Guilty or innocent, he's entitled to justice. Same as you or me."

Liz groaned as if hearing a joke for the hundredth time. He knew that she knew that for most of his criminal clients, conviction was an occupational hazard. And once more tonight, after the drawn-out sequence of questions and lies, bluffs and denials, the ritual had ended with the man's signature scratched on the statement that would send him to jail, enabling everyone else to go home, their jobs done. Chances were that tomorrow or the next day he'd have a change of heart and solicitor and some cowboy from Ruby Fingall's firm would try to get his name in the papers, building a case on police brutality.

"I know what you're going to say." He mimicked her old refrain: "'How can you defend those people?' But it's my job, remember?" Fishing in his pocket for a pack of Player's, he said, "So why have you turned up after so long?"

"I thought you might want someone to celebrate with. Thirty-two today, or is it Thursday morning already? Only a couple of birthday cards up, I notice," She hiccupped. "Sorry I haven't brought a present. You'll have to make do with the charm of my

3

company. Many happy returns, anyway." She raised the tumbler and added as an afterthought, "Am I right in thinking you've put on weight?"

In the background, Woody Allen was soliloquising. Harry strode over to the television set and switched it off with a force that almost snapped the knob.

"You bastard. I was enjoying that."

"You didn't tell me what brings you here."

She shifted in the chair, stretching her slim figure like a self-confident cat. "Aren't you glad I'm here? Surely you've missed me, just a little?"

He sighed. "You were my wife, for God's sake."

"Still am, Harry."

"Yes."

He watched her finish the drink. Curious, he said, "Have you run out on Coghlan?"

"Sort of." She bit her lip. "But - I'm frightened, Harry."

The smile had vanished and her eyes, large and luminous, held his. Liz hadn't forgotten how to hypnotise him. To break the spell, he got to his feet and walked to the window, pulling the curtains apart. The flat was on the river side of the Empire Dock building, a converted warehouse which had once stored tobacco and cotton, with walls built to withstand fire, tempest and flood. In the distance, he could hear teenage delinquents shouting unintelligibly. Joyriders, hooligans or petty thieves perhaps. Tomorrow's clients, anyway. A police car siren wailed and nearer by, the site security guard's Alsatian began to bark. Meanwhile, the Mersey below snaked away into the shadows. A string of lights gleamed along the water's edge, trailing beyond Empire Dock as far as Harry could see. On the opposite side of the river, he could make out the angular outlines of the shoreside cranes, looming like creatures on an alien landscape. It was a Liverpool night, like any other.

He swiveled to face her. "I don't believe you've ever been frightened in your life."

The long-lashed lids were lowered now. "Harry, it's the truth."

"Convince me."

She studied her crimson fingernails. "Mick and I have drifted apart. He's back in his old ways, hanging around with his cronies up at the gym. Keeps making mysterious phone calls and throwing a fortune away on the horses. Sometimes I don't see him for days on end. I'm on my own so much, I even started working again. With Matt Barley at the Freak Shop."

"So I heard."

"You did?" She sighed. "Poor Matt, he's always been kind."

"You work part-time, he told me."

"Yes." An evasive look flitted across her face. "It fits in well with - other things. And it's a break. I'm not made to be the little lady, sitting at home whilst my feller spends every spare minute with a bunch of Second Division crooks." She resumed her scrutiny of her hands. "I've finally decided to ditch him, Harry."

His stomach muscles tightened. He hardly dared hope that she was back to stay. Forget that idea, he warned himself: a re-make is never as good as the original movie. But he could not forget it. Not wanting to say anything, he gazed at a bit of the carpet which was free of his papers. It was patterned in grey; he had chosen the colour that would best hide the dust.

Liz began to speak rapidly, the words running into each other. "I know you think I'm reaping my desserts. I can't blame you, there's no excuse for the way I behaved. I'm not asking for sympathy. But these past two years haven't been easy. I reckon I loved Mick once, but now I hate him and he hates me. He's mean and he's selfish and his temper is vile."

Harry waited.

Head bowed, she said, "And I've met somebody else. I need him badly. Don't wince - I'm serious. I've made all my mistakes. This is for real."

He closed his eyes, said nothing. There was nothing to say.

She talked on, though he hardly listened: "I thought Mick had no idea. I was afraid of how he might react. We've been so careful to keep it secret. But Mick's been too quiet lately, it isn't natural. Withdrawn, scarcely bothering to rant or rave if I burn his meal . . . as if he's planning what to do with me. He's even had me followed. I'm scared, Harry, I swear it. I believe - I believe he wants to kill me."

Liz always had a flair for melodrama, he thought. Like a heroine from one of those soap operas that used to glue her attention to the TV screen. Why did she never go on the stage? No actress could match her talent for fantasy. Long ago in their married life he'd learned that she would never be content; she had a child's thirst for new excitements.

Eventually, she said, "Well?"

"What are you asking for, Liz?"

She stifled an exclamation of impatience. "Your advice, of course. That's your job, isn't it? Giving the lawyer's impartial view. Solving problems. I don't know why you never made more money." She flushed. "Sorry. Me and my big mouth. But I do need your help. I trust you, Harry, always did. Tell me what to do."

He made a don't-care gesture with his shoulders. "If you're worried about Coghlan, move in with your new fancy man. He'll protect you."

"That's difficult." She licked the tip of her forefinger; an old, unconscious mannerism. "Trouble is, he's married."

Typical, Harry reflected. Aloud, he said, "And his wife?"

"His wife is - well, let's just say she's neurotic. He needs to pick his moment to break the news that he's walking out."

That struck a chord. He recalled the slow torture of those last few days before she finally left him one winter's evening. The skirting round of conversational no-go areas. Meaning less small talk at the dinner table. Silence in bed. And the awareness of a marriage rotting like so much dead grass.

"I get the picture."

She averted her face. "Mick's away at present. Down in London, or so he says. All the same, I can't go back to that house tonight, can't take the risk that he might turn up. Harry, he's violent! Dangerous. I daren't imagine what he intends to do. It's best to hide until everything's worked out. So - it occurred to me - I mean, would you mind if I stayed here for a day or two?"

Only Liz would have the nerve to ask, he thought. Her gift for making an outrageous request seem logical would be envied by any lawyer who ever made a speculative application for bail. The darkness of her hair, the height of her cheekbones, were the only clues to her Polish ancestry: in her instinct for the main chance, she was Liverpudlian through and through.

Wryly, he said. "Are you sure you'll be safe here?"

She treated him to her best knee-melting smile. "As safe as anywhere in the world. And I won't give you any hassle. I'll be out of your hair soon, I promise."

He stubbed out his cigarette and immediately lit another. She frowned and asked, "When did you start smoking again?"

"Day after you last saw me." He blew a smoke ring and waited for her to make a know-all comment about lung cancer or the nicotine stains on his hands. But for once in her life she had the sense to keep quiet and eventually he said, "Okay, you can stay."

"Thanks. That's wonderful." Almost to his surprise, he sensed that her gratitude was genuine.

"Where are your things?"

"I travel light, remember? I have a bag with me. Tomorrow I'll pick up the other odds and ends, if I'm sure Mick's still out of town." She smiled. "Let's talk more in the morning. I've so much to tell you, you wouldn't believe it. But there's plenty of time. Tell you the truth, right now, I feel as if it's my birthday, not yours, and there are a hundred candles on the cake."

Yawning, she stood up. Even her simplest movement was invested with that feline grace. He couldn't help saying, "You look no different from the woman I married."

"Flattery will get you anywhere." Their eyes met for a moment, before Liz moved away and said, "Well, maybe not everywhere. I went on a tour whilst you were out. You only have one bedroom."

The bed was their old kingsize. "It's all I need."

An I'm-not-to-be-tempted look flitted across her face. Her tone was gentle but firm. "The last few weeks have been hell for me, Harry. Truly. I must have a good night's rest. So what are the options?"

He weighed up her expression for a moment and then said, "The sofa folds down."

"Would that do for you? I mean - you know how it is?"

When he didn't reply, she leaned forward and kissed him lightly on the cheek before disappearing into the bathroom. Already she was at ease with the geography of the flat, gliding around as if it were home. He heard the shower running and said to himself: That's your wife in there, this is your chance to make it happen again. But he knew that he, too, was in danger of succumbing to fantasy and all he did was pour himself a whisky and settle back in his chair.

Soon she re-emerged, a towel wrapped round her hair. She had stripped off the jeans; her bare legs were as smooth as ever. "I'd forgotten what a mess you make of the toothpaste," she said. "You need a woman to take charge."

"My trouble is, I attract the wrong type."

She laughed. "I deserved that."

"You deserve much worse." He couldn't help grinning. For all her faults, Liz had always been able to make fun of herself, as well as of those around her.

"I like this flat," she said gently, "but it's lonely. You don't have anyone special?"

Only you, he wanted to say.

"No."

"That's ridiculous. You're not a bad-looking feller in a poor light."

Reaching for an ashtray, Harry said dryly, "My next door neighbour thinks all I need is a little female company. She keeps inviting me round for coffee and I'm running out of excuses."

Liz beamed encouragement. "Get together with her. It'll do you good. The bachelor life is fine, but if you don't relax, you'll never make it to thirty-three." Her left arm reached out and stroked the heavy stubble on his chin. For a short while, neither of them spoke, but at last she said, "Goodnight, Harry." Her tone was soft, almost tender, and the words hung in the airless emptiness of the room as the bedroom door shut behind her.

Harry remained motionless, staring through the picture window into the darkness outside. Despite the heat of the room, a chill of fear had suddenly touched him for when he had looked down at her slender wrist, he had seen the angry red stitch marks which criss-crossed it - marks that he recognised as the stigmata of a failed suicide.

Chapter Two

Sleep eluded him for hours. The sofa was too narrow to allow him the insomniac's self-indulgence of tossing and turning as he raked over the conversation with Liz. His mind was a junkyard of discarded emotions and he could not be sure if he was glad or angry that she had returned to him, merely to say goodbye. As consciousness drifted away, he had a fuzzy recollection of a question he had forgotten to ask.

When he awoke, the wall clock reminded him that he hadn't retrieved his alarm from his bedroom. Eight o'clock already and he was supposed to be back at the Bridewell by half-past to complete his stint of twenty-four hours as the city's Duty Solicitor, as confidant of the thieves and muggers, drunks and vandals who were picked up by the police and had no one else to turn to. Cursing, Harry struggled to his feet. He yearned to stay and talk to Liz; even if she was no longer his, he could think of no one with whom he would rather be. For a moment he contemplated phoning in to say he was sick and unable to come in today. But the work instinct won and he shambled to the bathroom instead.

After a hasty wash and shave he looked in on Liz. So many times, waking first, he had watched her exactly like this. With the duvet tucked beneath her chin, her face seemed as peaceful as a child's, and as innocent. No make up, no worry lines, no hint of any suffering. Why should she want to cut her own wrist?

Shaking her, he said, "I must go. There's food and drink in the kitchen for breakfast. Okay?"

In a slow ceremonial way, like a monarch bestowing attention on a humble subject, she opened her eyes. It took a second for them to focus on him and then she smiled. "Thanks for looking after me."

Harry wasn't sure if she was teasing him. "You might call me," he said, trying to be off-hand about it. "We could have lunch."

"I'd love to be your honoured guest. No, seriously."

He could feel himself tense as her fingers touched his hand.

"You all right, Liz?"

"Fine." The green eyes widened. "I feel safe here." Her arms dangled negligently by the side of the bed and once more he saw the damaged wrist.

Flinching, he turned to go. "See you later."

Outside, rain smacked the pavements with sadistic fury. For once it was worth taking his car the short distance into the city centre. He drove an M.G. convertible, twenty years old and still lively beneath a rusting exterior. The only car he had ever owned; he was comfortable with it and didn't believe in change for the sake of it. Glancing every so often at his watch, he weaved through sodden one-way streets, squeezing past roadworks and imperilling pedestrians who took a chance.

The riddle of why Liz might want to kill herself continued to nag at him. Might he have been mistaken in interpreting the marks on her wrist as the legacy of a failed suicide bid? He didn't think so. In the past he had seen similar scars disfiguring his clients. One had been the victim of a messy divorce, another a kleptomaniac with a heroin habit: both had tried to kill themselves. Could Coghlan's vicious streak have caused Liz comparable despair? Anything was possible - and yet the Liz he knew loved life, would never bring it to an end a moment too soon.

He arrived with less than a minute to spare. The Magistrate's Court was not yet open but he turned into Cheapside and banged on the heavy black door round the corner. A taciturn constable let him in, jangling keys in his pocket as if to taunt any sharp-eared ruffians incarcerated in the holding cell with the sound of freedom. He unlocked the iron gate leading to the cell and motioned Harry through.

The Bridewell sergeant was perched on his high chair like a pre-war schoolmaster, while a pack of his subordinates lolled on a bench opposite the holding cell, engrossed in the racing pages of the *Sun* and *Mirror*. On an oblong of white card suspended by string from a hook in the wall, someone had written: please do not ask for bail, as a REFUSAL MIGHT OFFEND.

"All right, mate?" enquired the sergeant. He peered at Harry's shiny-elbowed suit and scuffed Hush Puppies. "You really must give me the name of your tailor some time."

"Piss off, Bert," he said without malice.

No matter how many times he came here, it always took him a moment to adjust to the Bridewell's purgatorial atmosphere. He blinked in an effort to adjust to the harshness of the artificial light before striding over to the other side of the room, where Ronald Sou was waiting for him.

"How are you, Mr. Devlin?"

Harry said he was fine. Almost every day he tried to persuade his clerk to call him by his first name. But Ronald Sou, the son of a Chinese seaman who had married a girl from Toxteth, remained inscrutable as if, like his forefathers, he had been born in Canton rather than Liverpool Eight, and when speaking to his employer he always maintained the respectful distance appropriate to a bygone age.

"An interesting night?" enquired Ronald politely.

Harry pursed his lips. "You could say that." After a moment he added, "One call out, nothing more."

One of the constables coughed and said, "Been busy since you left, Harry. Must be a score of customers for you inside." He jerked a thumb in the direction of the holding cell and said, "Junkies, an arsonist, two blokes we picked up in Sefton Park wearing skirts and suspender belts. You name it, all human life is there."

Harry went to the cell door and peered through the spy-hole at the bleary faces of the captive men. Most were slumped on

12

the bench that ran around the walls. Several wore suspects' space suits, the off-white, thin as paper, all-in-one garments which the police supplied to those whose clothing was taken away for forensic tests. The interior of the cell was dimly lit, its gloom matching its occupants. Harry settled himself in the first interview alcove while Ronald Sou went into an identical cubicle next door.

The job took an hour and a quarter. As each detainee's surname was called out in alphabetical order by one of the constables, the individual concerned shuffled over so that Harry could log the details of the offence and the name of the miscreant's lawyer in the ruled lines of the large red diary that was the Liverpool Duty Solicitor's book.

Every now and then the atmosphere of grudging resignation was poisoned by incoherent screams of rage from within the holding cell - drug addicts growing restless as they came to end of their latest fix. Occasionally someone would beat a tattoo on the metal door that set them apart from the outside world, prompting the youngest policeman on the bench to wander over and mutter a few warning words beneath his breath. His colleagues had seen it all before and continued to read undisturbed.

When the last detainee returned to captivity Ronald was still ringing round the city's criminal advocates to inform then of their clients' latest misdemeanours. Harry yawned and went back upstairs.

The room set aside for the Duty Solicitor was off the main hall of the court building. There would be another ten minutes or so to wait until the first of the morning's clients arrived. Idly, he leafed through the newspaper. Trouble everywhere, of course. Renewed fighting in Beirut. The I.R.A. expressing its regret to the family of a child killed in Belfast when a bomb had gone off an hour early by mistake. A Cabinet minister denying a homosexual affair with his constituency agent. A big bullion raid in Leytonstone and three people dead after a gas explosion in Leeds. Harry kept turning the pages.

With the task of sifting through the morning's crooks finished, he could not keep his mind off Liz. Why, if Coghlan's behaviour had caused her to attempt suicide, had she failed to mention it to him? Liz always found it hard to resist ending any story with a histrionic flourish. He would have expected her to play for more sympathy, to point to her wrist and exclaim. "Look, this is what he drove me to!" Even if she had taken good care not to injure herself too severely, even if it was nothing more than a half-hearted cry for help of some kind, it would be unlike her not to exploit the drama of a brush with death. The inconsistency bothered him more than that nonsense about Coghlan wanting to kill her. Provided, he thought with a pang of unease, that it was nonsense . . .

Ronald Sou poked his head around the door, scattering the litter of Harry's speculations. "Have you seen the listing details, Mr. Devlin?"

"What? No, I was just about to."

"I had a word with the court clerk," said the Chinese man. "You're on in five minutes. The Benjamin case."

They had jumped to the head of the queue. "Ronnie, how do you manage it?"

The clerk smiled and held the door open. The hall outside had become congested with people and more were flooding through the main doors with every minute that passed. Everyone was talking at once. Newly arrived solicitors elbowed their way towards the notice board on which was pinned the computer print-out with its list of the morning's defendants and the times of their cases. Mutterings of disgust came from those facing a long wait as they turned to complain to anyone within earshot. There were no chairs anywhere, just wooden benches like those downstairs, screwed into the walls so as to deny souvenirs to the city's cheekier thieves. All around, lawyers were interviewing their clients, bellowing so as to be heard above the hullabaloo.

The sour smell of failure and decay was everywhere. The building reeked of it, with plaster flaking from green-grey walls and cobwebs spiralling down from the ceiling. Solicitors bustled this way and that, directing helpers laden down with files, seeking out the courts where they were supposed to appear, checking to see if their clients had arrived, calling out names, arguing with anyone who got in the way.

"Mr. O'Shaughnessy?" piped a clerk from Windaybanks in Harry's ear.

The youth's boss, Quentin Pike, put a clammy hand on Harry's shoulder before he could reply. "Sorry, old chap. You're a dead ringer for my unlawful sexual intercourse. Wouldn't happen to have a twin with a penchant for schoolgirls, would you?"

"Pike, you utter shit." The rich bass belonged to Reuben Fingall, doyen of the local legal fraternity, who had appeared behind them. He smelled as if he had bathed in after shave. "You touted a rapist from my clerk on Monday." Flicking back into place a single errant strand of grey hair, he raised his eyebrows in contempt. "Is business so bad that . . . ."

Harry caught sight of a tall West Indian wearing a suede full-length coat and standing at the other side of the hall. He raised a hand in greeting and left his colleagues to their professional bickering.

"Peanuts, there you are."

The black man showed shark's teeth in a lazy grin and drawled, "Man, this place give me the heebie-jeebies. Shouldn' regular customers get preference? A chair, maybe even a private changing room?"

In fact Peanuts Benjamin looked as if he had already devoted a couple of hours to dressing for the occasion. Beneath the unbuttoned coat he wore a pale fawn suit with matching silk tie and handkerchief, as well as a white shirt that one of his ladies had ironed to perfection. Jewellery glinted from his cuffs and Harry could see his reflection in the shine of the Italian leather shoes. Peanuts had been bailed twenty-eight days previously to appear today on a charge of living off immoral earnings. The prosecution evidence was so strong that not even the time-honoured option of asking for a trial in the Crown Court and relying on a Liverpool jury's narrow conception of criminal guilt could be expected to result in an acquittal. Peanuts' best hope of avoiding imprisonment rested on the Home Office's directive to magistrates not to add to prison overcrowding.

They went into court number three and as they waited their turn, Harry's mind obstinately drifted back to Liz. He kept telling himself that it was pointless to worry about her and absurd to put any credence in the idea that Coghlan would care enough about his mistress's infidelities to want her dead. All the same, he was glad when Peanuts' case was called, robbing him of any further chance to dwell on what his wife had said the previous night.

The trial, as ever, proved less of an exercise in nerve and temperament than in the hassle of coping with bureacratic routine. The plea of mitigation was no different from hundreds of others. Harry explained that his client had obtained a new job with prospects, starting Monday. To jail Peanuts, he suggested, would serve no useful purpose to society; the man had learned his lesson.

"Judging by the number of people who come before us claiming they will be starting work the day after their trial," said the chairman of the bench, a middle-class sceptic, "unemployment in this city ought to be a minus figure."

But the result was what mattered. The three magistrates conferred briefly and announced the sentence, without bothering to adjourn and ask for further assessment reports on the accused. Twelve months' imprisonment, suspended for two years, and a fine. Harry didn't tempt fate by making the customary request for time to pay.

When they got outside, Peanuts punched the air in jubilation. "Man, my girls can earn that much in a night!"

Harry winced. Sometimes he wanted to forget he was a defence lawyer, paid to protect his clients, not to sit in judgment.

Peanuts responded with a shameless wink. "Yeah, yeah, I know. But if you can't be good, be careful. Don' worry, man. I learned a lot from this. I'll watch my step. They won' catch me again."

They said goodbye. Harry watched the tall black man push through the crowd, heading back to Toxteth and his twilight world. Again he thought of Liz and his anxieties flooded back. She was someone else who couldn't be good. The trouble was, she never managed to be careful either.

Chapter Three

By noon Harry was walking back to the office. He had sent Ronald Sou ahead with a message to the switchboard girl that if his wife called, he would be free to see her at one o'clock.

"At the usual place," added Harry.

Ronald bowed. "I will tell her."

The usual place - Mama Reilly's in Harrington Street. During their marriage, they must have snatched lunch there a hundred times, but Harry had never returned after the separation. It would be good to go back together. He made up his mind to ask her about the damage to that wrist. However determined she might be to step out of his life, he still had the urge to discover what had happened to her during their two years apart.

The firm of Crusoe and Devlin occupied a cheap slice of a three-storey building in Fenwick Court. It was a turn-of-the-century building, still blackened by grime from the years before the clean air laws and unredeemed by any hint of architectural merit. Property agents' signboards festooned the exterior; half the floorspace in New Commodities House was to let. Steps at the front led down to a scruffy second-hand record shop where Harry spent too much money and time. His firm shared the ground floor with a lottery company and a place where you could heel your shoes or get keys cut. Scratched nameplates on the wall recalled past tenants who had failed to make their businesses pay.

Harry slipped in through an unmarked door at the rear. Turning sharply at the end of a corridor, he cannoned into Jim Crusoe and staggered backwards. It felt like walking into the side of the Liver Building and the collision took Harry's breath away.

"Not so fast," said the big man. With his mane of brown hair, shaggy brown beard and lumbering gait, he resembled a huge grizzly bear. Stretching out a great paw, he tapped Harry in the ribs, an amiable gesture which elicited only a gasp.

"You could carry a week's shopping in those bags under your eyes, old son. Been burning the candle at both ends?" The craggy features split in a grin. "That rapacious neighbour of yours broken down your resistance at last? Careful now, you're not as young as you were."

"You'll never guess," said Harry quietly. "Liz came round last night."

Jim Crusoe's brow darkened. Harry was aware that his partner had always had a blind spot about Liz, had never seemed at ease in her company or susceptible to her charm. Jim was a conveyancer by profession. He bought and sold properties, drafted wills and handled probates: steady work, well-suited to a man for whom reliability was as instinctive as breathing. The black-and-white certainties of a bundle of title deeds appealed to him; he distrusted litigation as a game of chance. With erratic, unpredictable Liz, he had as much in common as the Rock of Gibraltar with a rolling stone.

"Don't get the wrong idea," Harry said. "It's only a flying visit. She's leaving Coghlan for some other fool."

But the easy jocularity had been wiped from Jim's features, as though by a damp cloth. "Watch your step, Harry. The woman's nothing but trouble."

"No sweat. She'll be off in a day or two."

Jim shrugged and set off towards the reception area. "The sooner the better, if you ask me," he said over his shoulder.

I didn't, Harry was tempted to retort. But the big man always spoke his mind and there was no point in arguing for the sake of it. Their partnership too was a marriage of sorts. They had worked together for the past eight years, having met as solicitors on the staff of Maher and Malcolm, a large practice which acted for Liverpool's upper crust. Over a pint one evening they had talked themselves out of their comfortable rut into becoming masters of their own destiny, no longer wage slaves hired to pile up profits for senior partners who spent half their time yachting or out on the golf course. The following day they had written their resignations and the firm of Crusoe and Devlin had kept its bank manager nervous ever since. In that time, both of them had learned the need for give and take.

Harry wandered over to his room, a claustrophobic box which might have been purpose-designed to deter clients from overstaying their welcome. From the walls, paint peeled almost before his very eyes, although the worst blemishes were hidden by a cartoon of a solicitor milking the cow of litigation and framed certificates which helped him to remember that he was a respectable professional man. Bulging buff files were strewn across his desk and cabinets, on the carpet and the window sills. He tore yesterday's date from the calendar that had been a building society's routine Christmas gift. Each day's sheet bore an unctuous motto; he crumpled up *The secret of happiness is to admire without desiring* and threw it into the wastepaper bin. Today's offering was *The mystery of women is largely the product of men's imagination.* Shaking his head, he picked up the telephone.

"So you're back," snapped the switchboard girl. "Just as well, there's a client waiting." Her attitude had been foul since Monday, when he had interrupted her in the midst of a lengthy call to a boyfriend she had met in Marbella last summer. When Harry asked if there were any messages for him, she rattled through half a dozen before adding, "And a woman called."

"Yes?"

"She wouldn't give her name. Said she was your lodger and she was sorry she'd missed you. She didn't think she'd be able to make lunch with you since she was just going out." Harry could sense the girl curling her lip; her tone was that of one who suspects sexual impropriety and considers it the sole prerogative of those as young as herself.

So the message he had sent via Ronald would not have got through to Liz. He tried to bite back his disappointment. "That would have been my wife," he said, more briskly than usual. "If she calls again, Suzanne, put her straight through."

With an effort, Harry pushed Liz away from the centre of his thoughts and leaned back in his seat, trying to compose his face into the unshockable expression with which he aimed to greet his clients' tales of bad luck, infidelity and crime. Giving advice was easy, not like believing all that he was told.

One gross indecency and a case of car theft later he made his way to reception, where a young couple were arguing about the new house Jim was buying for them. Swings and roundabouts, Harry reflected: we may lose the property deal and get the divorce. He tapped the window which separated the switchboard girl from the clientele. Suzanne was immersed in a Mills and Boon about an amorous sheikh. With a reluctant pout, she slid aside the glass partition.

"Any more calls for me?"

She leafed through a wad of pink telephone notes. "The Magistrates' Court - please call before noon. Your accountant's chasing after your tax return. A new gross indecency, Lucy's booked him in for three o'clock." Smirking, she added, "Nothing from your lodger."

"Just my wife's idea of a joke," he said, feeling defensive and resenting it. Suzanne sniffed and returned to fictional romance.

From his own room, he dialled the flat number. No reply. After waiting three full minutes he banged the receiver down on its cradle. Perhaps she had gone to Coghlan's house to pick up her things and would ring back shortly. The frustration of having missed speaking to her gnawed at him like an ulcer. Ploughing through the files, with their commonplace tales of greed and confusion, seemed as tedious as reading out-of-date tide tables. He lit cigarette after cigarette, only to find that smoking did not have its usual calming effect, and he kept stubbing the ends into his ashtray before he had finished. Now and then the phone would trill; each time he snatched at it only to be connected to clients fretting about their alimony or industrial injury claims. He uttered the necessary words of reassurance and ended the conversations as soon as he could.

Had Coghlan returned home earlier than expected? A worrying thought. Harry had never met the man who had destroyed his marriage, but knew a good deal about him. Mick Coghlan's name cropped up as often in gossip down at the Bridewell as it did in the columns of the city's Press. He ran a gym on the edge of Chinatown and liked to portray himself as a pillar of the community, forever raising money for charity, a local scally made good. Liz had talked of his generosity when she had broken the news to Harry that she was moving out. But whispers in the city had long had Coghlan down as the most ruthless scion of an old Liverpool family of villains, a man suckled on crime. People said his money had come from a series of armed post office raids in the mid eighties but his C.V. included nothing more damning than a couple of minor convictions for wounding. From time to time, a client or policeman would mention Coghlan in conversation, unaware of the quickening interest with which Harry listened. A hard man, they would say, and ruthless. Harry found himself shivering. If Coghlan came back to find Liz packing her bags, might he go berserk? Perhaps that wild story about his wanting her dead was no exaggeration.

He took a full audio tape to his secretary, whose desk was in a glassed-in cubicle they called the typing pool. It was Lucy's lunch break and she was listening to pop music on Radio City. Her grey eyes filled with concern. "You look terrible," she said.

"A late night and a lousy morning, that's all."

As she was shaking her head in gentle reproach, Jim looked in and said, "Lunch?"

Harry joined him outside. "Thanks, but I'm busy today."

"You're worrying about that woman, aren't you? Take it from me, she's just not worth it."

"Let me be the judge of that."

"Do me a favour. Coghlan may play at being a businessman, but he's still a crook and Liz had her eyes open when she shacked up with him. That's how she is, old son. Give her an outfit by Zandra Rhodes plus a fortnight on the Côte d'Azur and she won't worry too much about where the money came from."

Harry grunted and walked towards his room. At his retreating back, his partner fired a parting shot. "You should have divorced her long ago, can't you see? Start afresh, it's the only way."

Slamming the door behind him, Harry sat down to work again. But his concentration had gone and he was reduced to shuffling the papers around on his desk. Liz had not lost her capacity to strip him of both emotion and common sense. His fear that Coghlan might have hurt her, his sense of utter powerlessness, had started to stretch his nerves.

By two o'clock he could no longer ignore the hunger pangs. He wandered out to the Ancient Mariner's, a corner cafe near the waterfront where buxom girls who couldn't care less about cholesterol served thick wedges of ham with eggs and mugs of steaming tea. Harry listened to the waitresses' chatter about lovers past and present, jealous friends and trouble at home. Perhaps all our problems are the same, he thought, it's just the packaging that differs.

While paying for the meal, something occurred to him. Liz had a part-time job; she might simply be working. Outside, the rain had turned to sleet, but he folded the collar of his coat and hurried in the direction of Harrington Street. The Freak Shop was sandwiched between a wine merchant's and a florist's full of drooping daffodils.

One window of Matt Barley's emporium was filled with distorting mirrors, Hallowe'en masks and a rail of fancy dress costumes. A display of just-about-legal porn videos, exotic lingerie and thigh-length leather boots crammed the other. Harry didn't know how Matt had persuaded Liz to help him out this last time. An up-market fashion shop might have offered at least the surface glitter for which she yearned - but going back to a dump like this, run by a temperamental dwarf? He shook his head, unable to fathom it.

In any event, she wasn't here today. A handwritten card on the door said that the Freak Shop would be closed this afternoon. The truanting schoolkids who were pressing their noses to the glass, admiring the naughty nighties, could goggle to their hearts' content. Further down the road, he paused for a moment outside Mama Reilly's. But there was no reason to go inside and it was time to return to Fenwick Court.

Back at New Commodities House, Suzanne's sheikh had presumably got his woman and the switchboard girl was now tackling a thousand-pager about sex in Hollywood. Without looking up, she said, "Your lodger - sorry, your wife - called again. She said she'd be out this afternoon, but she hopes to see you tonight."

Relax, Harry told himself, nothing's gone wrong after all. Coghlan isn't a teenage hoodlum: losing Liz wouldn't be the end of his world. Follow Jim's advice and don't look back. Yet like a client urged to be calm in the witness box, he found it easier said than done.

He chain-smoked his way through the rest of the afternoon and rang the flat a couple of times without result. Shortly before six, Jim came into the tiny room.

"I'm off to the match." An F.A. cup-tie at Anfield, already twice postponed due to the snow last week. "There's a spare ticket here. Ronnie can't make it. Want to come?"

"No, thanks, not tonight." Ridiculously, the tone of the invitation, too deliberately casual, irked him: it resembled a treat for a matrimonial invalid.

His partner's face was a blank. "Suit yourself. I'm in tomorrow."

Since the break-up of his marriage, Harry had developed a habit of stopping off at the Dock Brief on his way home. In the absence of Liz there was no need to break the routine. The pub was tiny and invariably packed to overflowing. Above the counter was a sign which said in GOD WE TRUST - ALL OTHERS PAY CASH and its walls were covered with photographs of Liverpool in days gone by: the old Lyceum, Exchange Station and the overhead railway known universally as the dockers' umbrella. The real name of the place was the Anchors Aweigh, but its popular title was ingrained into city folklore and seemed appropriate to its mix of customers: professionals and businessmen at lunchtime and in the early evening, ship-workers and assorted locals as the night wore on. As he often did these days, Harry outlasted the other men in suits, propping up the counter whilst in the background deals were struck and pint pots occasionally shattered.

As Harry drank, questions about Liz's whereabouts swam around in his mind. Where had she been all day and would she be waiting for him at the flat when he got back in? The alcohol didn't help him to find any answers and in the end he banged the glass down and pushed through the mêlée round the bar out into the drizzling night.

The walk to Empire Dock took ten minutes. In the lobby, he ran into Brenda Rixton, the woman who lived next door. She had been chatting with the porter, but joined Harry as the lift arrived. Although he wasn't in the mood for casual conversation, there was no escaping it.

"Miserable evening, isn't it? And turning so cold, too!"

"Sure is, Brenda."

"That's better! At last you've dropped that Mrs. Rixton nonsense. Neighbours ought to be on first name terms, don't you agree?"

Within the enclosed space, her perfume was overpowering. Harry hated lift travel and the lack of a sensible place to focus his eyes. Unwillingly, he looked straight at his companion. She was tall, almost his height, with fine blonde hair and a willowy figure encased within a pink sweater and matching slacks. Although she was in her forties, Harry reckoned, she had the inquisitive smile of a young girl who is anxious to know everything. Only the fine lines etched into the skin around her blue eyes hinted at age and a loss of innocence.

With gentle irony, she said, "I gather you've taken a lodger."

Liz must have been amusing herself again. He forced a non-committal smile.

"I met her this evening when I got back from work," said Brenda, adding, "I admire your taste. She's extremely attractive."

They had arrived at the fourth floor. Stepping out, Harry found himself saying, "That's no lodger, Brenda, that's my wife."

"Your wife? But I thought . . ."

"Yes, well, she has a strange sense of humour. We're separated, but she may be around for a couple of days till she sorts herself out."

"I see," said his neighbour, although her baffled expression made it clear that she did not.

They stopped at her front door. "Mustn't loiter," said Harry with fake breeziness. "Plenty of paperwork to tackle, I'm afraid."

She wagged her index finger. "All work and no play. It isn't good for you."

He was already unlocking his own flat. "Goodnight, Brenda."

Tonight no Liz awaited him. Her return must have been brief. He could detect no signs that she had eaten here, but in the bedroom he almost fell over a couple of heavily strapped suitcases left behind the door into the hall. There was a carrier bag full of cosmetics and odds and ends of clothing bought from George Henry Lee's. So she planned to use the flat as a hotel for one more night at least. But where was she now? He changed into a sweater and jeans and flicked the television on. A choice of a repeated sitcom or snooker, a chat show or a documentary on AIDS. He groaned and went to examine the contents of his fridge freezer.

As he was lighting the gas on the cooker he caught sight of half a sheet of paper resting against the coffee pot. A note from Liz. Scrawled in her flowing hand, it said: *Missed you again! I'll be at the Ferry Club by eleven. Come over why don't you?*

Her easy assumption that he would come running after her angered him. During their time apart, he had found it easy to forget that the centre of Liz's universe was herself. Screwing up the piece of paper, he fed it vengefully to the gas flame. But he didn't bother to deceive himself. When Liz called, he had always followed. Sometimes he was afraid he always would.

Chapter Four

The Ferry Club was hidden at the heart of a maze of side streets behind Lime Street Station. Harry walked past empty burger bars and curtained Chinese restaurants, shuttered shops and barricaded redevelopment sites whose walls were covered with fly-posters advertising a political rally at the Pierhead. As the minutes ticked away towards eleven, Liverpool was quiet. Even the Ferry looked almost discreet as he approached. No neon lights, just a notice confirming that Reginald Anthony Gallimore was licensed pursuant to Act of Parliament for singing, dancing and the sale of intoxicating liquor, plus a yellow placard pinned to the door which said that Angie O'Hare, Hit Recording Artist, and Russ Jericho, Popular Comedian, were starring tonight.

At the entrance, a drunken tramp was about to pick an argument with a couple of bouncers, mean and muscular in their ill-fitting dinner suits. Their sniggers suggested they were hoping that he would provoke them into violence. A sign by the pay desk said MEMBERS AND BONA FIDE GUESTS ONLY - BY ORDER, but when Harry handed over his money he was allowed straight through with no questions asked.

The interior of the club was a raucous contrast to the desert calm of the city streets. The queue at the bar was three deep and dozens more people sat at tables grouped in a semi-circle facing the stage. Drinking, talking, a few even listening to the Popular Comedian, a flabby elephant of a man who was tossing old mother-in-law gags out of the side of his mouth in a treacle-thick Scouse accent.

"Y'know, I'm not saying she's ugly," Harry heard him mutter, "but I've seen better faces on clocks. And the size of her! Bleeding hell, she could eat a banana sideways. Y'know, I reckon she could sing a duet on her own."

Now and then members of the audience got up and walked straight in front of the act to the bar, but no one seemed to care, least of all Russ Jericho. It gave him the chance to paper over the cracks in his act. When a fat girl in a mini-dress plodded by he interrupted a racist joke about a bald Pakistani to say, "Last time I saw an arse like that, it was being whipped by Lester Piggott."

Harry's gaze travelled around the room. Glittery pillars supported a plasterboard ceiling on which pin-point lights flickered in rotation, red, green and blue. Two overhead fans whirled in a doomed attempt to dispel the fug of cigarette smoke and cheap scent. Young girls chatted to each other, feigning not to stare at the leather-jacketed lads sinking pints in silence near the door. Within easy reach of the bar, painted women in short black skirts and fish-net tights watched out for men who might pay for the pleasure of their company.

Liz was nowhere to be seen. Harry stifled a grunt of irritation and looked at his watch. Five past eleven. Perhaps she would be along in a minute. He decided to buy a drink and as he waited for service he reflected that the Ferry hadn't changed much since his last visit with her. They must have been married eighteen months then and he had already discovered the fascination which clubland held for her; as with so much else, he didn't share her point of view. The place had probably not been cleaned in the meantime, but in the dim lighting you couldn't tell.

Harry's turn at the bar coincided with a scabrous punchline about a lunatic and a lesbian. Harry ordered a pint of Ruddles from a barmaid with dyed blonde hair that was dirty brown at the roots. Large spiky hoops hung from her ears like offensive weapons. Her blouse was cut low, her fingers were heavy with rings. As she took Harry's money, she stared over his shoulder.

"Froggy, at last! Where were you?"

A small man jostled past Harry, catching his elbow and causing him to spill some of the beer that the blonde had poured a moment before. Without a sideways glance or an apology, the newcomer said in squeaky indignation, "Had things to see to, didn't I?"

"The boss was chasing after you. As soon as he turned up, her ladyship threw a fit. God knows why, he wasn't back as late as he said he would be. Anyway, you should have been here at half nine, so if he's searching for someone to kick, you're favourite."

The man had protruding eyes and a forehead wrinkled as if with the effort of years spent making up excuses. It was a petty rogue's face, of the sort Harry encountered every day of his working life. Standing by his shoulder, Harry caught a whiff of a foul smell, distinctive even in the Ferry's murky atmosphere.

After a pause for thought the man said, "Anyone asks, Myra's been took sick. They've rushed her into hospital and I'm only just back from the Royal. Okay, Shirelle?"

The barmaid shrugged. A bulging eye twinkled at her as a new line of self-defence evidently occurred to the man. "And I'll keep me mouth shut about yer job at the Apollo. Promise."

Shirelle tossed her blond mane in contempt. The earrings jangled with menace, but she spoke resignedly. "All right, I'll cover for you. Now sod off."

The small man blew her a kiss and shoved back through the crowd, vanishing from view. Liz still had not turned up. Harry spotted a trio of young girls slinking through the double doors at the other side of the concert hall. Off to the disco. Liz loved to dance and it occurred to him that she might be jiving the night away. He followed the girls downstairs. On the dance floor half a dozen women were swaying to the beat thudding from head-high speakers in each corner of the room. The dancers gazed into space, while the strobes painted them in ever-changing colours. Liz was not amongst them. Harry took a long draught from his glass and went back upstairs, in time to hear Russ Jericho wind up his act with a mumbled platitude about a terrific audience. The applause was patchy and Harry didn't join in.

A compère in a black velvet suit with flecks of dandruff sprinkled like snowflakes around the shoulders strutted on to the stage. As he gabbled about the quality of the entertainment, more people gravitated towards the bar. Harry scanned their faces in the hope of seeing Liz. No luck.

He turned to the man standing next to him, a stocky figure sales-rep smart in jacket and tie, and said, "I'm looking for a woman. Tall, dark, she . . . "

The man interrupted him with an ironic wink. "Aren't we all, pal, aren't we all?"

Harry finished his drink in silence. Where was she? The old frustration at her thoughtlessness began to burn within him: had she stood him up? For all he knew, she might be at the Demi-Monde or Huskisson's with some new bloke she'd just picked up. Of course, he should blame himself for succumbing to the temptation of her note like an addict craving for another fix.

"Well, that's enough from me," said the compère and a slurred voice from the audience bellowed assent. "Now is the moment you've all been waiting for. The highlight of our show, our very own hit recording artiste." He rolled off the last word with a Gallic flourish before rising to a new crescendo: "Yes, ladies and gentlemen. The enchanting. The talented. The lovely. The one and only - Miss Angie O'Hare!"

The keyboard player and drummer in the background burst into life with a Lennon and McCartney number. The people at the tables started clapping and someone cheered. A woman swept on to the stage, microphone in hand, singing about all the lonely people.

For Harry, her sound belonged to the distant past and the pop music of his youth when once or twice she had made it to the lower reaches of the record charts. Sixties ballads had always appealed to him and he still had an Angie O'Hare album somewhere at home. The song brought Brenda Rixton back to mind. Lack of companionship must cause her to contrive their regular meetings in the corridor or lift at Empire Dock. Where the lonely people all come from, he thought, matters less than where they find to go. And, suddenly, he felt Liz's failure to turn up as keenly as a nettle sting.

Angie O'Hare took a bow and as her head rose again, for a second he fancied that he saw a glimpse of sadness in her sapphire eyes, as though she too identified with the lyric. But within moments he realised that he must have been mistaken, for a smile of triumph spread across her face as she said, "Thank you all so very much," and started talking about the next number that she was going to sing. Feeling cheated, Harry reached for a cigarette and looked away once more.

The drinkers' queue had thinned and he traced a path towards the serving blonde. She was lying to a tall, tanned man in a slickly tailored dinner jacket whom Harry took to be the manager.

"Froggy? He only arrived half an hour ago, poor lamb. His wife's sick and they've whipped her into the Royal. He shouldn't really have come at all, but he didn't want to let you down."

"Do me a favour." The man tugged at the ends of his dark moustache. His mind seemed to be elsewhere, but you could tell from the gesture that he thought himself handsome. Even the barmaid, concentrating on her trivial deceit, let her eyes linger on her boss a little longer than necessary before she spoke again.

"Honest," she insisted, "you only have to ask him. But mind what you say, he's been under a lot of pressure lately."

Worthy of an Oscar, Harry thought. He coughed and shuffled, drawing attention to the fiver in his hand. Ignoring him, the manager said, "He'll be under more pressure if I find that he's been spinning me a yarn." But he turned away as he spoke.

After being served, Harry stayed by the counter, sipping the beer and telling himself that Liz would not be coming now. Why she had bothered to summon him here was anyone's guess. It would have made more sense to listen to Jim's advice and steer clear, but where Liz was concerned, logic was as scarce as love in a brothel. Today had been reminiscent of their marriage as a whole, as he twitched at the end of whatever strings she cared to pull.

From the stage, Angie O'Hare was crooning the chorus of *Don't Make Me Over*. He looked around the concert room. Everywhere, men and women were pairing off, like chess players easing through a well-tried opening game. Through the crowd, he could see the man called Froggy deep in conversation with a customer who had his back to Harry. Spinning another tall story, no doubt. But then the customer's girlfriend, a sulky blonde with a tart's wiggle, interrupted them and drew her man aside. Froggy resumed his desultory collection of disused glasses, casting a surreptitious glance at the manager as he did so. Harry saw the little man relax visibly as he spotted his boss at the rear of the room, standing with arms folded, looking abstractedly towards the stage.

Angie was in full flow: no matter how many times she had wrapped herself around the lyric, she still managed to give it everything. Harry could vaguely remember fancying her when she was in her prime. Women had been a mystery to him then. Come to that, they still were. But tonight, in a shimmering silk dress slashed from the waist and with her auburn hair fashionably frizzed, she looked as good as ever. There was a strength there, a sense of power, that he found as attractive as the curves of her body. Unexpectedly, he experienced his first stirrings of desire for her that he could recall since long-ago schooldays and when the number spiralled to its climax, he found himself applauding with the rest of the Ferry crowd.

Breathing hard, she inclined her head in acknowledgment, and this time Harry could detect no hint of anguish in her eyes. Softly, she said, "Tonight is very special for me, so I'd like to dedicate this next song to the man in my life." She sent a secret smile into the sea of faces. "I sang it to him on the night we met. It means so much to me - and, I hope, to you."

Absurdly, it was as if for Harry the words had broken a momentary spell when Liz was forgotten and for an instant the singer was in tune with him. The keyboard player struck up with the opening chords of *The Look of Love* and Harry started to edge towards the door. Liz would not be seen in the Ferry Club tonight.

On the way out he felt a hand brush against his leg. He glanced round and found himself looking at the grinning face of a woman in an unflattering tight red frock. She might have been any age between twenty and forty. Her freckled face was as used as an old bus ticket and somehow familiar.

"Looking for company, darling?"

Harry paused, trying in vain to place her in his memory. At the sight of his hesitation, she said, "No need to be shy. Mine's a vodka and lime. Or - we could take a walk if you like. I'm not too fussed about her voice, are you?"

Bony fingers dug into his arm. Decisively, he shook his head and said with a rueful grin, "Sorry, love. Not tonight." Or any night, please God.

"You don't remember me, do you? I'm Trisha. Peanuts Benjamin is my friend."

Of course. He had defended her on a soliciting charge eighteen months ago. Result: a fine, paid off no doubt by her going straight back on the streets again. As far as he could recall, she had still been in her teens at that time, but women aged rapidly in Trisha's business. He said hello and asked how she was.

"All right. You know. I'm having a night off, as a matter of fact. Peanuts had to sort out some bother at the Ludo Club. Pity, we was going to celebrate him getting off. In court, I mean. You did a good job, he's really made up."

"I'll get you that vodka and lime."

"Don't bother, I was only messing. Anyway, I'm sick of this place. Might as well catch a taxi and go back."

They went outside together. One of the men on the door treated Harry to a knowing smirk. Trisha stuck her tongue out at the bouncers and put her arm in Harry's, a gesture of camaraderie rather than a come-on. For him, it was a relief to get back into the open air.

As they walked down the road, looking for a cab she said, "So what are you doing in the Ferry? It's not where you expect to find posh solicitors, a dive like that."

"Long story," he said. "Would you believe I was just looking for my wife?"

"Oh yeah?" She giggled in incredulous merriment. "And I'm an Avon lady. Never mind, you didn't meet anyone this evening, but there's always tomorrow."

A black Corporation taxi pulled up in front of them. "I suppose you're right," he said. "Goodnight, Trisha. Give my best to Peanuts."

She climbed into the cab and then lowered the window. "Call him if you want. He'll fix you up, no problem. Specially after what you did for him in the court today."

He smiled without answering and waved her off. Left on his own, he suddenly felt overcome by exhaustion. Drink and disappointment had made his limbs heavy and his every movement a battle against fatigue. Trying without success to think about work rather than his wife, he dragged himself back once more along the city streets that led to the Empire Dock.

The flat seemed quieter than ever. Liz wasn't there, nor had he expected her to be this time. Pulling his clothes off sleepily, he noticed the suitcases and plastic bag which she had abandoned in his bedroom. Then he remembered that scarred wrist, the stupid tale about Coghlan wanting to kill her and how sold she seemed to be on her latest lover. Since they had split up, her life had changed in a way that he did not understand. And through an alcoholic blur, he realised that tonight the two of them were further apart than ever.

35

Chapter Five

The insistent wail of the doorbell woke him. Harry opened his eyes a little. Everything was dark. The throbbing inside his head seemed always to have been there, though he tried to tell himself it was only an early morning hangover. Ignore the racket, he told himself. Wait for it to go away.

Again the bell rang, for a full minute without a break. Impossible to sleep through that. Swearing, he peered at the luminous digits of the radio alarm. Five-fifty. There must be some mistake. But after a brief pause came another ear-piercing summons to the door.

"All right." He admitted defeat with a dehydrated croak. Climbing out of bed wasn't as easy as usual; his legs might have been those of a rheumaticky pensioner. Struggling into a dressing gown, he padded into the hall. The noise ceased as he put a filmy eye to the spyhole. A man's face, bleak as a mountain range, filled his line of vision.

In a hoarse whisper, Harry said, "You realise what time it is? What's this all about?"

"Mr. Devlin." A statement of fact, rather than a question, uttered with glum authority.

"Correct. And who are you?"

"Police. Will you let us in, please?"

Harry unlatched the door, but didn't release the chain. Outside stood two men in suits. The man who had spoken was heavily built and aged about forty. He had sandy hair, thinning on top and going grey. The corners of his mouth turned down to give him a lugubrious look. Harry recognised his accent as West Yorkshire. His companion was a generation younger, lean, lithe and wary as a soldier scanning a street in the Bogside. But what struck Harry most was the colour of his skin. In Liverpool, a black cop with a sergeant's stripes was still unexpected, like a mermaid rising from the murky depths of the Mersey.

"Detective Chief Inspector Skinner," said the first man. His melancholic tone matched his appearance. He indicated his colleague. "This is D.S. Macbeth."

"I don't care if he's Banquo's bloody ghost. What's the big idea?"

Skinner ignored the question. "You'd like to see our I.D., I imagine."

He flipped open a card and his colleague did likewise. Harry tried to focus on the documents.

"Okay. So why . . . "

"May we talk inside, please, sir?"

Skinner's manner precluded contradiction and Harry was unable to think of a reason for not doing as the policeman asked. He couldn't think of much at all. Leading the intruders into the lounge, he motioned them towards armchairs, more than glad to sit down himself. He saw their quick professional glances around the room, taking in the mess of books and papers, the crumpled jacket draped over the arm of a chair and the leaves of the unwatered cheese plant just beginning to yellow.

"I gather that you're a local solicitor," said Skinner. He spoke as if diagnosing an illness.

Harry nodded. He wasn't acquainted with either of this pair; nothing odd about that in a large city, but why the black sergeant was glowering at him with scarcely concealed hostility was impossible to understand. Crusoe and Devlin didn't have a bad name down at the Bridewell; they weren't thought of as bent. Nevertheless, it wasn't customary for the local force to pop into the homes of defence lawyers in the early hours to chat about their current caseload.

Skinner leaned forward. "I believe you are married to a Mrs. Elizabeth Devlin?"

Harry scarcely recognised the name. It must have been years since he last heard it. Anyway, it didn't fit Liz. She had always been her own woman, never a possessed spouse. But he grunted assent.

"I am afraid I have some bad news for you, Mr. Devlin."

Harry sensed that he was expected to respond, but the ache in his head blotted out rational thought. He glanced at Macbeth, but the dark face was now stripped of expression. Both men were studying him intently. After a short pause, Skinner coughed and spoke again.

"Mr. Devlin, I have to tell you that your wife died last night."

Harry stared, first at one man, then at the other. Their features betrayed nothing. They were two detectives, watching him watching them. And waiting. Time passed. Seconds, minutes, hours? Harry neither knew nor cared. The silence made his head hurt more and his stomach began to churn.

Skinner cleared his throat and said, "I'm sorry."

Harry's shoulders twitched. "But isn't . . . I mean . . ." He couldn't frame what he wanted to say. He had no idea what he wanted to say.

Softly and with no emphasis, the chief inspector said, "Your wife's body was found last night. We are treating it as a suspicious death, Mr. Devlin."

Harry was conscious of the detectives' unwavering gaze. Vaguely aware that there were questions which he should be asking - though if Liz was dead, how could any answers matter? - he clutched like a shipwreck victim at the first which entered his head.

"How did she die?"

Skinner said in the same flat tone, "She was stabbed, Mr. Devlin."

Stabbed. The word twisted in Harry's guts like the blade of a knife. He shut his eyes. A hundred memories surged into his mind, like unwelcome intruders breaking down the door.

Liz on the night of their first meeting, at a fireworks display within a stone's throw of here at the Albert Dock. She'd told him then how much she loved to see the river lit up by the exploding showers of colour, had laughed and introduced herself: Liz Wieczarek. He couldn't pronounce her Polish surname and she had teased him about his ineptitude.

Their wedding day when she'd promised to honour and obey, while a trace of humour had sparkled in her eyes and he'd tried not to grin at the provocative touch of her fingernails running along the back of his hand while the vicar droned on about the nature of their sacrament.

The evening when his cross-examination skills had drawn out the admission that she was sleeping with Michael Coghlan. When Harry asked if she loved the man, she had spread her arms and simply said, "I think so. But even if I don't, I do know that I want him."

Eventually he again became aware of the unblinking scrutiny of the policemen. Their watchfulness as they assessed his reaction to their news made him think of physicists noting the outcome of a laboratory experiment.

"I realise that this must come as a shock to you," said Skinner. He coughed once more. "Even so, I wonder if you could help us by answering a few questions."

Harry felt as if every muscle in his body had melted. This is the same room, he told himself, in which you talked to her thirty hours ago. That's where she sat. Through the door is the bed in which she slept. Yesterday morning she was alive and said thank you, for making her feel safe.

"Perhaps I could start, sir, by asking when you last saw your wife."

Harry's lips were dry. "Yesterday. Yesterday morning."

The policemen exchanged glances. They had not expected that reply. Macbeth seemed to be breathing harder, although he continued to hold his tongue. His superior kept the next question casual.

"At what time?"

"Shortly after eight in the morning."

"And where was that?"

"Here, in this flat."

Skinner scratched his nose, perhaps to conceal his surprise. "She visited you here?"

"Yes. She stayed the night."

The chief inspector frowned. Sitting opposite, his sergeant's eyes began to gleam with that brooding hostility which Harry could identify, but not comprehend.

"Am I right in believing," said Skinner, "that you were separated from your wife, but not divorced?"

Harry nodded.

"An amicable arrangement?" asked the policeman softly.

There was something here which Harry didn't understand. A secret from which he was excluded. He fumbled for a cigarette and found an old pack of Player's in his dressing gown pocket. His hands trembled as he lit up. Instinct urged him to choose his words with care. Cautiously, he said, "Is any separation amicable?"

"That's a lawyer's reply, if you don't mind my saying so, sir." Skinner was curt. "Now - were you still on friendly terms or not?"

"I hadn't seen her for two years. We weren't on any terms at all."

"Yet she called on you," said Skinner, "and spent a whole night with you."

"Not *with* me."

Skinner's eyebrows curved like question marks.

"I mean, we didn't sleep together. She took the bedroom, there's only one, you can see how tiny this place is. I had the sofa."

"I see."

"I doubt it," said Harry. Anger began to surge inside him, providing an anaesthetic against pain and giving him strength to confront the puzzle. What in God's name had happened? And what were they withholding from him?

"Tell me, then."

Harry exhaled and with a jerky movement stubbed out the half-finished cigarette. "Liz was waiting for me the night before last. I arrived back at midnight. She'd talked the porter into letting her in."

"Why had she come?"

"She'd started an affair with a married man. Unfortunately her other boyfriend found out. That frightened her."

"Why?"

"The boyfriend is Mick Coghlan. Runs the gym in Brunner Street." He moistened his lips. "Your people must have a cabinet full of files on him."

Skinner inclined his head.

He already knows about Coghlan, thought Harry. Christ, what's going on?

"You're sure - I mean, you are definite that Liz is dead?" Harry looked quickly from one man to the other. "There hasn't been - some sort of a mistake?"

He knew the answer before it came. For the first time the sickening realisation hit him that he had been here before. Eighteen years ago, when staying at a friend's house, the adults had taken him to one side and told him his parents would not be coming home again. Harry had not believed it then, and it had taken weeks - no, months, surely? -for the truth finally to sink in. Trouble was, he had always had a secret faith that a mistake had been made, some bizarre error of identification. Forcing himself to admit that there had been no such mistake had been the hardest lesson of his life. Since then he had blotted out the memory of the breaking of the news. Until now.

His parents had died through the randomness of fate, hit when crossing the road by a fire engine which had burst through red traffic lights. The driver hadn't been to blame, they had simply been in the wrong place at the wrong time. And afterwards, he had felt lost, for there had been no scapegoat for him to hate, except for the never-to-be-identified hoaxer whose false alarm had sent the engine thundering to disaster that foggy November night, now so long ago.

Skinner's voice jerked him back to the present. "I'm afraid there's been no mistake, though I am going to have to ask you to provide formal identification of the body shortly." Skinner fished inside his jacket and offered him another cigarette. Harry took it with an unsteady hand. "I am sure this must be difficult for you, sir, but would you be good enough to tell me what happened, from when Mrs. Devlin came to see you onwards?"

In a daze, Harry described his discovery of Liz in the flat on Wednesday night. He gave a fragmented account of their conversation and of how he had missed her on the phone during the following day and responded to her written summons by making his fruitless visit to the Ferry Club. He spoke dully; his mind was elsewhere as he tried in vain to reconcile himself to the fact of her death. When he mentioned her fear of Coghlan, he noticed the chief inspector exchange a glance with his sergeant, but the combined effect of hangover and shock made him uncaring about anything other than his loss of Liz. After he had finished talking, he bowed his head, as if to say: What does any of it matter now?

But Skinner wanted more. "This note that she left for you. May I see it?"

Harry tried to recall what he had done with it. "That's . . . yes, I remember now. I burnt it. In a temper, I admit."

"Why do that? It seems an extreme reaction."

"I was angry, that's all. She was taking it for granted that I would chase after her."

"Yet that is precisely what you did," pointed out Skinner. "Very well. Did you go to the Ferry Club right away?"

"Not immediately. I made myself something to eat first, read a little, then went out. I must have left here about twenty to eleven."

"And did you bump into your wife on the way?"

"Of course not."

"Talk to anyone whilst you were out?"

Harry hesitated, then told the detective about his conversation with Trisha. Skinner nodded, Macbeth made a note. Yet neither of them seemed interested.

"And you say you left at about twelve?"

"Give or take ten minutes. I can't be precise. Look, do you mind-"

"You came straight home, you said. Anyone see you arrive back? Or depart?"

"Not as far as I can recall. The porter may have been on his rounds."

Skinner appeared to reflect on Harry's answers for a moment or two before saying, "What were your feelings towards your wife, Mr. Devlin?"

Harry scoured his mind for a suitable reply. But how could he give a sensible response to someone who had never met the woman? What were his feelings for Liz: love, hate, devotion, fury? All in equal measure at every hour of the day? He stretched out his arms helplessly.

"You're speaking in the past tense," he said at last, "I don't think I can cope with that at the moment. Any minute now Liz will walk through the door and tell me this is all some gigantic joke. An out-of-season April fool."

Skinner's pale pink tongue appeared between narrow lips. "I'm sorry, Mr. Devlin, but I have to ask you this - did you kill your wife?"

43

Harry lit another cigarette. Although he avoided the detectives' eyes, the prickling of his skin told him that they were weighing him up like ratcatchers examining their prey.

"Liz tempted me to murder from the hour when I met her, Chief Inspector. She was impatient and impulsive and infuriating. I never came across a woman who could goad me with such ease. I won't pretend she didn't sometimes drive me crazy with rage. But I'd sooner lose an arm than cause her a moment's misery. If you're scratching round for a culprit, count me out."

Macbeth said, "Mind if I look round?" After his superior's low-key questioning, the sound of the black detective's voice came as a shock. The accent was deepest Kirby, the tone unambiguously insolent. Even before Harry could reply, the young policeman was on his feet, prowling about the room, his whole body taut with expectation. Harry noticed that he touched nothing.

"What were you wearing last night?" As an afterthought, Macbeth tossed in a "sir" that added to the insult.

Trying to steady his voice, Harry described his clothes and, turning to Skinner, asked, "Where was she found?"

"Didn't I tell you?"

Unsubtle, thought Harry. "No, Chief Inspector."

"One of our patrolmen discovered the body on his rounds. In Leeming Street, at the bottom of an alleyway running down by the tyre centre, Albiston's."

A mean place for anyone to die. A liver-rotted wino would be ashamed to finish up there. For an instant Harry thought he was going to vomit. Only with a heart-straining effort of will was he able to conquer the feeling of nausea.

"When was she killed?" he asked.

Skinner shook his head. "Too soon for us to say, sir."

And even if you could, you'd keep that card up your sleeve, thought Harry. He noticed Macbeth push open the bedroom door and step inside, but made no objection. Instead, he pressed for more information and the chief inspector painted in a few background details.

There was, said Skinner sombrely, no indication of a sexual motive for the attack, although pending the post mortem it was too early to draw a firm conclusion. The murder weapon had been a Stanley knife, of the kind sold in hardware shops on every street corner. So far it had not been found. Liz's handbag had been stolen, but picked up two streets away. No money or credit cards - just the empty wallet - but the driving licence had identified her. Ironic, as she never cared to drive; being chauffeured was much more in her line.

Slowly, Harry said, "Presumably it was some kind of street crime? A mugging gone wrong."

"We can't rule out any possibility at this stage." Skinner's melancholic face offered no hint as to whether he considered it likely or not. Yet Harry's years in the law had taught him anything could happen in this city. A kid desperate for money to feed his taste for heroin perhaps, setting on a woman alone, messing up a bag snatch, then grabbing for his knife in a spasm of panic.

"As I mentioned, sir," continued Skinner, "I'm afraid I'll have to ask you to accompany my sergeant to the mortuary."

Before Harry could speak, Macbeth strode out of the bedroom, barely able to contain a savage smirk of triumph. To his superior he said, "A couple of suitcases in there, sir. Also a shopping bag full of women's things. The luggage is marked with Mrs. Devlin's name."

"You failed to tell me about that, Mr. Devlin."

Harry shrugged. "I forgot, that's all."

"Really, sir?" The corners of Skinner's mouth seemed to turn even further down than before.

It took Harry's last reserves of self-discipline for him to respond evenly. "Liz dumped them there yesterday when I was out. I think I told you, my neighbour exchanged a word with her in the early evening."

"If you don't object, sir, we'll have to carry out a search of your flat. A routine precaution, I'm sure a man with your background will understand."

Harry nodded, as for the first time this morning his mind began to work. From the moment they'd learned Liz had spent Wednesday night here, he'd been in the frame. Skinner's attitude made it clear that his time at the Ferry, his speaking to Trisha, gave him no alibi. Liz must have been killed earlier in the evening. If it was much later, the police wouldn't have arrived so quickly. And if he objected to their making a full search, a warrant would materialise like an ace from a conjuror's palm.

"Go ahead, Chief Inspector." He hoped he sounded more relaxed than he felt.

Skinner nodded and Macbeth walked over to the door. As he got up to leave, Harry had to choke a bitter laugh in his throat as a thought sprang into his mind. Never mind about a mugging - hadn't Liz in this very room, not forty-eight hours earlier, expressed her dread of meeting her death at Mick Coghlan's hands? And he had dismissed it as an absurd flight of fancy. Perhaps to be suspected of murder was the start of his punishment for having disbelieved her.

Chapter Six

"Yes, that's my wife."

The sweet, sickly stench of the mortuary was everywhere. Instinctively, Harry knew that he would never escape it. No matter if it faded from his nostrils or was cleaned from his clothes. At any moment in the years to come, he would recall this grey morning and again be haunted by the odour of the place of death.

He stood with D.S. Macbeth as the attendant, a silent white-coated man, pulled the sheet up to cover Liz's face. Seeing her again in this tiled, windowless room seemed unreal. Yet there was no denying that the cold corpse was hers; the last self-deluding prayer, that the police had blundered over identification, had gone unanswered. The dark hair curled as crisply as ever over closed eyes and for all their bluish tinge, the lips had a twist of self-satisfaction. As if to say, "I told you so." The mortician's skill almost fooled Harry; it looked as though she were only sleeping. But a second glance at the pale waxy cheeks that he had so often kissed made him realise the spirit had gone. All that was left of Liz on earth was an empty, lifeless shell.

He felt dazed. For a second he thought his legs were going to buckle beneath him, but he summoned up the last of his strength and managed to straighten up. He dare not let himself sink into a quicksand of despair. He must reach for solid ground, try to make sense of the cruel absurdity of what had happened to his wife.

The attendant wheeled her away on a squeaking trolley. Harry did not watch her go. Instead he demanded, "Have you interviewed Coghlan yet?"

His expression unreadable, Macbeth said, "I understand he's out of town."

"Liz was terrified of him," said Harry. He could not help brooding about Wednesday night. "I should have listened instead of thinking it was all an act."

The policeman said nothing. He led the way into the raw air outside and directed Harry to his unmarked Montego. Macbeth was a good driver, swift and certain, and within ten minutes they were back at Empire Dock. Two squad cars were parked by the entrance and Harry had to walk past the morning porter and relief security guard, who had stared with naked curiosity when he got out of the car, but averted their eyes in embarrassment as he approached, finding themselves unable even to offer a good morning. He could imagine their fascination at the police activity and their ghoulish speculation about whether he was implicated in the death of his wife.

Inside, the police were taking the flat apart. Not a book remained in place, nor probably a speck of dust. The cheese plant had collapsed on to its side and no one had troubled to restore it to the vertical. Strangers tramped backwards and forwards through his home as if on the concourse at Lime Street Station. What were they searching for? Something to pin him to the murder scene, Harry presumed. A photographer was carefully gathering together his gear and an acned constable who seemed anxious to please was flourishing two large polythene bags for Skinner's inspection. The packages were sealed and bore blue-inked labels stating their contents and the date. Inside were the jacket and trousers Harry had worn the previous night.

In his West Riding monotone, the chief inspector said, "We'll need to remove one or two personal items for forensic tests, Mr. Devlin. You'll appreciate, in a case of this kind we have to take a number of routine steps of this sort. I'm afraid I also have to press you for some further information about her background, sir."

At Skinner's prompting, Harry sketched a picture of the past. Family details. Liz's parents had died years ago. Her father was a

Pole, who had settled here after the Second World War and found himself an English girl who worked in a bakery in Bootle. There were two children. The older sister, Maggie, nowadays lived in the best part of Blundellsands. Her husband was a partner in the local branch of a country-wide firm of accountants, a dust-dry character with a flair for figures and as much sense of humour as a computer system. Liz had loved to poke fun at him.

Job details. Liz had left school at sixteen, hoping to make it as a model, but her looks weren't fashionable that year. After a few photo sessions with sweet talkers who may not have had film in their cameras, she'd hauled herself off the slippery slope and settled for shop work and finding a man. She'd graduated from one-night-stands with fumbling teenagers and married men whose wives didn't understand them to an on-off affair with a boutique owner who made her his assistant manageress. But after a couple of years of dithering, he'd decided he preferred the company of his own sex. Yet Liz hadn't let the experience sour her. She'd taken a job with Matt Barley, and when Harry met her as fireworks lit the sky at Albert Dock, had betrayed no hint of past disappointments, confident as ever that good times were around the corner.

Marriage details. At first, life together had been full of promise. Liz had always wanted to squeeze the maximum pleasure from life, and for a time he could deny her nothing. Not swish clothes, not holidays in the sun, not all night parties, not clubbing it till the early hours. But the time came when a summons to the Bridewell interrupted a romantic dinner that she had slaved over for hours, and when the free flow of money had to slow down. Slowly, slowly, the cracks began to show. He was content simply to be with her, but she had grown frustrated, impatient for something more than he could give. Harry realised she could never change, and for all the rows that had torn them apart, secretly he had never wanted her to.

"Finished in the bedroom, sir." A uniformed flunkey attracted Skinner's attention. They conversed in low voices over by the entrance hall, whilst behind them a walkie-talkie crackled.

Harry absorbed the scene. The unhurried comings and goings were grimly compelling to watch as the team of men approached the end of their task. The frustration he had felt when seeing them pore over his clothes and furniture was submerged by curiosity as they made vague efforts to restore a semblance of order in their wake, stuffing books back onto shelves and righting the wretched cheese plant at last. Only doing their job, he told himself, it's a necessary evil. And yet he already understood that this place - no, more than that, his whole life - would never be the same again.

Skinner returned to his side. "Nearly ready, sir."

"Found anything of interest?"

When the chief inspector failed to reply, Harry pressed him about the murder. Skinner let a few more droplets of information trickle out. There had been, he said, half a dozen separate wounds in the body. Harry felt his gorge rise in his throat as he tried to visualise what had happened in that darkened alley, but he kept his voice calm as he asked if that meant that the murderer was certainly a man. Impossible to be definite yet, said Skinner, but undoubtedly someone possessing very considerable physical strength. How much had the Press been told? A statement had already been made, the detective told him, but it would be sensible to prepare for their questioning.

"I can handle them," said Harry, as much to himself as to Skinner. He clenched his fist, as if glad of an outlet for his anger at having lost Liz. "No way am I having a bunch of journalists camping on my doorstep day and night, trying to grab a story." He glanced at the clock. "I must ring the office, let them know why I haven't arrived."

He got through to Jim Crusoe at the first attempt and in two or three clipped sentences explained that Liz was dead. At the other end of the line, his partner's shock was almost tangible.

"It's - my God, I heard on Radio City that a woman's body had been found, but I never . . . " Jim's voice trailed off into nothingness.

"Tell Lucy I'll be in later."

After a pause, Jim said in amazement, "You're not coming in to work?"

"What else should I do? The police are all but through with me. I just have to talk to Maggie about all the arrangements, but the inquest's bound to be adjourned. There's nothing else for me to do but sit and mope. The way I feel at present, I'll be better off in the office than sitting here with my head in my hands."

"Look, I - I want you to know . . . Christ, this is terrible."

Harry could picture his partner going back over the past and all his gibes about Liz, her greed and unfaithfulness. Too late now to apologise, he thought savagely, but all he said was a brusque "See you later" before ringing off.

Skinner was back. "I think we can leave you in peace for the time being, sir."

Harry gazed at the room. It still bore the indelible marks of unwanted intrusion.

"Where do you go from here?"

"We have plenty of inquiries to make in a case like this, sir."

"Your sergeant told me Coghlan's still out of town." He hesitated for a moment, then added impulsively, "Make sure the bastard doesn't slip through your fingers. I don't want him to get away with this."

"I wouldn't jump to conclusions if I were you, sir. As a solicitor, you don't want to find yourself on the receiving end of a libel writ."

"For saying that he killed her? That's slander, not libel, Chief Inspector, and anyway there's a defence of truth."

"I'm keeping an open mind, Mr. Devlin, and I'd advise you to do the same. You'll be available if I need to speak to you again, sir?"

"I'm not thinking of doing a moonlight, if that's what you have in mind. But I've told you everything I know and that isn't much. Liz and I had become strangers. So until you have some news for me, you don't need to call round again. Having half the police force here all morning is bad for business when my job is to keep clients out of trouble. The neighbours must have had their eyes out on stalks since your lads turned up with their fancy cameras and their two-way radios."

Getting that off his chest made him feel a little better. Concentrate on the trivia, he told himself, like what the woman next door might think and how to cram a day's work into four or five hours. Bury your darker imaginings, that's the way to stay sane when the world seems full of madness.

The detective scratched his chin and said, "I can't guarantee that I won't have to trouble you once more, sir, as the inquiry develops. We have to do our job, you understand."

Surely they couldn't now regard him as suspect? They had turned the flat upside down and found nothing; Harry was certain of that, for there was nothing to find. Even so, Skinner's attitude bothered him as the invaders finally left, abandoning him to the flat's solitude.

He slumped on the sofa whilst the events of this dreadful morning swirled around in his head, defying his attempts to impose the discipline of rational thought. Eventually he made himself a black coffee. Too bitter. Pushing the cup to one side, he forced himself up and into the stinging chill of the outside world.

Liz is dead. Repeating the words over and over would not, he knew, explain anything, but perhaps doing so would help his protesting brain to assimilate the truth.

Liz was dead. That lovely selfish woman whom he had adored. No more would she tease or taunt. The great green eyes wouldn't captivate again. That disconsolate pout when she failed to win her way belonged to history. Liz was dead and his hopes of a reconciliation had died with her. For at last he was beginning to acknowledge the truth: he had spent the past two years as a sleepwalker, dreaming that one day she would return to share with him the silly moments that had made existence seem worthwhile. And there had been many such moments. Making love beneath their own Christmas tree, the December after they were married, her slender body basking in the soft glow from the fairy lights. The Rhine cruise of their honeymoon, their hands clasped as they sailed around the Lorelei. Skiing in Austria and her radiance as she exclaimed for all the world to hear, "I feel so free!"

Liz was dead. And a primitive rage started to burn within him. Someone in this city owned the hands that had crushed out so much life. Perhaps a mugger or a maniac, but possibly the man of whom she had expressed so much fear: Mick Coghlan. Might her murder so soon after she had begged for shelter from her lover's wrath be nothing more than a macabre coincidence? Harry's mind rebelled against the idea. It was not simply that he didn't believe in such quirks of fate, but more that nailing Coghlan with the guilt had about it a rightness and classical inevitability. That the man who had wrecked his marriage should be responsible too for the final act of brutal destruction seemed as logical to Harry as his own rapidly rising hunger for revenge.

The wind from the Mersey chewed at the bare flesh of his face. The riverside walkway was deserted save for a couple of elderly dog-walkers kitted out in anoraks and fur-lined boots who glanced at him nervously before scurrying on. The noiseless moving of his lips might have disturbed them, or it may have been his wild appearance. Lacking a jersey or coat to guard against the bitter cold, with his patched jeans and thin shirt he must have looked like a ravaged scarecrow, but he didn't care.

Harry kicked a pebble over the side and heard it splash into the waves that slapped against the breakwater. They used to call this the Cast-Iron Shore, where granite warehouses towered above iron quays and the world traded through the port of Liverpool. Jesse Hartley, the no-nonsense architect who had built the Albert and Empire Docks, was said to have had a contempt for beauty, but the austere grandeur of his monuments remained now that the buildings had out-lived their original usefulness to become traps for tourists and the leisure cult. Times had changed. Gone were the days when the Mersey was crowded with big square riggers arriving on every tide, bringing cargoes of cotton from the New World. The only vessels to be seen this morning were the two river ferries, chugging back and forth from the Pierhead to the landing stages at Seacombe and Woodchurch.

After passing the Tate Gallery, he stopped as he always did at the sight of the Liverpool waterfront, with the Cunard, Dock Company and Liver Buildings towering above the stick men and women who strolled around. Why, he wondered, did he love Liverpool when behind the Victorian splendour of the Pierhead there was so much about the place to hate - the dirt and the poverty and the crime? It occured to him that, as with his ceaseless yearning for Liz, his affection for his birthplace remained strong enough to survive the worst: it could not simply fade away. The city and the woman, they would always be part of him.

In the pocket of his jeans he had thrust, out of habit, a box of matches and a handful of cigarettes. He was about to light up when, for no reason that he could understand, he changed his mind. All at once, he wanted never to smoke again. A ridiculous time for such a decision. But it was a small token of the need he had to commit himself to one objective in life, at least, that might be attainable. He hurled the matches and fags in a single movement out into the river. They bobbled on the surface for a second or two, then disappeared from view. A woman passing by tutted in disgust at this latest pollution of the Mersey.

Increasing his pace, he walked towards Water Street. As he passed the equestrian statue of Edward VII, a pigeon, Scouse-irreverent, defecated on the monarch's head. Harry grinned for a moment, but then his jaw set again and he made a silent vow. Of course it would be harder than denying himself a smoke. But Liz had trusted him to keep her safe and he had failed her. Now he would not rest, could not rest, until he had found her murderer.

Chapter Seven

"I can forgive a man anything," said Ken Cafferty, waving a chunky hand magnanimously, "provided he has a sense of humour. But Ned Skinner, now - typical bloody Yorkshireman! Miserable as a Monday morning in Middles-borough."

He lifted a chipped mug to his lips, oblivious to the ring it had left on the surface of Harry's office desk, and beamed with pleasure at his own phrase-making. Then he sucked in his cheeks and added, "But he gets results. By God, Harry, he gets results."

Ten minutes earlier Cafferty had put his notebook away and they had started speaking off the record. Chief crime reporter on one of the city's local rags, with Harry he had a you-scratch-my-back relationship of the kind that went back years and suited them both. Like most journalists and lawyers, they remained wary of each other, conscious of the conflict between the public's right to know and the client's craving for confidentiality. Yet within the constraints of their irreconcilable objectives, Harry was willing to feed Cafferty with as much information about a case as common sense permitted and trusted the man not to print more than was needed to make a story that didn't sink like a stone.

This time Harry was cashing in a few old favours. He wanted the minimum hassle from the Press and as much inside information as Cafferty could provide. The reporter was willing to oblige; after probing for half an hour, he seemed satisfied that he wasn't interviewing a credible murder suspect. Positive leads, though were in short supply and he'd been able to tell Harry no more than Skinner had already divulged. The Coghlan angle, as Cafferty persisted in calling it, held his interest, but as Harry had kept quiet about Liz's fear for her life - he knew better than to show all his cards at the outset, even when seeking help - there wasn't much meat on the bones of an exclusive yet.

"It comes down to this . . ." said Cafferty, furrowing his brow. Harry knew the cherubic face and cheerfully mundane small talk masked a shrewd intelligence. ". . . was your wife simply in the wrong place at the wrong time? Or did she know her killer?" He paused, as if hoping to provoke a response, but when none was forthcoming, said, "Did Skinner drop any hints to you about the way he sees things? Without prejudice, as you legal bods would say?"

"Not a thing," said Harry slowly. "I can't make out what the man is thinking."

"Sniffing round for a motive, isn't he? What can it be if not sex or money? There are no stray lunatics out on the loose to take all the blame. At least, no more than usual. By keeping you guessing, he's taking no risks. After all, you wouldn't be the first lawyer in the past few years to have flipped and turned to murder. And remember, my friend, most killings are domestics. That can't surprise you, you handle divorce work."

"Maybe you're right." Harry stood up. "Thanks for coming in, anyway." He tried to make it sound like a dismissal. Cafferty had not responded to an invitation to chat; he had simply been hanging round outside New Commodities House waiting for the chance to catch Harry for a one-to-one talk about Liz's death. But he took the hint and got to his feet.

Offering his hand, Cafferty said, "Appreciate your time. "Specially on a day like this. It's rough for you, it won't have sunk in properly yet. Doesn't matter how long the two of you have been split up, she was still your wife." For an instant his face clouded. "Believe me, marriages have deeper roots than people realise. Jenny, my first, she buggered off fifteen years ago with some snotty-nosed kid on an assignment from the *Mirror* and I dream about her to this very day."

Harry showed him out and agreed to call if there was any further news. Suzanne on the switchboard, shiny-eyed at being involved

- if only at one remove - in a case of violent crime, attracted his attention. "Message for you, Mr. Devlin." She had abandoned her surliness, no doubt as a mark of respect for the bereaved. "Your sister-in-law, Mrs. Edge."

"Ring back. I'll take it in my room."

The phone was trilling as he walked through the door. He hadn't spoken to Maggie for eighteen months, since they'd bumped into one another in the Playhouse bar during the interval of a Willy Russell play, but it might have been yesterday as she came on to the line. Her voice was as warm as ever, although it faltered a little as she commiserated with him. For a short while they exchanged words inadequate to express their shared sense of shock, before Harry said, "I must see you soon, there are things we ought to discuss."

"Yes," she said. "Yes, of course. When would suit you?"

"I was hoping, right away. Can you manage that?"

"Where, Harry?"

"You know the Traders' Club in Old Hall Street? We have a firm's membership there. At least we'll be able to talk without being disturbed. Meet me there in forty minutes and I'll sign you in for lunch."

Someone rapped at the door as he put the receiver down. Jim came in and sat on the edge of the desk. His rugged features were darkened by dismay.

"Nothing I say will be right," he began, his manner diffident for once. "But I am sorry. I understand what she meant to you."

"Thanks."

"Have the police said anything much about what happened? Do they have any ideas?"

"They spent most of the morning turning my flat upside down because Liz stayed overnight with me. They give the impression I'm suspect number one."

"Only routine. You know that better than me."

58

"I suppose so. As to the rest, it's early days yet. At least they don't think it was intended as a rape. A mugging, maybe, but it's far from clear. I have my own views on the subject, for what they're worth."

"Which are?"

Harry told him about Liz's fear of Coghlan. Each time he recalled their conversation, Liz's anxiety seemed no more justified than before. But for the fact that now she was dead. The bitterness of self-reproach darkened his voice as he said, "I was so sure she was fantasising. But now I look back, I realise that she was telling the truth about the way she felt. And I didn't lift a finger to help! Christ, I was married to her. I should have been able to tell the difference between her ideas of fact and fiction."

"I doubt it," said Jim. "Liz didn't know the difference herself."

Harry felt stung. "Easy for you to say that."

"True, though."

"Coghlan's a vicious bastard. If she walked out on him . . ."

"He's a robber and a thug, by all accounts. Not necessarily a murderer."

"Not until now."

His partner jabbed his midriff with a gentle punch. "Look, old son, I know you hate Coghlan. Don't blame you for that, you have good reason. But don't let hatred get a hold of you. It's a cancer, it'll do you harm. And don't start convincing yourself that anything you could have done might have saved Liz's life. Odds are, she was just unlucky. This is a dangerous city, the same could happen to anyone. Sickening, I know, but you mustn't let yourself become smothered by what might have been."

Examining the worn areas of the office carpet, Harry said quietly, "Of course, you're right."

"Yes." Jim climbed to his feet. "You ready for a late spot of something to eat?"

"I'm meeting Maggie at the Traders'. There are things we have to talk about."

Jim nodded. "Understood. When's the funeral?"

"Not for a while, I gather. Skinner will want the inquest over first."

On his way out, Jim stopped at the door. "Look, anything I can do . . ."

"Yes. Thanks."

"Why don't you come over, spend the night at our place? Longer if you like. Heather would be glad if you did; in fact, she'll give me hell if you don't. Help the boys with their homework - they reckon the two of us are as thick as planks."

Harry shook his head. "I appreciate it, really do. But at present I think I'd feel better on my own, making an effort to sort some sense out of this mess."

"Up to you, old son. The offer remains open. Anytime you'd like to take advantage, shout."

Left alone, Harry shuffled rapidly through the papers on his desk. Jim and Lucy had already organised his work so that Ronald Sou and the articled clerk, Sylvia, were handling the more urgent matters. A couple of court cases had been briefed out for barristers to deal with and there wasn't any pressing reason for him to come back to the office in the afternoon. Except that he wanted to. The run-of-the-mill workload at least offered the reassurance of familiar territory: arguments between neighbours and shoplifting from department stores, far removed from the finality of death in a bleak back alley.

The Traders' Club was five minutes' walk away, tucked in the shadow of the huge ochre-faced insurance building that Scousers called the Sand Castle. As he reached Old Hall Street, he caught sight of his sister-in-law, standing by the steps that led up to the double oak doors. Her slim figure was wrapped in a huge white fur coat, her elfin features scarcely visible beneath an engulfing scarf of hand-painted silk. She moved forward and clasped him to her in a gesture that was as sudden as it was welcome. He felt the warmth of her breath on his cheek and for the first time since Skinner and Macbeth had rung at his front door he was able to lose himself in the hug, clinging to her, reluctant to let go.

Maggie took his hand in hers and stepped back. "It's been a long time."

"Too long." He returned the pressure of her hand. "You're more attractive then ever." It wasn't an appropriate comment to make on this occasion, but he meant it and had never quite mastered the lawyer's knack of not saying what came immediately into his head. Maggie had never matched Liz for glamour, nor had she attempted to, but her small, up-turned face had a natural charm that the dismay in her grey eyes could not diminish.

"Shall we go inside?"

The Traders' might be only three-quarters of a mile distant from the Ferry Club, but it was a world apart. A uniformed porter whose name was Alfred and who had been there for upwards of twenty years, saluted and held a door open for them. He greeted Harry by name, as if his last visit had been the previous day rather than in the height of the summer. To walk through the hallway was to step back in time. Heavy, gilt-framed portraits of past presidents of the club lined the walls; stern, long-dead shipping magnates and cotton dealers, many of them, men who had prospered during Liverpool's years of greatness. Extravagant crystal chandeliers hung above their heads and in an alcove a cabinet displayed ivory ware and exotic sailing ships in bottles, trophies of a bygone age. Harry signed his sister-in-law into the visitors' book and they allowed a uniformed porter to take their coats.

"The Trafalgar Room, sir?" It was the politest reminder that the presence of ladies was not tolerated in the members' private dining room.

"Please." Harry allowed the man to shepherd them into the guest lounge. More oak panelling, more maritime artefacts, few people and none of them other than members of staff awake.

Harry whispered to his sister-in-law, "Do you know, even the cockroaches in the kitchen have to wear a jacket and tie?"

A trace of a smile eased the strain on Maggie's face as they helped themselves from the salad bar. For a couple of minutes they picked at their food in silence before she put down her knife and fork and said in a voice that quavered slightly, "They asked me to identify the body. I had only been back in the house a few minutes when you called."

Harry glanced at her sharply. "Me too."

"God, why put both of us through it? Surely one identification is enough?"

Harry didn't answer directly, but the explanation was obvious. Skinner was covering his back. It wouldn't do to have to call for identification evidence at a murder trial from the man accused of the crime. He shivered. Merely for the thought to have crossed the policeman's mind was disturbing.

"What did they tell you?"

"Not much." She gave him a brief account of her visit from the police. No new facts, but they had questioned her closely about the men in Liz's life. Coghlan. Harry. And the latest lover.

"Who is he, Maggie?"

Spreading out her arms, she said, "I honestly have no idea."

"She must have told you something about him."

"Less than you might imagine. Don't forget, we'd gone our separate ways."

True enough. Maggie had followed an orthodox path. Secretarial college as a prelude to five years working for a firm of accountants. Marriage to the boss six months before he became a partner and could point to his name on the notepaper. Two kids and a plush detached house overlooking the sea. An upwardly mobile existence with money no object. It lacked the glamour for which Liz yearned, but he found himself wondering whether all her scathing comments about Derek Edge and her sister's dinner party lifestyle might in truth have been a cover for the envy that she felt.

"Didn't she confide in you at all?"

Maggie shook her head. "Not where men were concerned. She was a tease, Harry, you know that better than anyone. She loved to hint and tantalise. Even as a kid sister, she always made a parade of keeping secrets. Anything to be a touch out of the ordinary or to convey an aura of mystery. She would have you believing her latest feller was a member of the aristocracy, but he'd always turn out to be an office boy with the gift of the gab." She laid down her knife and fork. "Poor Liz. She thought she knew everything there was to know about men, when all the time she didn't have a clue. You were the only worthwhile one of the lot. She had the sense to catch you and then she threw it away. Crazy."

"So what did she say about her latest conquest?"

"He was rich and handsome, but of course. Then, so were you at one time of day - you might not have been aware. The money that you were going to make out of the law game . . . there was no end to it. You should have been Lord Chief Justice by now. Anyway, I asked if he was married and she said yes. She anticipated my disapproval. I think she liked to try to provoke me."

"His name?"

"She never told me. We only spoke about him once and that conversation didn't last long. I couldn't hide what I thought about it."

"When was this?"

"A couple of months ago, possibly longer."

He was surprised. "Surely you've seen her since then?"

"No. Not even at Christmas." She bowed her head. "The fact is, Liz and I have drifted miles apart since the two of you split up. I told her she was a fool and she didn't care for that, reckoned I was jealous. The sun shone out of Mick Coghlan then. She worked him out eventually. Too late, as usual."

"Did he beat her?"

"She wouldn't have admitted it to me if he had. And, as I say, we saw less of each other. Of course, she used to mock Derek, as you know. After she left you, there was no reason for me to put up with that. We only met Mick Coghlan once and that was plenty for both Derek and me."

Harry found that easy to understand. Strait-laced Derek Edge's only acquaintance with crime would be on the fringe of his clients' insider trading and elaborate tax dodges. For him to small-talk with Mick Coghlan would be like an archbishop's wife asking a call girl round for tea.

"So Liz and I just met for a cuppa once in a while. Our lives ran on different tracks. I didn't see any future in her being some kind of gangster's moll and I dare say my prattling on about the kids bored her to tears." Her face creased in recollection of lost opportunities. "And now there won't be another chance to put things right between us."

Harry waved to a waiter for coffee. "Did she seem frightened when you saw her last?"

Far from it. She kept saying how hard it was to be separated from the man you loved. I gave her a piece of my mind, told her this time she'd better make sure it was for keeps. Naturally, she made a few snide remarks about Derek. Poor man, he can't help being an accountant."

The coffee arrived. As they sipped from delicate china cups, Harry studied his sister-in-law. He had always been fond of Maggie. No fads or fantasies for her. Liz had poked fun at the Edges' well-dusted home and their immaculate square of garden. Boring, boring, boring. But although Maggie could never equal Liz for looks or style, she had the gift of knowing her limitations. She had worked out exactly what she wanted from life and seemed to have acquired it. And yet - there was an indefinable difference in her from the Maggie that he remembered. A streak of ruthlessness, perhaps? Or possibly he'd expected her to seem a little more devastated by Liz's death. But he reminded himself that he was trying not to let shock and despair take over. Maybe Maggie was simply doing the same.

They talked for a few more minutes, going back over their shared past. The Guy Fawkes party on the anniversary of his first meeting with Liz when the bonfire had been too wet to light. A cousin's wedding when Liz had drunk too much and proposed to the bridegroom. The stripping-nun kissagram she had ordered for Derek's thirtieth birthday celebrations in the discreet restaurant where he used to dine his clients.

After he had signed a chit in lieu of a bill - the Traders' was not the sort of sordid place where members' money changed hands in the sight of guests - Maggie said, "Why did you ask if she was frightened?"

He gave her a brief resume of Liz's late night visit to his flat. When he had finished, there was a long pause before Maggie took a deep breath and said, "You don't think - there's anything suspicious about her death?"

Harry winced and she said quickly, "Sorry, that was stupid of me. But I meant, do you believe it was any more than a street attack that went horribly wrong?"

"It's possible. The police are being cagey but they certainly haven't handled it as though they're satisfied with the simple explanation."

Shaking her head, Maggie said, "You can't think that Mick . . ."

"I don't know what to think. But there's a great deal I want to find out."

She placed her small, white hand on his. The fingers were cool, the pressure firmer then when they had greeted each other. "Keep out of it, Harry. This is a dreadful day, but for all her faults, I won't accept that anyone would wish to do Liz harm. It's sure to have been an ordinary street crime. If killing a person can ever be ordinary. And if it wasn't . . . "

"Yes?"

"Then you shouldn't meddle." She closed her eyes for a moment. When she spoke again there was a harsh urgency in her tone. "Let the police sort it out. That's their job. Don't get involved."

He might have said: You don't understand, I was her husband, I am already involved. But instead he remained quiet, wondering why Maggie, too, now appeared to be frightened.

Chapter Eight

Instead of returning to the office, Harry wandered about the city for an hour, struggling against the dull ache in his head and the weakness of his limbs in a vain effort to marshall his thoughts. He yearned to act, to take some positive step towards achieving vengeance for Liz's death. It wasn't enough to wait for the police investigation to take its course. Yet his sluggish brain refused to tell him what to do.

His shoes slid on pavements greasy after another fall of rain and when he looked around he saw Liverpool with a stranger's eyes. Streets littered with discarded till receipts, rotten apple cores and polystyrene hamburger cartons. Illicit dealers flogging dustbin bags and cheap brooches from upturned crates. Teenage kids with green hair loafing at corners and men in leather jackets trying to sell socialist propaganda. Today everyone had a face as grey as the sky. Vandals had ripped up a row of saplings planted under the shadow of St. George's Hall and sprayed shop walls with slogans about football, sex and anarchy. Normally he took the shoddiness of it all for granted, but this afternoon the sight of the place hurt him as much as would a scar across the face of a friend.

Harry quickened his pace as he approached each newspaper stand; the early evening editions were already on sale. Hoarse relish filled the vendors' voices as they shouted their reminders that Liz was dead.

"Murder of City Girl!"

Harry flinched the first time he heard the cry, but soon it was commonplace, as much a part of the background as the smell of onions from the hot dog sellers' carts and the intermittent screeching of the buses' brakes.

"Murder of City Girl! Murder of City Girl!"

People were buying the papers; he could see one or two of them devouring Ken Cafferty's prose. Liz had always wanted to be the centre of attention and in death her wish had come true. He remembered her once quoting Andy Warhol's dictum that everyone should be famous for fifteen minutes and wondering aloud when her moment would come. Real life was never good enough for her; television and movies, the admen's images of a better life just over the rainbow, had seen to that. She would have revelled in her name being on everyone's lips. He could picture her grinning and with a careless toss of the black hair, saving only half in jest, "Maybe this makes it all worthwhile."

In the end he bought a copy himself and took it back to the office. Slumped in his chair, he could scarcely believe that he was reading about his wife. The newspaper told him nothing he didn't already know. The photo of Liz must have been taken years ago; probably some journalist had prised it out of Maggie. Liz had been looking straight at the camera, wearing the practised smile she had learned in her abbreviated modelling career. On the facing page was a smaller, smudged file photo of himself. It dated back to a much-publicised case when he had defended an enterprising Evertonian who earned a crust impersonating people summoned for jury service, but reluctant to perform their civic duty. Harry gazed at the rag for a minute or so, then threw it into the wastepaper bin.

Sighing, he contemplated the beer belly that bulged unmistakably beneath his shirt. A few years ago he had run in the Liverpool Marathon with the minimum of training; these days he used the lift in the Empire Dock rather than climbing the stairs. Cigarettes and booze were partly to blame, but so was the sense of futility that had dogged him since the marriage breakdown.

Thinking about keep-fit reminded him of gym-owning Michael Coghlan. There was no escaping the man; he muscled into any memory of Liz. Realistically, was it conceivable that Coghlan murdered her? The fingernails of Harry's right hand dug into his left palm as he was seized by the impulse to find Coghlan and beat the truth out of him.

Of course, the logical thing was to go home and wait for the police to act, but he no longer cared about the logical thing. On the calendar, today's saw was *There are situations in life when it is wisdom not to be too wise.* For once the message rang true. He pushed the remaining files to one side, said goodbye to Lucy and left.

Brunner Street was five minutes distant by car. He parked across the road from a Chinese moneylender's and walked down to the old brush factory that had been converted into Coghlan's Fitness Centre. A gaudy yellow signboard nailed across the building's soot-blackened exterior promised high quality facilities and a family atmosphere. Harry walked in past a ground-floor display of jogging gear and sweatshirts and a gum-chewing assistant who was chatting up some girl on the telephone. The place was quiet. Too far from the city centre to appeal to health-conscious businessmen who fancied a lunch hour work-out, thought Harry, and too close to Toxteth to make an up-market image credible. He went through a door marked members only. It led to a flight of steep stairs which he took two at a time out of some vague gesture of solidarity with the keep-fit clan, but by the time he reached the top he was puffing for breath.

Upstairs a red-haired woman sat at a small table reading the fashion page of a glossy magazine. She wore a tight tee shirt emblazoned with the legend: *My boss is a comedian - the wages he pays are a joke,* and an expression as bored as the voice in which she asked for his membership card.

"I'm looking for Mick Coghlan."

His eyes roamed around the gym. No evidence here of the family appeal of Coghlan's, just a handful of squashy-nosed men in singlets and boxer shorts working out on the punch bags and dumb-bells or pressing their hairy, hard-muscled bodies up and down with practised ease on the green mats that covered half the pine block floor. Grunts and curses punctuated the sweaty silence. On the far side of the room, a burly and balding man in a faded tracksuit stood, arms folded, watching the activity. A navy blue towel was slung over his shoulder. He caught sight of Harry and stared at him in a menacing, sleepy-eyed way, as if he fancied himself a Liverpudlian Robert Mitchum.

The woman said, "Mr. Coghlan isn't here." Her eyes narrowed. "Why do you want him, anyway?"

"I need to talk to him urgently."

"Arthur." She called to the burly man, who strode towards them. "What's the problem, Paula?"

"This feller wants to see Mick. Reckons it's urgent."

Arthur scowled at Harry. It was like sustaining the visual equivalent of grievous bodily harm.

"So who are you?"

"My name's Devlin. Harry Devlin."

The man looked puzzled for a moment, as if the name rang some far-off bell, then his brow cleared and he picked up a copy of the evening paper from the table, turning to the story about Liz's murder.

"Harry Devlin, eh? Well, pal, Mr. Coghlan isn't here and I don't think he'd want to talk to you if he was."

"Is he back at the house?"

"You deaf or summat? I said, he wouldn't want to see you. Now scram before my patience breaks."

Harry began, "Whatever you say, I'll be sure to . . ." But he got no further because the man laid a couple of shovel-like hands on his shoulders, spun him around and frog-marched him towards the door.

"Arthur," said the red-head in a warning tone.

"No problem," came the reply. "Simply seeing Mr. Devlin out." He released his grip and bent down to hiss in Harry's ear. "My

manners aren't always so good. Now fuck off and don't come back."
One push sent Harry tumbling down the first few steps and had
him clawing at the rail to regain his balance.

Downstairs the youth was still busy on the phone. Harry left
Coghlan's Fitness Centre without regret but with no sense that
it had been a wasted visit, either. He had the illusion of having
done something positive and he'd seldom experienced that kind of
feeling recently. The next move was to find out whether Coghlan
had yet arrived home.

Liz had phoned him a couple of times after going to live with
Coghlan, asking him to send on a few of the things she had left
behind on the day she moved. Harry remembered that her new
address had been in Woolton; he stopped off at a post office on the
way to check the details in the phone book. It was five o'clock and
darkness had fallen. He drove throughout the waste land of the
inner city towards the more affluent suburbs, trying to work out
what he would say if Coghlan was there. In truth, he had no real
idea of how he would handle things but that, perversely, was part
of the challenge.

Coghlan's place was a modern detached in spacious grounds,
worthy of a successful executive or a villain too smart for the police
to catch. More than likely there was a swimming pool at the rear.
That alone would have been enough to captivate Liz - she loved the
water and used to say that as a kid she'd had a recurrent dream of
being a mermaid. Harry pulled up outside, walked to the door and
pressed the bell.

Behind him, someone boomed, "Harry Devlin - what the hell
are you doing?"

The unexpected familiarity of the voice was bewildering. Harry
whirled round and snapped, "Who's there?"

"You shouldn't be here, you daft sod." A man with a chest as
broad as a coal barge emerged from the gloom. The gravel rasped
beneath his feet; there was nothing subtle about his heavy tread.

71

For all his anonymous plain clothes, the man would never be mistaken for anything but a policeman.

"Dave."

Detective Constable David Moulden nodded. "Long time no see."

"Why are you . . . ?"

"I asked first. This is the last place I thought I'd run into you, Harry."

"Last place I would have intended to come if . . ."

With a gentleness surprising in a big clumsy man, Moulden interrupted again to say, "Sorry about your missus, Harry."

Harry looked at the detective. They hadn't met since one night the previous summer when a client of Harry's had taken it into his head to crash a stolen taxi cab into a police car. "Am I right in assuming Coghlan hasn't turned up yet?"

"Correct."

"Significant, don't you think?"

"You know me, Harry, I'm not paid to think." The good-humoured expression was as effective a mask as any.

"Any idea where the man is?"

"Your guess is as good as mine. All I know is that we'd like to talk with him when he does show up. Result is, two of us have been sent to keep an eye on this place. My mate's in the car down the road. But you've no business here, you're well aware of that."

Harry said grimly, "I'd dearly love to speak to Coghlan myself."

"Forget it. This is a murder inquiry, Harry, not some piddling burglary. You're personally involved. Do yourself a favour and keep out of it."

Harry fished for more information, but landed nothing. Moulden might not have been told much about the case by his superior officers and in any event was too good a policeman to let anything slip.

On his way back to the city centre, Harry asked himself what the journey had achieved. Coghlan's continuing absence was hard to understand. Had he done a flit? The first signs were that Skinner was right in implying that Liz's death had not been a straightforward case of a mugging or rape that had gone murderously wrong. More than ever, Harry wanted to find out for himself exactly what had happened to her. But how could he do that?

Tonight of all nights he couldn't go to the Dock Brief. Too many people who knew him frequented the place and he wasn't in the mood for repeated condolences. Instead he chose the Lear, a free house in Lime Street which took its name not from the Shakespearean king but from the Victorian rhymester who under Lord Derby's patronage had written many of his poems over at Knowsley Hall. Pictures of luminous-nosed Dongs and toeless Pobbles decorated the walls, strange companions for the seamen and tarts who packed the bar.

Harry sat at a table by himself for hours, drinking slowly and turning the day's dreadful news over and over in his mind. Quite apart from the traumatic news of Liz's death itself, the way in which Jim, and especially Maggie, had reacted to the crime was somehow unsettling. And where was Coghlan? Was the nagging thought that the man might have murdered Liz prompted by logic, loathing or merely his own reluctance to accept that she might have met her end at the hands of a teenager doped out of his senses by smack?

In the corner of the snug, a couple of prostitutes were conducting a drunken dispute about a customer beneath a framed print which depicted the Owl and the Pussycat in their beautiful pea-green boat. And as the evening wore on and alcohol, fatigue and consciousness of what he had lost fuzzed his mind, the murder of Liz began to seem more ludicrous by far than a simple piece of nonsense verse.

Chapter Nine

At eight the next morning, the alarm's buzz woke him. The coldness of the day made him shiver; his restlessness during the night had thrown the duvet onto the floor. Already the memory of staggering home from the Lear was as hazy as a scene observed through a smeared windowpane. He had an idea that he'd taken the phone off the hook and ignored a tapping at the door accompanied by a voice that sounded like Brenda Rixton's asking if he was all right.

Nothing could be seen when he pulled the bedroom curtains apart. Fog had rolled over the Mersey, covering the water with its grey quilt. No hint of human life anywhere outside; he might have been marooned on an urban island.

He was drinking black coffee when the doorbell rang. Brenda again? No: when he put his eye to the spyhole, the sad face of Chief Inspector Skinner gazed back at him. It was a gut-wrenching repeat of the start to the previous day and for a moment he thought that he must still be dreaming. When he opened the door, he saw Macbeth was there as well.

"Sorry to disturb you again, Mr. Devlin," said Skinner. There was a faint snuffle in his voice, as if he had picked up a February cold. "We have a number of additional questions for you, I'm afraid."

Harry stood aside and they walked into the lounge. His grudging offer of coffee was accepted and as he poured two more cups from the jug, he sensed they were appraising his words and movements, on the look-out for evasions and inconsistencies that might suggest he intended to tell them less than he knew. Macbeth didn't take a seat. Sleek and immaculate in a leather jacket and slacks, he prowled the room like a panther about to pounce.

Skinner said, "We'd appreciate it if you could take us through your movements again on the day that your wife was killed."

Harry repeated his account of the events of Thursday. Already it seemed a lifetime away. Neither policeman took notes. Skinner listened intently; his sergeant radiated cynicism.

"Is there anything you would wish to add to your statement?" asked the Chief Inspector. "Or change?"

Harry shook his head. "Why should I?"

Macbeth spoke at last. "Why did you call at Coghlan's house yesterday?" He glared at Harry, daring him to deny the visit.

"I wanted to talk to the man. Simple as that."

"Why?"

How to reply when there was no safe, sensible answer? "Liz left me to live with him. I've never met Mick Coghlan, but he's still one of the most important people in my life. When she was dead, I thought I should at least speak to him."

"Mourning together?" The sergeant shovelled on the sarcasm.

When Harry said nothing, Skinner asked, "How did you react when your marriage broke up?"

"I celebrated with champagne, what do you imagine?" Even as he spoke, Harry regretted being provoked into a bitter, childish response. No good would come of it. He had counselled clients a thousand times about keeping cool under interrogation or in the witness box. Easier said than done.

"You must have felt wild."

Why deny it? "Of course, but at least I had enough nous to realise there was no way I could change her mind for her. If she ever wished to come back, it had to be her decision, taken in her own time. She-"

"Yes?"

"She was a strong-willed woman, Chief Inspector. Threats or pleading, neither would have achieved anything. They would only have made her more determined."

"Presumably you never lost hope that one day she'd tire of Coghlan and want to give the marriage another try?"

Harry grimaced. "In the back of my mind, yes, I suppose you're right. Liz and I shared some good moments. But she used to complain I spent too much time working for too little reward. She wanted something more from life."

"All the same, you never divorced. Exactly why not?"

"I had no urge to and Liz never asked for it. Neither of us bothered with the recriminations that make lawyers rich." He pondered for a moment and then said, "Some lawyers, at any rate. I put her in touch with a solicitor from Maher and Malcolm and we sorted things out as painlessly as possible. The money side was simple. We sold the house and split the lot down the middle. She wasn't greedy. She was confident Coghlan could keep her in the style to which she wanted to grow accustomed."

Macbeth snapped, "And what about Wednesday night?"

"What about it?" Despite himself, Harry could feel the sergeant's hostility beginning to get under his skin.

Stolidly, Skinner said, "You must have been aggrieved when your wife turned up, as you say, out of the blue. Let's face it, she was treating this place as a hotel, somewhere she could rest her head between lovers, isn't that so?" When Harry failed to answer, he continued, "Frankly, Mr. Devlin, I wouldn't have blamed you if you'd been furious with her. Only natural in the circumstances."

"Believe it or not, I was glad to see her again."

Macbeth moved forward, his lean body tense. "Did you sleep with her on Wednesday night?"

"I told you. She slept in the bedroom, I had the couch."

"Are you absolutely sure about that, sir?" Skinner conveyed disbelief without sacrificing a scrap of politeness.

"I'm hardly likely to have forgotten."

"You see," Skinner persisted. "Mrs. Devlin was obviously an attractive woman. Charming, vivacious. Everyone we've spoken to has agreed about that. And she was your wife, sir, come home after two years with another man."

"We didn't sleep together, Chief Inspector. I wish we had."

"You told us last time," said Macbeth, "that you hadn't seen her throughout that two-year period. Do you wish to change that statement?"

"No."

"Then it isn't true that you'd been meeting your wife regularly for some time?"

"Totally untrue." Harry was startled. The trend of the interview was puzzling him and he looked from one detective to another in search of a clue to their line of reasoning. Their faces were trained to yield no secrets, but he was conscious of frustration not far below their surface assurance. They were uncertain of their ground, he could tell. Important pieces were missing from the picture that they were trying to build and so they were pursuing a speculative enquiry in the hope of stumbling across a fresh signpost to the truth. He was well acquainted with how they must feel after years of cross-examining resilient witnesses - themselves policemen, more often than not - who refused to break down but whom he suspected of holding the key that he sought. The tricks of their trade closely resembled his own: the haphazard questioning, the dodgem swerves from blandness to provocation.

Might as well steal the initiative. "So what progress have you made with the investigation, Chief Inspector? Any prospect of an arrest in the near future?"

"Not imminently, I'm afraid, sir. As you can gather, our enquiries are continuing. We have received some valuable information, it's fair to say."

"Such as?"

"Well, sir, you'll appreciate that we have to limit what we disclose at this stage, even to the husband of the deceased."

The deceased. The words struck him like a slap on the cheek, a reminder of the fact of Liz's death. He said, "Have you traced her lover yet?"

Macbeth snorted. Skinner said calmly, "I'm sorry to say that my sergeant isn't finding it easy to come to terms with the existence of your wife's new lover."

No need to feign bewilderment at that. "I don't understand."

"I'll spell it out for you, sir. We've interviewed a large number of people who were on good terms with your wife, including several of the friends and relations you told us about. So far, none of them can come up with a name for this new man in your wife's life."

"Nothing odd about that, it's typical Liz." How to explain her to men whom she had never met? "She would like to dramatise the situation, make a mystery where none existed." A thought occurred to him. "And she certainly told her sister a little about the man."

"Together with one or two others, that's perfectly true. But it is a mite surprising that she played her cards so close to her chest, wouldn't you agree? I gather that she was a lady who liked to - if I may say so - talk about herself."

"The man's married. She didn't want his wife to find out."

"Could be, sir." Skinner's eyelids drooped. "Then again, there seems to have been a widely held opinion that one day the two of you would get back together again. Mrs. Edge thought that, for instance."

"As I said, it was my hope too. Forlorn, as it proved."

"Yes, Mr. Devlin. All the same, I can believe she was unhappy with Michael Coghlan - she'd made a bad move there. I can accept that she was having an affair. Yet there's no hard evidence of any other relationship. Obviously, you will say that she covered her tracks, but at present the man most people think she really cared for was you."

"I wish they'd been right." Harry felt the urge well up inside him to find a cigarette, have a smoke to ease the tension. But he suddenly realised that it was important for him to resist temptation. "I've already made it clear to you that I'd have been glad to have her back. She could have left Coghlan any hour of the day or night as far as I was concerned."

"Yet, sir, is that correct? The man's known for being violent. Would she have had the nerve to kick him into touch?"

Harry said, "Liz didn't lack guts."

Macbeth intervened. "What about her attempt at suicide?"

"What are you . . . ?" Too late Harry realised that he didn't know how to reply. In his confusion he allowed the sentence to trail away. The detectives were watching him closely. Taking a deep breath, he said, "She never discussed it with me."

"Yet you were aware of it?" This was Skinner.

"Yes - that is, I saw her left wrist on Wednesday night. I didn't mention it then. I imagined - in her own good time . . ."

"The wounds were only superficial, I'm told. But they appear to have been inflicted recently. Could you explain why you failed to mention the matter in your statement?"

Helplessly, Harry shook his head. "No reason. It didn't cross my mind. Or seem important. Obviously I only gave you the gist of what happened the other night. Not a verbatim report."

Macbeth said, "So you say that your wife arrived unexpectedly on Wednesday night after two years of playing away from home. You noticed that she had tried to kill herself but didn't utter a word. And the next day she was murdered. Is that what you're asking us to accept?"

"I'm not asking you to accept anything," said Harry. To his dismay, he found that he was almost shouting. "I've simply explained what happened."

Skinner said, "But are you telling us everything you know?"

"As far as I can recall. You must remember, this isn't an ordinary experience." Feeling the need for a prop, for something to do with his hands, he again felt that pressing desire for the comfort of a cigarette. It occurred to him then that Liz would have been amused by the thought that she had, indirectly, caused him to practise such self-denial when all her attempts to persuade him to give up during her lifetime had failed. He relaxed, but only for a moment.

Skinner finally lobbed his grenade.

"So it would come as a complete surprise, would it, for you to learn that your wife was pregnant?"

Harry stared at the detective, unable to utter a word.

"Yes, Mr. Devlin, about eight weeks gone."

Hoarsely, Harry said, "I know nothing about that. Nothing at all."

Skinner's gloomy face wrinkled with disbelief as he said, "Can we take it, then, that you deny being the father?"

Chapter Ten

The moment the detectives had gone, Harry telephoned his sister-in-law. Maggie's voice was anxious. Gone was her customary assurance, the quiet pleasure at having planned life as a series of attainable targets - marriage, children, money - that had irritated Liz and, perhaps, made her jealous.

Cutting short the conversational preliminaries, he said, "The police have been round again. They tell me Liz was pregnant."

"What?"

He repeated himself. From Maggie's faltering response, he had little doubt that the news stunned her just as much as it had him.

"She didn't tell you, then?"

"No, no. I - can't believe it."

"Hard to imagine, I agree, Liz as a mother. It hasn't sunk in with me either, yet." Nor had it. Their own talks about having children seemed to belong to a long ago era when being young meant that there was plenty of time, no need to rush. Liz had said, "Let's live a little, first." Unless she had grown careless, her outlook must have changed. The reminder of how far he and his wife had grown apart in the two years of their separation was like a punch to the solar plexus.

Maggie asked, "Do they know who the father is?"

"Apparently not. They were enquiring whether I was responsible."

"But that's ridiculous!"

"So I told them. Whether they believed me or not is another matter."

"Could it . . . could it be Mick Coghlan?" Strangely, it seemed to Harry as though she were hoping that he would say yes.

"Maybe. I gather that he's still missing. The man will have a lot of explaining to do if he shows himself."

"You still think he killed her, don't you?" Her question was curious, tinged with uncertainty, but still less sceptical in tone than she had been the previous day. Again, it almost seemed as if she were willing herself to believe in Coghlan's guilt.

"Who else would want to do her harm?" he asked. When she did not reply, he continued, "Take it from me, Liz was genuinely afraid the other night. I should have realised."

"Stop blaming yourself, Harry. You couldn't have guessed it would end up like this." She said, with nervousness that he found difficult to fathom, "What about her new boyfriend?"

He grunted. "It seems you and I haven't been able to convince the coppers that he was anything other than a figment of the imagination. Or, possibly, that Liz and I had got back together again, but she was too scared to tell friend Coghlan."

"Oh God, Harry, what a mess." Even at the other end of the telephone, her dismay was plain. "The police seem to be flailing around in the dark."

"Simply doing their job. Not easy. There's something else. I blotted my copybook by failing to tell them. Forgot to mention it to you, as well."

He told her briefly about the marks on Liz's wrists. She snorted with scorn.

"Suicide? That I will not believe. She simply wasn't the type."

"A week ago I'd have said the same, but the more I think all this over, the less sure I become about everything."

"I'm sure, Harry." He could hear the passion bubbling in Maggie's voice. "She was my kid sister, remember. And it's out of the question. Liz was in love with life, there's no way she would want to kill herself."

"A cry for help, perhaps?" Even as he made the suggestion, Harry realised how unlikely it was.

"Who was she crying to? No, Harry, face up to it. There's something here we don't understand."

"I'm going to make it my business to understand, Maggie. I owe her that. The trouble is, neither of us was in her confidence. Any idea who might have been?"

A few seconds passed before Maggie said slowly, "I can think of a couple of names. Matt Barley, for one. Liz always cared for him. And Dame, of course. She was her oldest friend."

"Right. I didn't have an address to give the police where they could contact Dame. Is she still around? And if so, where?"

"God knows. Frankly, I shudder to think."

Harry decided not to pursue that one. He was fond of both Maggie and Dame, but the two women had never hit it off: the one a paid-up member of the bourgeoisie, the other as cheerfully down-market as a fish and chip supper. "Anyhow," he said pacifically. "I ought to get in touch with them."

"Like I said yesterday, you shouldn't interfere. Leave it to the police to sort the whole thing out." Again anxiety caused her voice to tremble a little. "They'll unravel it all if you give them time."

With a vehemence that took even him by surprise, he said. "But they didn't know Liz! Don't you see? If this isn't a commonplace street killing, then Liz was murdered because of who or what she was. I was her husband, I lived with her day and night. I can cut corners that the police painstakingly plod round. And what's more, I won't waste time and effort wondering if I'm the bastard who stuck a knife in her."

His sister-in-law sighed. "You always were an obstinate devil. I suppose nothing I can say will change your mind. But if you really cared for her, you would remember Liz as she was, not trample over her grave."

That stung him. Sharply, he said, "Sorry, Maggie. I simply can't sit back waiting for something to happen when out there is a man who has stabbed my wife."

83

After hanging up, Harry checked the number of the Freak Shop and dialled immediately. After what seemed like an age, Matt Barley answered.

"Matt, this is Harry."

He heard a sharp intake of breath at the other end of the line before the other man said, "Harry, what can I say? It's unbelievable. I feel so sick that Liz should have died like that. I keep expecting her to walk through the door, late for work as usual. I phoned yesterday evening, but there was no answer. Just meaning to say - well, you know. I remember how much she meant to you."

They talked for a minute before Harry said, "Can I come and see you, Matt? There are things about the murder that bother me. You saw her regularly, you may be able to help. I'm sure the police have grilled you, but would you mind?"

"Okay," said Matt. Did Harry detect a shade of reluctance there? "If you think it's necessary. That is - I'd be glad to see you, of course, but I'm not quite sure what you're getting at. Some maniac killed her. Isn't that the top and bottom of it?"

"Maybe. Maybe not. Can I come over now?"

"Well . . . it's difficult, Harry. I'm rushed off my feet. Short-staffed at the moment. Won't tomorrow do?"

Harry kept pressing but ultimately had to agree to call at the shop the following morning. As a throw-away line, he asked if Matt knew where Dame could be found these days.

"She chucked her job in at the casino," said Matt. "Liz did tell me what she was up to, but I can't remember off-hand. Something barmy, as I recall. Let me think it over, it'll probably come to mind before we meet."

As he was saying goodbye, Harry heard the doorbell again. It seemed to him that the sound would forever be associated with the arrival of horrific tidings. He went to the door slowly, aware of an involuntary tensing of the muscles in his neck, arms and legs. This time, though, the visitor was innocuous. Brenda Rixton's carefully made-up face smiled at him through the spyhole.

When he invited her in, she seemed for once to be tongue-tied, almost embarrassed, "I came to ask - how you were coping," she said, after a couple of false, stammering starts.

He shrugged and said, "All right, I suppose, in the circumstances."

"I wondered . . ." she began ". . . I mean, you must be feeling pretty low. Yet at a time like this, you really need to keep your strength up. So I thought you might like to share lunch next door."

"I couldn't possibly put you to all that trouble," he said hastily. "Besides, I'm going out for a long walk. Clear my head."

"No trouble," she said quickly. "If you're busy - perhaps dinner tonight?"

He was about to refuse again, but something in her expression made him have second thoughts. It was a look of yearning for company that he felt he could not ignore. So he simply said, "That's very kind of you. What sort of time?"

"Shall we say seven?" She beamed. "Good. I'll see you then."

After she had left, Harry threw on a coat and scarf and went out to the waterfront. Walking along the path towards Otterspool, he mulled over the endless questions surrounding Liz's death. Where was Coghlan and was he the father of the child that the murderer had also killed? Was there something odd about the attitude of people like Matt and even the policeman Macbeth, let alone Maggie and Jim? Or was he being misled by his own over-stretched imagination?

At least he ought to be capable of sorting out what had been going on in Liz's life during the past two years. Learning of the loss of her unborn child had, if that were possible, strengthened his resolve to discover the man who had committed the crime. A night's sleep had at least helped to bring matters into perspective. He still wanted to strike out, to take revenge. But more than that: making an effort to contribute towards the killer's detection would help exorcise the guilt he felt for having ignored Liz's fear of Michael Coghlan.

On the way back home, he passed families enjoying a Saturday afternoon stroll, kids gambolling around their parents' feet. Might Liz and he have ended up like that, if he had handled things differently? No, he couldn't deceive himself. Their relationship had been a helter-skelter ride, not a journey on a long-distance train.

In the entrance hall of the Empire Dock, a rosy-cheeked figure in a raincoat which had seen better days was chatting up the porter. With a journalist's sixth sense, Ken Cafferty swung round, his face aglow with anticipation.

"The very man!" '

With a casual wave to the porter, Cafferty walked across the foyer. "I have a tit-bit which may interest you. The police have found Mick Coghlan. He's down south, apparently, being questioned at length. They haven't charged him yet, but they haven't let him go, either. Interesting, yes?"

An overwhelming sense of relief swept over Harry. "How did you find that out?"

Cafferty tapped the side of his nose. "A good newspaperman never reveals his sources."

But it did not require Sherlockian powers of deduction to work out that Ken must have called in here on the off-chance, on his way from the police H.Q. at Canning Place across the road. Harry dodged a dozen questions and ignored a hint that an offer of coffee would be welcome. Glad as he was that Coghlan had been located, he knew days might pass now before a confession was dragged out of the man or before Skinner and his cohorts decided they had enough evidence to make the charge stick. If, he meditated with a defence lawyer's instinctive search for the loophole, any link between Coghlan and the crime had the strength to survive critical scrutiny. Ten to one there was an alibi in the background;

that would explain Coghlan's sudden departure down south. And an alibi from a crooked crony might not be easy to break.

Escaping eventually to his flat, Harry switched on the box and yet again watched the video of *Don't Look Now*. Roeg's lush portayal of Venice retained its power to hypnotise and the moment when the psychopathic dwarf strikes that final, fatal blow had lost none of its horror. As the credits rolled, he thought of Matt Barley, the only person of restricted growth - Harry understood that that was the phrase to use these days - he knew. The little man was devoted to Liz. He'd lived next door to the Wieczarek family years ago; the same age as Maggie, he had more than reciprocated the girls' affection for him. Harry had always enjoyed Mart's sometimes savage humour and his refusal to allow the mere lack of size to interfere with a Scouser's birthright of making a dodgy living, selling joke masks to kids and sex aids to middle-aged men.

He showered and changed and rang the bell next door. Brenda ushered him in, saying twice how glad she was that he had come. Her hair was pinned back elegantly and, for all his ignorance about women's clothes, he guessed that the low-cut taffeta dress had come from the place in her wardrobe reserved for special occasion wear. Her flat was identical to his in design, but she had transformed the small box with subtle wall-lighting and so much greenery that a visitor almost needed a machete to cut a way through the hall. Her living-room walls were hung with oriental tapestries and a couple of icons of the kind advertised in charity gift catalogues.

They ate by candlelight. Brenda produced a bottle of Portuguese wine to complement a boeuf bourgignon which bore no resemblance to the packet version, stuffed with monosodium glutamate, hydrolysed protein and artificial colouring, which Harry often slung in the oven for half an hour and ate without noticing. During the meal, she chatted about her job as a sales negotiator for a firm of estate agents, spicing anecdotes about unscrupulous sellers and pernickety buyers with a touch of satire that he had not previously suspected in her. When the plates had been cleared, they settled down in opposite armchairs.

"I feel better for that," he said.

"I'm glad," she said. "If you don't mind my saying so, for the last day or two you've looked like a man going through a living hell."

He didn't reply. The wine had relaxed him, but he wasn't yet ready to chat about Liz's death to inquisitive strangers.

"The police came to see me, enquiring about your wife. They seemed interested in your movements on Thursday night. I explained that I'd seen your wife and yourself at different stages of the evening. They wanted exact times so I did my best to be accurate."

She studied him carefully, as though trying to gauge his reaction.

"Routine, Brenda," he said firmly, "I don't think I'm a serious suspect."

"Oh good Lord, naturally! I mean, I hope you don't think I was suggesting you were." She tried to cover her confusion by changing the subject. "I read the reports in the local rag. You've had a hard time over the years, from what I can read between the lines. They described your wife as fun-loving, I saw. I imagine," she swallowed hard but continued, "imagine that means she must have led you quite a dance."

"You could say that."

She looked straight at him. "I understand how it feels, Harry. You see, my own husband . . ."

The story spilled out with no encouragement from him. Nothing out of the ordinary. She had been married for fifteen years to a Lothario who flitted from job to job and business to business. Finally, he had set up a driving school and inside six months he'd sped off with one of his pupils. Brenda said that until then she had always regarded divorced women as failures; possibly that was right and she had failed with Les.

"One in three," interrupted Harry. He'd finished the bottle whilst she had been talking. "A third of all marriages end up in the divorce court. Not counting all those where the couple soldier on against their better judgment, because of the kids or habit or both. You can't apportion blame."

"I'd be glad to think so. Sometimes late at night, though, when I sit here listening to the radio or squinting at the television, I can convince myself I'm the only woman in the world who's on her own."

Neither of them spoke for a while. Harry thought: Perhaps fear of loneliness is even worse than the thing itself. This woman's attractive enough, she could find someone if she put her mind to it.

Brenda stood up and yawned. "Forgive me. I'm tired and yet I suffer from sleepless nights. Doesn't add up, does it?"

He rose too. "Terrific meal, Brenda. Very kind. Suppose I ought to be making tracks now."

She moved towards him. Her perfume was just perceptible, a discreet fragrance, different from the exotic muck which Liz used to daub on herself. "Stay longer if you can. Don't feel you have to go on my account." She smiled, showing even white teeth. "It's good to have someone to talk to. Although I'm afraid I've done all of the talking."

"I've enjoyed it as well." He could feel her warm breath on his cheek. Stepping back, he said, "I must go. Thanks again."

At the door, she said, "Thank you for coming. We must do this more often. Cooking for two is much more fun than for one." She closed her eyes and inclined her face in his direction. But he didn't want to kiss her; it would have seemed a betrayal, although of whom or of what he wasn't sure.

"Goodnight," he said softly.

As he locked his front door and settled down inside, he thought about the mixed emotions on her face as she had turned away and for a moment he experienced an unexpected pang of regret that he had rejected her invitation to stay.

Chapter Eleven

Next morning he rang police headquarters and asked to be put through to Skinner, meeting the switchboard girl's prevarication with the persistence born of years in the legal profession. After a full five minutes' delay, the Chief Inspector came on to the line. He sounded full of cold.

"What can I do for you, Mr. Devlin?"

"Found Coghlan yet?" Better not let him know that Ken Cafferty had already broken the news.

"Mr. Coghlan is in London at present. He is assisting our colleagues in the Met, yes." Skinner sneezed. "Meanwhile, our enquiries are continuing."

"When are you going to charge him?"

With an obvious effort at patience, Skinner said, "As you are well aware, Mr. Devlin, there's a limit to what I can . . ."

"Christ, Chief Inspector, the man killed my wife! I want to know."

Skinner said bleakly, "I've warned you before about these wild allegations, Mr. Devlin. You're under stress, I appreciate that, but you know better than most about being innocent until proved guilty. People in your line of business make a few bob out of that old principle, don't they? Well, for your information, we have no specific reason to believe that Mr. Coghlan was concerned in your wife's death and it is highly likely he will be returning home in the course of the next few hours. A free man."

"But . . ."

"And that, I'm afraid, is all that I can say at this juncture. Now, if you'll excuse me, I have a great deal of work to do. Rest assured, I shall contact you when I have something to say."

Skinner rang off, leaving Harry sick with dismay. What story had Coghlan been weaving? Why hadn't he been brought back to the local force for interrogation? By now, the questions that had arisen in respect of Liz's murder should have been finding answers. Instead, they were multiplying. A thought sprang into his mind: in a case such as this, could there be any justification for taking the law into one's own hands, if the system proved powerless to ensnare the man concerned? Harry had seen too many culprits go free - had participated sometimes in ensuring that they went free - to have too much faith that Coghlan would eventually be brought to book. Uneasily, he forced himself to think of other things.

He spent a tedious hour trying to restore order to his flat. Pulling an old tie into the back of a drawer, he chanced upon the album in which he and Liz had kept their wedding photographs. Souvenirs to look back on in years to come, they had agreed at the time. But there hadn't been many years to come and Liz had not claimed the pictures when she had left to start another life. He flipped through the book and its collection of memories. At the altar, signing the register, in the doorway of the church With Jim, his best man, with Maggie and Derek and Matt too. That reminded him. Checking his watch, he found that it was time to go. He shoved the wedding album back in the drawer. Sometime he must have a clear-out. But not today.

Outside, the red bricks of the reclaimed dock warehouses basked in the brightness of a February sun. The city streets were quiet as he walked briskly to the Freak Shop, casting his mind back to his first encounter with the little man, a month or so before that wedding day. Mischievous Liz hadn't revealed in advance that Matt was a dwarf, having taken care merely to describe him as a long-time friend of the family. Characteristically, she had relished Harry's attempt to conceal his bewilderment when introductions were made. Matt Barley was perfectly proportioned, but only forty-five inches tall. He had a mop of fair hair and a vice-like handshake. There was no need to indulge in excessive tact about his height; Matt joked about it often - so often that Harry came to realise that for Matt, humour was a shield, used to help him compete on equal terms with a world of tall people.

Yet Matt had no need to feel inadequate. He had a sharp brain and a flair for making a fool out of anyone crass enough to equate a lack of size with a lack of nous. From his father, an equally diminutive sales manager in the motor trade, he had inherited an entrepreneurial zest that had enabled him to start a market stall flogging Beatles memorabilia of doubtful provenance before setting up the Freak Shop. There was more than a trace of self-mockery in the name he gave to the shop which he had transformed into a cross between a fancy dress hire business and a pornographer's discount store. Liz had enjoyed working there. It suited her unshockable style.

The shop was protected by steel shutters and conspicuous burglar alarms. Harry rang the bell and heard bolts being slammed back before Matt's head appeared round door.

"Come in."

The silent, unlit shop seemed as eerie as a waxworks in a Hammer horror movie. To one side was a counter covered with tricks, toys and masks which caricatured people in the public eye, along the other ran a rail from which were suspended clowns' suits, Elizabethan dress and a score more examples of the costumier's art. Matt led the way past a sign which said private - NO RIFF-RAFF, through a bamboo curtain and into a sparsely furnished back room. On a table in the corner was a tattered paperback of *Zen and the Art of Motorcycle Maintenance* together with an opened bottle of Lambrusco and a paper cup. In one corner was a battered old Rock-Ola jukebox that Matt had been tinkering with for as long as Harry could remember. The walls were adorned with a dozen posters showing Matt's hero, John Lennon, at different stages of his career from the Cavern Club days to the self-indulgence of the seventies.

Matt swept a pile of Swedish magazines off a rattan chair and waved Harry into it.

"Tea, coffee? Beer, wine? Tequila, Bloody Mary? Cannabis, cocaine?"

Harry grinned. "Coffee's fine."

As Matt bustled, they talked of days gone by. Friday night at the Dock Brief or the Drum, Saturday afternoons spent watching soccer at Anfield or Goodison, whilst Liz went round to see Maggie or Dame. When the coffee was made, Matt perched on another chair opposite Harry. His face was suddenly screwed up with pain.

"This can't be happening, you know, Harry. I can almost believe she's here with us in this room, checking her make-up in the mirror and complaining about our grubbier customers." He switched to the past tense. "She had a genius for making me laugh, squeezing me out of a bad mood. Like I told you when we met in the pub the other week she turned up out of the blue just before Christmas. I was glad to take her back. You know how it hurt me when she took that job with Yes."

Harry remembered. During their marriage, she'd met at a party the director of a fashion concept retailer and he'd offered her the chance to run a store in the Cavern Walks. She'd packed that in at the time she met Coghlan; he was apparently the sort of man who felt his masculinity threatened if the woman in his life had a full-time job.

"She was beginning to find the life of luxury a bore?"

"Suppose so. Liz never talked much about the creep she was living with and I seldom asked. I gathered that he didn't care for her coming back here, but she'd made up her mind and once that happened she was an irresistible force. Even where Mick Coghlan was concerned."

"Any idea why she didn't simply walk out?"

Matt gave him a pitying look. "You think I didn't suggest it? There was a day when she came in with a mark over her right eye.

He'd hit her, I knew, although she denied it. But she simply said she'd make any move in her own good time and I knew her better than to act like a nanny."

Harry said tightly, "So the bastard did beat her?"

"Don't get me wrong, I'm not suggesting Liz was lilywhite. Matter of fact, she said she'd thrown a lamp at the guy and cut him across the face. A stormy relationship, you might say."

Harry bit his lip. Never once had he laid a finger on Liz during their marriage, yet come to think of it, she had once taunted him with that, while hurling pots and pans around in the kitchen after a row over something of no importance. "You never lose your temper!" she had shouted, "That's no way to behave, bottling things up. You ought to let yourself go once in a while. Like other men. Like me."

Matt said, "Not as if she had no one to turn to. There was Dame. Maggie, possibly, though the two of them had drifted apart. Or even me." He bowed his head. "I offered to let her stay at my place, anytime she needed to escape. But she never took me up."

Harry wondered why she had not gone to Matt, rather than himself, on Wednesday night. He said, "She was involved with someone new."

The little man compressed his lips. "I tumbled to that. There were signs. She'd spend half the day having muttered conversations on the telephone, pop out for a few minutes and be gone for an hour. Her mind wasn't on the shop this time around, I soon found that out. Anyway, she told me a week ago that she was packing the job in. The last few days, she didn't even come in to work. I didn't make a fuss. She was too busy with her Prince Charming, I suppose."

"Who was he, Matt?"

"She didn't say. And I didn't ask. Like I said before, it was all a case of in her own good time. I was willing to lend an ear if she wanted to talk, but there was no point in trying to discuss anything before she was ready. She wouldn't take any notice of me."

"Did she strike you as frightened?"

Matt considered. "On edge, yes. Jumpy, at times. But frightened - I dunno. I suppose the truth I don't want to face is that I was no longer close enough to her to tell."

"Yet she came back to work here, that signifies something."

"Does it?" His tone became unexpectedly sombre. "Dunno. It was almost as if - she had some ulterior motive. The job seemed like a means to an end as far as Liz was concerned."

Harry said suddenly, "Did you know she was pregnant?"

The question seemed to catch Matt off balance. He paled and said hastily, "Yes, yes, the police told me. First I heard of it."

"So you don't know who the father was?"

Frowning, Matt replied, "No, of course not, how could I?"

"What else did the police have to say?"

Slowly, the little man said, "When I heard that she was dead, I thought it must be a sex crime. They happen every day - though never, you expect, to someone you know. Yet the police seemed too keen to dig up the details of her life, as if they imagined there might be some clue to the thing buried in her past. Not as though she was simply another crime statistic. They wanted the dope on you, for instance."

Harry felt his cheeks burning. "Yes?"

"And Coghlan, too, of course. How did she feel towards the two of you? Did any friends call on her here? Did she have any enemies?" For an instant, the old humorous twist turned up the corners of his mouth. "I wasn't much help, I'm afraid, but I did make it clear that you at least were kind to animals and good with small children. Poor but honest, at any rate in comparison to every other lawyer I've ever met." He paused. "They asked who was to blame for your breaking up."

"And?"

"Drop the worried look, I said she was an idiot. When they suggested you might have harboured a grudge, I said no. I'm sure you must have kept hoping she'd come back to you once she'd flushed Coghlan out of her system." He lowered his voice. "Believe it or not, I envied you. Despite the way she messed you around, at least you had the memories. There was a time when she cared for you."

"You too, Matt."

To his surprise, the little man responded furiously. "Are you kidding? I was a convenience to Liz, nothing more. Christ, I'm only a midget. Someone to pat on the head from time to time, that's all."

For a minute, Harry was silent. Matt had been a volatile character for as long as he had known him, but this fierceness was unexpected. A nervous reaction to the death of a friend whom he had known for most of his life, or did it signify something more? In the end Harry collected the coffee jug and poured them both a second cup. After taking a sip of the muddy brown liquid, he said, "I think Liz was murdered by Mick Coghlan."

"What makes you say that?"

Harry explained about Liz's nocturnal visit and the fear that she had described. The anger rose within him as he recounted his conversation with Skinner a couple of hours earlier. "I swear to you, Matt, the man who killed her isn't going to get away with it."

Matt stared at him. "What can you do?"

"Leave that to me. At present, I'm trying to put the piece together. That was one of the reasons why I wanted to talk to you and Dame."

"That reminds me." Matt brightened a little. "A mutual friend called in yesterday, after we spoke. A girl who knew Dame from her time at the Playhouse. Lovely brunette, she wanted a Whore of Babylon's outfit for this party up at the University. Anyway, she told me that Dame's currently starring in the lunchtime show at

Franco's in Rumford Place. If you move yourself, you might catch her now."

"What sort of show?"

"That I leave to your fertile imagination. But you know Dame."

"On a Sunday?"

"So she said."

Harry shook his head. "What's the world coming to?"

The two of them walked towards the front door, exchanging commonplace conversation before Harry said, "You know, I came round here on Thursday, when I was trying to make contact with Liz. The place was shut up in the afternoon. It's not an early closing day for you, is it?"

The little man seemed discomfited. "No, not Thursday. I was out." He looked at the ground and said again, "Just out."

Chapter Twelve

Both women were smeared with mud from head to toe. They wore skimpy bikinis, one red, one blue, and enough bare flesh was visible to delight the watching men. The taller and heavier of the two girls had her opponent in an arm-lock and was threatening to dip her blonde head in the muddy bottom of the lime green plastic swimming pool that the management of Franco's had installed over the dance floor.

Cradling his pint in his arm, Harry pushed his way towards the front of the crowd. Had the city council's entertainments sub-committee really licensed this performance for the Sabbath? Most likely Franco's were just taking a chance with the law and raking in the profits. As he moved forward, a roar of approval greeted the emergence of the smaller girl's pert, pink-tipped breasts from her bikini top as her assailant tightened her grip.

Harry fixed his gaze on Dame, who now had the blonde in a parody of a half-nelson, to the accompaniment of boos worthy of a televised wrestling contest. Looking up for a moment, she spotted Harry and winked saucily at him before being diverted as the other girl managed to wriggle free. In the ensuing mêlèe, the blonde contrived to unfasten and then detach Dame's bra, which she waved in triumph above her head. Dame grabbed it back from her, but with a magnificent gesture threw it at another goggling teenager, to the noisy acclamation of his fellow lookers-on.

"Will you look at that," breathed a bespectacled youth standing by Harry's side. His glasses were in danger of steaming up. The sight of Dame's pendulous bosom, milky white but rapidly caking over with mud, became too much for him and he lapsed into silence.

The blonde beckoned at the boy who had caught the bra-trophy and a surge from behind pitched him headlong into the plastic pool. Alcohol had endowed him with bravado and, staggering to his feet,

99

he bowed to his friends before turning with a start when Dame flopped towards him and laid a hand on his shoulder. Diverted, he was no match for the other girl's nimble attentions to his belt and zip and within seconds his trousers were down at his ankles. As Dame started to unbutton his shirt, everyone bellowed with beery amusement. Soon enough, though, they had cause to groan as the man in the dapper get-up of a fight referee arrived from backstage to stop the bout and declare a dead heat. The two girls bowed to rapturous applause and exited arm in arm. Gathering his clothes and grinning inanely, the audience participant stumbled back to be swallowed up in the crowd.

The entertainment over, Harry and the others drifted in the direction of the bar. His second pint was nearly at an end when he heard a couple of ribald comments from the other men standing at the counter at the same time as a long arm snaked around his waist. At the same time, a husky voice in his ear said, "Mine's a Bacardi and Coke, in case you've forgotten, and take no notice of this ignorant mob, I only have eyes for you."

As he turned his head, Dame's cheek pressed against his. He found her hand and, clasping it, ordered drinks for them both. Moving back, he surveyed her virginal white blouse and black leather skirt, newly combed shoulder-length hair and wicked smile.

"I hardly recognised you with your clothes on."

"That's what all my men friends say," she said. "Cheers."

He took a draught from his replenished pint pot and said, "Congratulations. An outstanding display in every way."

She laughed. "I ought to try harder with the diet, be honest. Anyway, Franco's made up. It brings the punters flocking in on what would otherwise be a dead day. Specially you repressed office types. The fellers tell their old ladies they're just popping out to the local for a quiet Sunday jar and then they leg it down here for a bit of harmless fun."

"Almost a public service."

100

"You're not wrong." She emptied her glass. "Thirsty work, though."

As he tried to catch up with the barmaid, he said, "Been here long?"

"A fortnight. The money's good, but I'm just filling in. I've been promised an audition for the new Bleasdale at the Everyman. Besides, it's only a question of time before the scuffers catch up with us here. At present, we get one or two off-duty constables who keep their mouths shut, but word'll get round. I need to look to the future."

Ever since he had first met her, Dame had been on the verge of a breakthrough in her acting career. A few years back, she had managed a bit part in a TV soap, only to be wiped out in a hotel fire on the whim of a scriptwriter under pressure to boost the ratings. Her appearances in regional rep had been confined to stripping off in unfunny farces. Otherwise she led a twilight existence, working mainly in pubs and clubs, transferring her affections from one unsatisfactory man to another, not allowing the knock-backs to diminish her faith that fame was just around the next corner.

The drinks arrived. She said, "Thanks, Harry," and then, more sombrely, "Don't feel you need to talk about Liz if it hurts too much."

"Matter of fact, Dame, I didn't simply come here for the pleasure of ogling at your boobs. Lovely as they are. I wanted to have a word with you about Liz. You were as close to her as any of us."

"I feel as though a part of me was killed that night." She uttered the phrase simply, without any false dramatics. She had grown up with Liz, lived in the next street to her, gone to school with her, shared early boyfriends with her. After a moment a harder note entered her voice as she said, "Where's that shit Coghlan? There's a story going round that he's done a runner."

After Harry had told her of his most recent conversation with Skinner, he said, "Why don't we go somewhere quiet to talk?"

"Suits me." An impish grin spread over her face. "I know a place where we won't be bothered."

"Lead me there."

"You'll have to put up with a few more topless ladies though."

He studied her own conspicuous curves and in the same bantering tone said, "I'm intrigued. Let's go."

As they left Franco's, Dame entwined her arm in his. "The Olivier it ain't," she said, "but at least it pays the rent."

They chatted about inconsequential things as she led him through the labyrinth of city streets. Eighteen months or more had passed since their last meeting and she filled in the gaps with a panache that had him laughing every dozen yards. She told him of her ill-starred spell as a stand-up comic in Manchester cabaret and of how her last live-in lover, supposedly a company director with a fortune tied up in the futures trade, had done a flit with five hundred pounds from her building society account. The cash had supposedly been borrowed to tide him over a week-end until, he'd said, a hiccup with his bank due to a computer break-down had been sorted out. As ever she took her disappointments philosophically; hers was a life of easy-come, easy-go.

When they reached the city end of Dale Street, he asked "Where are you taking me?"

She squeezed his hand. "Losing your bottle? Trust me. I'll make you believe I'm a highbrow yet."

"Dame," he said. "I'd willingly believe anything of you."

Giggling, she said, "And you'd be right."

"So what's our destination?"

"You're looking at it." She stretched out a long arm and pointed up the incline that lay before them towards the stately buildings of William Brown Street, the Iron Duke's monument and the Corinthian bulk of St. George's Hall. "The art gallery," she explained, as though to a slow-witted infant. "Remember what I said about the bare ladies? They're two a penny in there."

Following her past the two statues which guarded the approach to the Walker Gallery; Harry was unable to resist a grin, "Do you come here often?"

"All the time," she said with a wave of the arm. She treated a young man at the bookstall to a seductive pout; he had been admiring her figure and now responded with a blush. "Take that disbelieving look off your face, Harry Devlin. I went to art college once, remember?"

He had forgotten that and assumed a contrite expression. She nodded vigorously and said, "I may only be a humble mud wrestler, but this place fascinates me. It has a magic I never found in any other gallery. Don't ask why, I could never explain."

Harry's last visit here pre-dated his marriage. He let Dame guide him, showing off her knowledge and occasionally revealing a love for a particular painting that had a passion as real as the eroticism of the show at Franco's had been fake. As he listened to her expound upon the merits of Augustus John, he reflected that, like Liz, Dame had never lost her capacity to surprise.

They stopped in front of *And When Did You Last See Your Father?* Harry stared at the little boy and said to Dame, "Corny, I know, but after undergoing a grilling from the police on Friday and yesterday, I realise how the kid must have felt."

"They gave you a tough time?"

"Only doing their job. Have they seen you yet?"

She shook her head. "I'm not easily tracked down."

"Had you seen much of Liz lately?"

"We met now and then, not as often as I'd have liked. Different from the old days, eh?"

"How was she?"

A wan smile. "Always the same. Something good, someone good, was invariably around the corner. Like me, except I don't really believe all the rubbish I talk."

Harry pressed her for details. Dame didn't try to disguise the depth of Liz's infatuation with Coghlan; but eventually it had become clear even to her that the man would never change his ways. "Women are strange. You must have noticed, love. Men tread on us, drain us of every last penny and ounce of self-respect and still we beg for more. No sooner did Liz suss Mick out than she was spending nights on the town, hunting for someone new. That's how she got involved with this other guy."

"Did she talk much about him?"

"Hints and innuendoes mostly. You know how Liz liked to weave a web of mystery around her life. Being special, that's what appealed to her. Reality was second best. So I wasn't surprised when she told me he was rich and handsome and blessed with a neurotic bitch of a wife who didn't understand him. Tony, his name was. For all I know, he was a fat forty year old called Percival who was on the dole with half a dozen kids but could shoot a smooth line of chat."

"She was pregnant, Dame."

Her face suddenly grim, she nodded. "She told me about ten days ago, the last time I saw her alive. Thrilled to bits, she was, and so was I for her. Careless to get lumbered, but it may have been deliberate. I wouldn't be surprised. Help her bloke make up his mind to ditch the old lady . . . it's the oldest trick in the book."

"Coghlan wasn't the father?"

"Liz said not. I got the feeling that he had his hands full with other women and that was beginning to suit her fine. No, the new boyfriend was the culprit, or so she led me to believe. But you know what Liz was like. A lovely lady, but she couldn't always tell the difference between her dreams and real life."

"That's a nice way of putting it," said Harry wryly.

"Don't you speak ill of her," she said fiercely. "Liz had her faults, we all knew that, but she was still my best friend. We had so many laughs together over the years. Even when she poked fun at someone, like that stuffy brother-in-law of hers, she never meant to be cruel. And she never once let me down."

"Think yourself lucky." Harry spoke lightly enough, but Dame still turned on him, flushed and angry.

"It's the truth." She lowered her voice, spoke with urgency. "Look, I've never told anyone this before. When I was fourteen, I was careless too. Understand? Things were difficult at home. My boyfriend was a soldier, I never saw him again. I had to have an abortion. Liz covered for me with my mum and dad, no one even guessed what had happened. And more than that - she never told anyone else. Not even you, am I right?"

Harry nodded, abashed.

"She kept my secret when it mattered," said Dame softly. "I'll never forget that. Never."

They were in the Impressionists Room now. Harry halted in front of a painting of two men, bending over a woman's prostrate body. A sordid killing in a back street. *The Murder* by Paul Cezanne. The darkness of the artist's vision mesmerised him and he did not move until Dame led him gently by the hand towards the sweep of stairs.

"Tea," she said firmly.

When they were installed at a table, he rested his elbows on the formica and asked bluntly, "Did Liz tell you why she slit her wrists?"

Dame spilled some of her tea into the saucer. "What do you mean?"

Harry explained. There was no doubting the genuineness of her shocked reaction and he placed his hand over hers by way of comfort. "If she was so glad to be having the baby, I can only assume that she cut herself in a moment of desperation when she thought Coghlan wanted her dead. Or maybe this happened a while ago. I simply don't know. And yet . . ."

"And yet that doesn't sound like Liz? I agree, but how else can you account for it?"

He shook his head. "I dunno. All I'm sure about is that she was telling the truth when she confided her fears in me and that I should have listened."

"You shouldn't reproach yourself."

"Don't you start," he said bitterly. "You above anyone else know what Liz meant to me. And you can't imagine that I'll let it rest there. No, Coghlan was responsible, must have been, there's no other candidate. I owe it to her to make sure he doesn't get away with murdering her."

Dame leaned across the table. "Listen, speaking as one obstinate bugger who loved Liz to another, I wish you well. But don't forget, this isn't one of your courtroom games where you give the other guy hell then go off to the bar together afterwards, the best of friends. The only law Mick recognises belongs to the jungle. Watch out for man-traps."

"I'll take care."

"Good." Her strong fingers laced around his. "So how are you spending the rest of this cold Sunday? Out on the warpath or has the lunchtime entertainment sapped you so much that you need to recoup your strength?"

He pushed his cup to one side and said with a glimmer of a smile, "Late afternoon on a February Sunday in Liverpool? Not much more I can do till tomorrow morning, so I'm at a loose end. How about you?"

Dame laughed, a raucous sound coarsened by years of coping with crumpled dreams. "I'm all dressed up, with nowhere to go. This outfit cost the thick end of three hundred quid and that was in the January sales. But when I go back home tonight there'll just be one ring working on the gas hob, one bar of the electric fire glowing. I rent a flat in Aigburth the size of a broom cupboard. I'm not exactly desperate to rush back. Why don't we have dinner together? I won't insult you by offering to pay. How about it?"

"Dame, that's an offer no man could refuse."

She laughed so loudly that an old lady at the adjoining table turned round and stared. "Oh, Harry, if only that were true. If only that were true."

Chapter Thirteen

"My name is Fingall," said Harry into the handset of his office telephone. "Reuben Fingall."

The words rolled off his tongue as smoothly as if spoken by Ruby himself. The accuracy of the impersonation, the unexpectedly precise capture of that characteristic note of smugness, gave Harry a small surge of pleasure. In his schooldays he had amused himself and others with his amateur mimicry. Harold Wilson and Tony Hancock had been favourite targets, but he hadn't been sure that he had retained the knack sufficiently to deceive Paula from the gym at the other end of the line.

"I'm afraid Mick isn't expected in today, Mr. Fingall," she said in a cloying tone evidently reserved for her employer's close friends and professional advisers.

Harry already knew that from Ken Cafferty. This morning Ken had told him that Coghlan had been released by the Metropolitan Police uncharged and was supposed to have returned to Liverpool, although he could be found neither at the Woolton house nor at the gym. Meanwhile, Fingall was in the Crown Court attending on another case and remaining unusually tight-lipped about the whole affair, having declined to reveal his client's whereabouts. Skinner was saying nothing either and Ken had given up the hunt, having decided to wait for his quarry to emerge in the fullness of time. Harry wasn't so patient.

With the audible click of the tongue that conveyed Reuben's disapproval of any response that didn't suit, Harry said firmly, "I must contact him today, Paula - it is Paula, isn't it? You will appreciate that my call concerns urgent legal business. Michael would be most anxious that I speak to him."

"Hold on," said the woman, "I'll check with Arthur." Harry waited. After a single early night, he felt fitter and more relaxed, ready to continue his quest for Coghlan. He had taken Dame to a bistro in Penny Lane, where they had relaxed and talked for three hours about good times shared in the past. After driving her home, he had declined her invitation of coffee, even when she had solemnly assured him that seduction wasn't on her mind. He'd gone straight back to the flat, resisting also the temptation of a stop-off at the Dock Brief and an invitation from Brenda to come round for a drink. He suspected she had been awaiting his return and her downcast expression caused him a moment's remorse, but the prospect of drifting into a cosy routine of evenings shared with his next-door neighbour failed to entice him and he had politely but firmly pleaded a splitting headache.

"Mr. Fingall, so sorry to keep you," said Paula sweetly. "It seems Mick may be out playing golf."

In this weather? Harry stared out at the rain teeming down upon Fenwick Court. Nearly forgetting to maintain Ruby's exact elocution, he said abruptly, "And which club might he be playing at?"

"The West Liverpool." A pause, during which mental cogs must have whirred. "Weren't you actually the person who proposed him for membership, Mr. Fingall?"

Ring off, Harry instructed himself, before you make a mess of it. "Thank you very much indeed for your help," he said in a Rubyesque purr and put the receiver down. The West Liverpool, no less. One of the most prestigious courses in the country, he believed, although in truth he scarcely knew the difference between an eagle and an albatross. Ruby had certainly introduced Coghlan into high society.

Picking up his coat, Harry spotted *The Professional Conduct of Solicitors* in a dusty corner of his bookcase and wondered whether passing oneself off as a fellow lawyer was a specific disciplinary offence. Better look it up sometime.

Driving through the city, Harry listened to a cassette of early Beatles hits. The young Scouse voices sounded fresh and alive: hard to believe that of Matt's hero had been silenced by an assassin's bullet. Somehow the energy of the rock 'n' roll music complemented Harry's morning mood. Eight hours' sleep was partly responsible, but so was the satisfaction of at last having the chance to confront the man who had changed his life. It was like embarking upon the first steps of recovery after a long, wasting illness.

The West Liverpool Golf Club occupied one hundred and fifty acres on the suburban fringe, five miles further up the coast than the most northerly dock. The links stretched out towards the sea from the end of a cul-de-sac lined with opulent Victorian villas. Nowadays the club was said to be the haunt of the nouveau riche, the marketing men and finance directors who ran what was left of the city's industry.

Undeterred by a large signboard bearing the canard that all trespassers would be prosecuted, he parked outside the clubhouse, a sturdy Victorian edifice topped by a clock tower and disfigured by a low post-war extension apparently constructed out of the remnants of a giant Lego set. Even on this foul February morning, a dozen other cars were lined up again the grey brick wall: they included a Merc, an Alfa, three BMWs and, discreetly at the far end, a white Escort with a man inside who seemed more interested in Harry's arrival than the newspaper ostentatiously propped up on his lap. Whilst manoeuvering, Harry had caught sight of a square face before it had disappeared behind the *Daily Mirror*. Harry thought he recognised the man as the pock-marked constable who had helped to carry out the search of his flat on Thursday.

The rain was easing as Harry marched in. When in doubt, display confidence. Observing a tweedy gentleman of retirement age in the lobby, he called out in an old-school-tie-voice, "I say, wouldn't happen to have seen Michael Coghlan, would you?"

110

The elderly man didn't seem impressed by the mention of Coghlan's name. A twitch of his lips implied that he deplored the need to admit the uncouth to this noble place merely because they cultivated the right people and could afford the course fees. "Saw him going towards the show room," he said grudgingly.

Harry decided to wait. An encounter with a naked Coghlan was more than he was ready for. Assuming a proprietorial air, he strolled into the cocktail bar and ordered a beer. Two walls of the long rectangular room were adorned with oak boards recording the names of past winners of a host of golfing competitions and a row of faintly ridiculous portraits of former captains, each of them wearing a red and yellow striped blazer with matching tasselled cap. On the far side, rain-blurred glass doors led on to a verandah from which one could view the eighteenth hole. A couple of hardy soul in waterproof gear were visible, putting out on the last green. Harry took his glass to a table near the door and was idly flicking through an ancient copy of *The Field* when Coghlan walked in.

Recognising Liz's lover was easy. Coghlan wasn't shy of seeking publicity for the gym and from time to time the local paper carried his photograph in connection with some sponsorship or other. He was built like a stevedore and dressed like a football star. An open-neck designer shirt revealed a hairy chest and a gold medallion. A Rolex glinted on his wrist. With his blond blow-waved hair and a pair of Italian sunglasses that probably cost more than Harry's entire wardrobe, he was as out of place here as a Sumo wrestler in the Long Room at Lord's. Bitchily, Harry decided that Coghlan's nose was too beaky for him to qualify as handsome, but no imagination was needed to see why he had appealed to Liz. Subtlety had never been her strong point. Yet Harry also saw the strain-lines etched around Coghlan's eyes and the tense hunching of shoulder blades beneath the fawn blouson. For all the glitzy exterior, the man was troubled.

A smaller, older man in an Aran sweater accompanied Coghlan. Bald and snub-nosed, his too was a familiar face. Harry searched in his mind for a name. Wasn't he a jeweller, another local businessman who liked to see his name in the news? Yes, Raymond Killory, that was it. He had a chain of bottom-of-the-market shops throughout Merseyside. He too had a worried look and although their conversation was indistinguishable, his muttered remarks to Coghlan sounded squeaky and querulous. They kept talking as they moved to a table by the window, not looking as one of the golfers three-putted, to his evident disgust.

For an instant, doubt submerged Harry's determination. What could he say? He had turned up here unrehearsed, with no more than a vague idea of how to challenge Coghlan or what to do if the man simply laughed in his face. It wasn't too late to slip away undiscovered. But he choked back the thought and strode over to where his wife's former lover was sitting.

"Coghlan."

The blond head jerked in his direction. "Who are you?" The voice was gritty, the accent local.

"Harry Devlin. I want to talk to you."

Coghlan surveyed him from head to toe. He might have been a cannibal, encountering a missionary. The uncertainty on his face slowly gave way to calculation. "I can spare you a couple of minutes," he said. "Raymond, would you excuse me?"

The jeweller looked nervously from one man to the other. He coughed and said, I'll be at the bar when you're ready." Neither Coghlan nor Harry spared him a glance as he sidled away; Harry sat down in his place.

"I heard you'd been to the Fitness Centre," said Coghlan. "What do you want?"

"Don't you think a conversation between us is long overdue? We have something in common, after all."

112

"Get to the point. You may be a brief, but you're not charging me by the hour."

"Liz tired of us both, you as well as me. I know how it feels, Coghlan, the fury of losing what you thought you had forever." Harry leaned forward. "There comes a moment, doesn't there, when you want to scream? Or, perhaps, to take revenge?"

Coghlan bared strong, white teeth. "You're not making sense. Don't piss me about."

"Liz betrayed you, Coghlan." The unpractised words began to pour out. "You treated her like the rest of your common tarts. She stood it for a while, but you couldn't quench her. She met some other man. Hid it from you, for fear of what you'd do, but not well enough. You bullied her, terrified her. She slashed her wrists in a fit of despair. But then she learned she was going to have a kid and that changed everything. So she gathered up the courage to walk out." Harry took a deep breath. The man he hated was gazing steadily at him now, brow furrowed, but giving nothing away. "You caught up with her, isn't that right? I don't know who killed her. You or one of your sidekicks, possibly, whilst you set up an alibi. The police haven't been able to pin it on you yet, but they know that you're their man. And I know too."

Coghlan stretched out an arm across the table and grabbed Harry's tie with a movement so smooth and economical that no one in the cocktail bar noticed it. "You're crazy, Devlin. You've called at my house as well as the Fitness Centre. Oh yes, I'm well aware of what goes on in my absence. And now you interrupt me at a private club to pour out a load of garbage that I'd sue for if it wasn't all so sick. You're becoming a nuisance and that's a risky thing to do." He yanked the tie once, then let it go.

"You took Liz. There's nothing else you can do so far as I'm concerned."

"Don't you believe it. I don't take this crap from anyone, let alone a cheap brief from a back street without two pennies to rub together."

"My wife is dead. And you're responsible."

With a snort of laughter, Coghlan said, "Wife in name only. Plenty of water under that bridge since she packed you in." The contempt was unvarnished. "I'm not surprised you couldn't handle her. You're nothing much. You amused her, that's all, like a child's toy. When she wanted a man she had to try elsewhere."

Harry's beer glass stood on the table. He gripped the handle, tempted for an instant to grind it in Coghlan's face, see the glass splinter and the jagged edges tear into the flesh, transforming the scorn to pain. But as he lifted up the pint pot, a hand was laid on his shoulder and a plummy tone enquired, "Michael, old chap. Long time no see. What's your handicap these days?"

Blinking hard, Harry turned round. A tall man, gin and tonic in hand, was standing over them, smiling in an amiable, fellow-member's way. Harry rose to his feet and said, "Guilt." Then he walked out of the building without a second glance at either Coghlan or the interloper.

Outside, a thin drizzle had returned. The constable was still waiting patiently in the unmarked Escort. Harry got in at the passenger side of his car and sat down heavily. He could feel his heart pounding as violently as if he had completed a marathon. Against his expectations, the encounter with Coghlan had left him not so much angry as confused. Not because of anything that Coghlan had said, but as a result of realising, at the very moment of making out his case against the man as Liz's murderer, that he did not wholly believe it himself.

Chapter Fourteen

"Harold, a word in your ear."

Only one person in the world ever called Harry Harold. It wasn't the name on his birth certificate, as Reuben Fingall was well aware, but for years the old rogue had kept pretending to forget. Like Lewis Carroll's little boy, Ruby only did it to annoy, because he knew it teased. Adding insult to injury he put an arm round Harry's shoulder and a smooth palm over the hairs on Harry's hand.

They were in the hall outside the solicitors' room in the Dale Street magistrates' court. The corridor was airless and crammed with criminals and their defenders. A solitary, hard-backed chair was occupied by a stubbly drunk who was trying to contort his face into an expression of respectability deserving of one last chance. Harry had just said goodbye to the reckless driver whose licence he had somehow managed to save and was about to return to the office; he had come here from the West Liverpool via a sandwich shop in Fenwick Court which specialised in sardines and salmonella.

Detaching himself from Fingall's clutch, Harry said, "What do we have to discuss?"

A smile looped around Ruby's small mouth. He was in his early fifties, plump in a pinstripe, suit complemented by twinkling silver cuff-links and, on his index finger, a signet ring which bore his initals in curlicued lettering.

"A matter of mutual interest, shall we call it? Come now. I won't detain you for long." It was a remark with which he often prefaced lengthy closing speeches.

"Go ahead."

"Really, Harold, I would prefer to speak with you in private. Perhaps I should add that this concerns my client Michael Coghlan."

"Has he confessed yet?"

"Harold, please." A hint of exasperation lay beneath the cajolery as he waved a hand in the direction of the exit. "May we?"

Harry shrugged. "Okay, where do you suggest?"

"My office is only a stone's throw away."

True enough. Ruby and his minions occupied three whole floors above a pizza parlour across the road from the court. For Fingall and Company, crime paid. The firm had been built up from nothing in the space of twenty years, its success attributable in equal measure to Ruby's industry and his lack of professional scruples. Rumours about how in his early days he had paid a handful of crooked policemen to recommend newly arrested miscreants to use his services had hardened over the years into a thick crust of legend about legal aid fiddles and sharp practice inside and outside the courtroom. Ruby's Porsche lifestyle fuelled plenty of saloon bar tittle-tattle, but most people were careful not to let him learn of it. He had sued for libel three times and slander twice in the past two decades and defamation damages had helped keep him in the style to which he had become accustomed. Meanwhile, his clients mostly survived to mug or steal another day and amongst the criminal fraternity it was a status symbol to boast that Reuben Fingall was your brief.

Ruby directed Harry towards a door at the rear of the building, unlocking it and clambering up the steep stairs two at a time. "This way," he said breathlessly, "we avoid the hoi-polloi in reception, whining for their compensation and fretting over their latest summons."

His office was on the third floor. Panelled in mahogany, it was sixteen feet square. Hockney prints hung on the walls and heavy blue velvet curtains lined the windows. Taking a seat behind a huge desk on which stood a notice saying SILENCE! LE PATRON TRAVAILLE!, Ruby waved Harry into a leather-upholstered chair, picked up the telephone and said, "A pot of Earl Grey for Mr. Devlin and myself, Veronica."

Harry said, "You wanted to speak to me about Coghlan."

"Michael, ah, yes." The beam faded. "It does seem, Harold, that you have been making a nuisance of yourself so far as my client is concerned. Calling at his home, his place of business, even interrupting him during a snatched hour of recreation at the West Liverpool this morning, I gather."

"Don't worry, I'm not trying to poach one of your clients."

"I can assure you there's no danger of that. You appear not to appreciate, however, that Michael is not some sort of street hoodlum. He's a respected member of the local business community and your behaviour - I might almost say, your harassment of him - is naturally a source of considerable distress."

Harry pretended to wipe a tear from his eye. "My heart bleeds."

Ruby gazed sadly at one of the Hockneys. With the heavy patience of a schoolmarm urging a recalcitrant pupil to mend his ways, he said: "Michael is not a man to trifle with."

"I'm not trifling."

"You've antagonised him, Harold, and that isn't wise."

A matronly woman brought in the tea on a tray. Fingall thanked her lavishly and said, "Shall I be mother?" Without waiting for a reply, he started to fill the delicate china cups and, when the secretary had closed the door again, he asked, "Can I take it, then, that you won't be troubling my client again?"

"Surely you know me better than to imagine I can be warned off. Not like you to be naive, Ruby."

Few people used the nick-name to Fingall's face nowadays. His plump cheeks coloured and he said, "Don't trespass on my goodwill, young man, or my client's." The careful elocution began to slip, the vowel sounds shortening with his temper. "You know about his background. Enough said on that score, I think. I've put in a word for you, explained that you've had a rough ride. But don't push him any further."

"Thanks for your kind support, but I can take care of myself."

Fingall banged his cup down upon the desk, splashing a few drops of tea onto the polished surface. "You ought to snap out of this, Harold. Your wife's dead and nothing you can do will bring her back again."

"You think I've overlooked that? But I told Coghlan that I'd find the man who murdered Liz and nothing you can say is going to make me change my mind."

Ruby contemplated Harry's fixed expression for a full minute. When he spoke again, he had regained his composure, although there was a hard edge to his reproving tone. "You're no detective, Harold, don't let one or two past successes in that respect deceive you. You mustn't let this tragedy take hold of you. The way I hear it, you're behaving like a man obsessed. Take care not to interfere in things that are no concern of yours."

"Liz's death is my concern."

"Michael Coghlan had nothing to do with it."

"Where was he last Thursday night? Not down in Leeming Street, by any chance?"

Triumphant as a politician scoring a point in debate, Fingall said, "My client wasn't even within one hundred miles of Merseyside."

"So the alibi is standing up to scrutiny at present?" Harry rubbed his chin. "How much did it cost him?"

The older man puffed like a steam train. "That will do. I make allowances for you, Harold, you've suffered a grievous loss. But your credit's running out fast, young man. I won't have you hurling these slanderous accusations at a client of mine."

"Coghlan killed my wife. Everything points that way."

"You're an experienced lawyer," Ruby brayed. "Yet a novice would have more sense than to jump to ridiculous conclusions like that. Assumptions piled on top of prejudice. Why don't you act your age?"

Harry raised his eyebrows and after a moment Fingall said more gently, "There's no proof of Michael's guilt for the very good reason that he did not murder your wife. He hasn't been charged in connection with the crime precisely because he did not commit it."

Standing up, Harry said, "See you in court."

Fingall wagged a well-manicured finger. "Harold, I've given you fair warning. If you persist with this absurd vendetta because Michael Coghlan once hurt your pride - I won't answer for the consequences."

"Thanks for the tea, Ruby." And Harry walked out, leaving his host staring angrily after him.

He took the stairs to ground level two at a time. This latest attempt to dissuade him from pursuing his quest for Coghlan's skin had achieved nothing but the hardening of his resolve. Harry could accept that, for what it was worth, Ruby Fingall might not believe that his client had stabbed Liz. Harry had, when accusing Coghlan, sensed - whether from professional experience or superstitious instinct, he was not sure - that there was something about the case which he did not himself yet understand, some missing link without which guilt could never be proved. But it was plain that Fingall was acting under instructions, presumably phoned through from the West Liverpool, to pressurise Harry into abandoning his campaign. And Harry's reaction to pressure was always to resist it.

Arriving back at the office, he looked in on Jim Crusoe, who was poring over a bundle of title deeds, sheaves of heavy parchment scripted in copperplate and yellow with age. The craggy face glanced up and eased into a smile. "Rights of way, I hate them! Wish I did litigation, the easy life. Lucy tells me you were out in the Magistrates' this afternoon. Successful?"

Harry shrugged. "The boy got off through lack of evidence. Whether that counts as a success, I'm not sure."

"Course it does."

"You reckon?" Harry perched on the edge of a desk half the size of Ruby's. This room was no bigger than his own, though it was more orderly, with its neat piles of pre-contract enquiry and land registration forms and window sill array of law reports bound in blue buckram. Pensively, he said, "Ever think much about justice, Jim?"

"How do you mean?" Jim was too instinctive a lawyer to respond directly to a question as wide as that, even in casual conversation.

"Everyone knows my client was responsible for the crash with the motorcyclist. It was a miracle that no one was killed. Yet he walks out of the court without a care in the world. Is that just?"

"Keep talking like that and you'll only be fit for prosecutions."

"You disagree?"

Crusoe pushed the folded deeds to one side, using as a paperweight a mug bearing the legend *Old Lawyers Never Die - They Just Lose Their Appeal.* "Life isn't so simple. You're not paid to act as judge and jury. It's the oldest rule in the solicitor's book. You weren't a witness to your client's supposed crime. He denies responsibility. You're hired to defend the lad and the Crown's case falls apart. That's justice, even if it does stick in your gullet. Nothing to trouble your conscience there."

"Although the crime goes unpunished?"

"Face it, most crimes do."

"And you're satisfied with that?"

"No, but I'm not here to change the world. Besides, what did Blackstone say: 'Better that ten guilty men go free rather than one innocent suffer'? That's the system we have, pal, like it or not."

Harry slammed his fist down on the desk top, scattering a wad of telephone notes. "I always agreed with that old idea, but now I'm not so sure. How can you allow a man who has killed in cold blood to go free?"

Jim Crusoe gathered the bits of paper together and said, "So we're discussing Liz? Thought as much. Let me give it to you straight - stay out of this thing, Harry, you're too close to it. You're sure Coghlan murdered her. I don't know . . . you may be right, or totally wrong. In either case, leave it to Skinner. I've asked around, Harry, he's good. He'll nail the bastard if he can."

"You're singing the same tune as Ruby Fingall, do you realise? It's not so easy. I can't let go."

Jim's eyes became disapproving slits. "Not thinking of private vengeance, are you? Because if you are, forget it. Down that road, madness lies."

Getting to his feet, Harry said, "I'll see you later."

"Don't bother. Go home, take a holiday. This place can run without you for a while." Beneath the brusqueness of the words was an undertow of genuine concern.

At the door, Harry turned. "Maybe. But can I survive without it?"

Stepping into the corridor, he encountered Lucy, who was carrying a mound of letters she had typed for him. "Here you are," she said. "I was hoping you'd be back. There's something I have to tell you. I went to buy a loaf of bread from the delicatessen at lunch-time . . ."

He grinned at her earnestness. "Congratulations."

"No, you don't understand. I don't know how you'll react, but this is something I'm sure you'd want to know."

Gently, he took her arm and guided her into his room. "Start again, love."

"Like I was saying, I called at Beardshall's. Gillian served me. You must know her? The girl with the carroty hair and the big brown eyes. Reminds me of a red squirrel."

The accuracy of the comparison made him laugh. "Okay, so that's Gillian."

"She was talking about your wife. How terrible it was and everything. And she told me she knew one of her man friends."

Harry tensed. "Mick Coghlan?"

"No. This chap was involved with her step-sister until recently, that's how she came across him."

He cast his mind back to what Dame had told him. "Was his name Tony?"

She said no, the man was called Joe Rourke. Gillian hadn't said much about him, only that she was glad that Jane Brogan, her step-sister, had seen the last of him. He was a scally.

Harry was intrigued. Another boyfriend? No one had mentioned him before, not Maggie, not Matt. Not Dame. He wondered why. Perhaps Rourke had been a one-night stand, someone Liz had picked up before becoming involved with rich and handsome Tony? Jealousy flamed inside him for a moment, but almost at once it was doused by the urge to find out more, to put together a few more torn scraps from the picture of Liz's life during the past two years.

"Thanks for telling me." He pressed her hand.

Simply, she said, "It matters to you, doesn't it, to understand what happened to her?"

At least Lucy realised what Jim, Maggie and the rest of them seemed unable to grasp. He signed the letters with an illegible scrawl whilst she waited and, when she had returned to her room, checked his watch. Five to four. The deli would still be open. Might as well see what Gillian had to say. He grabbed his coat and hurried out to Beardshall's.

The food store served the city's business community, but Fortnum and Mason's it wasn't. Busy during the lunch hour, it was quiet at other times and now deserted save for a couple of assistants in drab brown overalls. They were languidly shifting tins from one shelf to another. He walked up to them and touched the shorter girl on the arm. She spun round, her squirrel-features wrinkled in enquiry.

"Gillian?"

Evidently recognising him, she flushed. He was an occasional customer here and the printing of his photograph in Friday's paper would have put his identity beyond doubt. Apprehensively, she said, "Yeah?"

Harry beckoned and, unwillingly, she approached. When he was satisfied that the other assistant was out of earshot, he said quietly, "Lucy told me you know a man who used to be involved with my wife."

"Women's gossip," she said. "That's all. She shouldn't have said nothing."

"Who is he, this Rourke?"

Lowering her voice to a whisper, she nevertheless managed to pack violence into her reply, "He's a shit, that's what he is."

"Tell me more."

"He was shacked up with our Jane for the best part of eighteen months. They had a kid, poor little mite, he treated it rotten."

He stepped over an abandoned wire basket to get closer to her. "Where does your step-sister live?"

Vigorously, the girl shook her head. "I don't want her messed about. She's had a lousy time, she's on her own now after that bugger left her. I shouldn't have said anything to your secretary, should've kept me gob shut."

Harry gripped her by the wrist. "Gillian, the man who stabbed my wife is still on the loose. I want to find him. Rourke's a new name to me. I'm not saying he was involved, but he may be able to help, point me in the right direction."

"You'll be lucky," she said, trying to wriggle free. "Anyway, Christ knows where he is."

"Then it's Jane I'll have to see. Tell me where."

"Let go," she hissed, "you're hurting."

He glanced across to where the other assistant was sweeping the floor aimlessly, displaying no interest in either the job or her colleague's conversation. Then he realised that the girl was tuned into a personal stereo; her eyes had a faraway look and her lips moved noiselessly to the words of some pop song. Suddenly releasing Gillian, he said, "Please, where do I go?"

The squirrel-faced woman sighed and came to a decision. On a discarded sell-by sticker she wrote in an unformed hand an address in South Liverpool. Harry knew the place as a notorious example of urban blight; these days architects held conferences to discuss how to avoid repeating the design mistakes which had created ghettoes like the Keir Hardie Estate. When he thanked her, Gillian said, "Jane has no idea where he's slunk off to. Good riddance, I say. But don't give her any hassle - okay? She's suffered enough already."

Harry promised. There was no more to be gleaned here and he returned to the office. Halting by the door of the glassed-in cubbyhole where Lucy did her typing, he said he expected to be out for the rest of the afternoon.

She followed him to his room, ostensibly to finish the day's filing, but closed the door immediately behind her. "Discover anything?" she asked in a conspiratorial undertone.

"The more I learn, the less I know."

"You're like a child picking at a sore tooth, Harry. But I hope you find what you're looking for."

He pointed to today's calendar adage: *Persistence is the mother of miracles.* "If only I believed it," he said.

Chapter Fifteen

Aneurin Bevan Heights - the Nye, locals called it - was a thirteen-storey carbuncle in concrete. Had it housed prisoners, they would have mutinied long ago. Harry walked towards it from the main road. After leaving Beardshall's, he had gone home to change into jeans, an old zip-front jacket and dirty plimsolls before jumping on to a bus at the Pierhead. It wouldn't be wise to turn up in this part of inner city Liverpool dressed in a pinstripe suit, however shiny at the elbows, and driving an unstolen car on which he wasn't anxious to have to claim the insurance.

The block of flats loomed above a landscape of despair. Shops that, though open for trade, had their windows boarded or barred. The busiest were the second-hand stores with their black and white signboards proclaiming free social security estimates given. Unlettable maisonettes straggled along the side of streets that lacked pavements. Bent Lowry-women, bare-legged despite the cold, gathered in small nattering groups. You would only come here for a compelling reason, or if you had nowhere else to go. Harry took a short cut through a patch of waste ground, glancing over his shoulder when shouts of glee attracted his attention. A gang of boys was throwing pebbles at the bus as it started up again. Harry's feet squelched through tufts of muddy grass, treading from time to time on rusted cans and empty packets of condoms. He passed a Ford Cortina, wrecked and burnt out, probably by kids too young to be prosecuted even if they were caught.

He reached the quadrangle of dusty asphalt which passed for a communal garden at the foot of the Heights. Looking up, the building appeared to reach to the heavens, but when he walked through the double doors with their cracked panes, he realised that he was stepping into an earthly hell. Someone had run riot with an aerosol paint spray, extolling in fuzzy blue the virtues of Everton

Football Club. Both lifts were out of order. Climbing the stairs quickly, he tried to ignore the stench of urine that hung in the air. On every landing windows were broken, with unswept fragments of glass still scattered on threadbare carpet tiles. Once or twice he saw discarded scraps of silver paper and polythene bags, the tell-tale spoor of heroin addicts and glue sniffers. His breath was coming in jerky gasps by the time that he reached the ninth floor. As he walked down the corridor in search of Jane Brogan's flat, an old woman in pink cardigan and hairnet emerged from a doorway and accosted him.

"You the man from the Corpie?"

"No, love. Sorry."

Her wrinkled face corrugated in a frown and she leaned confidentially towards him. "They send people to spy on us, you know."

"Not me, I promise you. Can you tell me where number nine-one-three is?"

She drew the cardigan more tightly around her thin frame, as if her virtue had been impugned. "That scrubber?" A thought occurred to her and her watery blue eyes shone with interest. "You checking up on her, then? Fiddling her Social, like all the rest of them here. The way she's been throwing her money around, like Lady Muck, about time you lot cottoned on."

When he located flat 913, his rap on the door provoked an outburst of juvenile wailing from inside. Muffled scolding noises were followed by the sound of footsteps.

"Who is it?" The woman's voice was wary, as if she believed that no news was good news.

"You don't know me, Jane. My name's Harry Devlin, I'd like to come in for five minutes. I need to speak to you about my wife."

Keeping the chain on, the woman opened the door an inch. His first impression was of lank fair hair and a face drained of hope.

With a shake of the head, she said, "I don't know no Mrs. Devlin." But Harry caught a note of apprehension in her reply.

"Maybe not, but your ex-boyfriend did - Rourke."

She studied him with a mixture of caution and curiosity before saying in a grudging tone, "You mean that woman what got murdered?"

"Yes."

"I don't know nothing about her."

"Please let me in, Jane."

Thrusting out her lower lip, she said, "Piss off and leave me in peace."

"Listen, Jane, I met your step-sister Gillian. She told me about Joe Rourke. I want to get the story first hand, simply so I can believe it. And I won't go away till you let me in. No matter how long it takes. Come on now, let me in."

She glared at him, but started to fiddle with the chain and security lock. Finally the door was pulled back to reveal a tall girl whose carelessly buttoned blouse displayed ample portions of white breasts. On a good day, Harry thought, she might be attractive, but this was far from being a good day. Her hair needed a wash and her eyes and cheeks were dull enough to suggest that she had packed a lifetime's misery into her - what? - perhaps twenty years. The resignation implicit in the way she said "Come inside" made it plain that she didn't expect his visit to herald a change for the better.

The flat was a mess of cigarette ash and baby's things. Weeks must have passed since it had last seen a vacuum cleaner. The damp stain which spread across one wall of the room into which she steered him was enough to rob anybody of the incentive to tidy up, though the place was at least equipped with telly, video and stereo system. A smart sheepskin coat, incongrous as the Koh-i-Noor in a cabbage patch, had been thrown over the arm of a chair. A single bar of an electric fire glowed dimly, failing to give off any warmth.

He perched on the edge of the two-seater settee and looked at the stain, trying to conceive what it would be like to live here day after day, month after month, year after year, with no prospect of parole. Anyone could go stir-crazy in the Nye.

She stood opposite him with folded arms, still weighing him up. "Smoke?"

"I'm trying to give them up," he said.

"Life's too short for that," she said, fishing a cheap cigarette from a pack lying on top of one of the hi-fi speakers. "Reckoned you was from the Social. They hound you these days, the minute you get a quid or two." Lighting up, she added, "Word's got round, Joe isn't here any more. Kids broke in at the week-end. They used to keep their distance when he was around. No one would've dared to do this place over while he was living in it. I'd only gone downstairs to empty the rubbish. I'd left it over a week, thinking the Corporation would fix the lift. I heard Wayne screaming and ran back in, but they'd already scarpered, hadn't they? Didn't get away with much, just a handful of me records. Little bastards."

When Harry muttered sympathetically, her response was a casual toss of the matted hair. "Happens every day, dunnit? It's this dump, the kids know there's nothing down for them. You could die in this hole and no one would know the difference. I should've listened to me dad."

"Yes?" Get her talking, thought Harry, take it slowly. Let her feel relaxed.

"He hates me, does me dad." The girl's face suddenly burst into life, blazing with pent-up fury, as if she were challenging Harry to contradict her. "He'd never let me back in the house. His wife, me step-mum, keeps it spick and span. They both think I'm a slut - maybe they're right. They were about Joe."

"They didn't care for Joe?"

She snorted. "Wouldn't have him in the house! They told me he was no good, they soon found out he'd been inside, I was never much of one for keeping things secret. Me dad said he'd chuck me out if I didn't drop Joe. Worst threat he could've made, wasn't it? By then I was expecting Wayne. I told the old sod where to go. Typical me, pig-headed. I never listen until it's too late."

"When did you find out that Joe was seeing my wife?"

She considered. "Fortnight ago, three weeks maybe." With a harsh laugh she said, "Caught him good and proper, didn't I?"

"How?"

"Found her photograph in the pocket of his jeans. I was only after a few bob to pay of the 'leccy bill before they cut us off. I knew he was flush, he'd just brought that coat and the stereo. Fell off the back of a lorry, I suppose. Anyhow, I found three hundred in fifties and this woman's picture tucked away. A real looker. The bastard! I thought."

"What did you do, Jane?"

"Took the money, didn't I, what else?" A smile flashed for a moment, lighting up her face. "And then I screamed at him, asked who the bloody hell she was. He flew into a rage, cuffed me good and proper." She brushed the fair hair off the side of her face. "You can't see the bruises now, they've faded, but there's the mark where his knuckle cut me, it's not healed up yet." A red groove ran down from the base of her left ear.

Harry felt sick in his stomach. Another violent thug with a criminal record . . . had Liz been out of her mind? He said grimly, "Rourke admitted he was seeing her?"

The girl snorted. "He'd had flings before. I can put two and two together."

Harry looked around again at the room. It was as cold and dismal as a crypt. Why would Liz have got herself hooked up with Joe Rourke, who lived in a slum like this, when she already had Tony, that elusive paragon with money, looks and style? As he asked himself the question, an idea began to form in his mind. Was Tony a myth? Might Rourke have been the father of her unborn child?

"So what happened?"

"After he hit me, he told me to shut up, it was none of my business. I raved at him. Then all the noise woke up Wayne and he started shrieking too. All three of us was going at it hammer and tongs. When Wayne wouldn't quieten down, Joe's temper really blew. He cracked Wayne, hit him across the face to make him calm down. Poor little mite, it only made him scream worse." She paused, scowling at the memory. "That finished me, I can tell you. I scratched Joe across the cheek - you can see the bloodstain on the cushion there where he wiped himself. I made a real mess of his face, really tore into it. I was glad. He was a vain bastard, it served him right. I thought for a minute he was going to kill me, but then he backed off. Decided I wasn't worth it, I suppose. I told him to get out and he said he'd been meaning to anyway. He'd get himself a real woman, not a boring cow with a whining kid."

As if in shared recollection of that quarrel, the child next door began to cry. The girl swore. "You'll have to go," she said. "Me hands are full here."

"All right," he said. "But tell me this - where does Rourke work?"

"You kidding? Joe's never had a job."

"So where did he get his cash?"

She looked at him as if he wanted to know if babies were made in heaven. "Never asked, did I? You don't ask too many questions if you want to sleep at nights, do you?"

"Listen, did Joe know a man by the name of Mick Coghlan?"

The wailing of her son increased in intensity. "Okay!" she yelled. "I'm coming!" Turning her attention back to Harry, she said, "No idea. He didn't tell me what he used to get up to. All the same, Joe was real bad news but I did care for him. Still do, in a funny sort of way. I know he was a shit, but it wasn't always like that." She grinned artfully. "Even this last time, he let me keep the money."

"Did he tell you anything about my wife?"

Jane shrugged. The baby was still howling, distracting her all the while. Harry hoped it was well wrapped up. She said, "He wouldn't admit to nothing. Typical man."

"How can you be sure the photo was of my wife? Did you hang onto it?"

"No, the bastard kept it, didn't he? Snatched it back off me. Fond of his fancy piece, y'see. But it was her, all right. Gill came over on Friday, she brought the paper with her. That's where I read about your wife being murdered and that. I told Gill. I said, "She got what was coming, the . . . " The sentence trailed off as she saw a spasm of pain convulse Harry's face. "Sorry," she said brusquely, "I know you was married to her."

When he didn't say anything, she asked, "Have they got the bloke what did it?"

"Not yet."

"Some nutcase, that's what it'll be."

"Perhaps. All the same, I'd like to have a word with Rourke. Where can I find him?"

"Forget it. You don't know the sort of man he is. He's an animal, sometimes. I could handle him, just about." She surveyed Harry sceptically. "He'd eat you alive."

Her unseen child began to cough. She edged towards the door and he noticed that her shoulders were prematurely sloped, as if two heavy hands were pressing down on her.

"Jane, my wife was murdered. Stabbed to death. There's a lot that I don't understand about the way she lived after she and I split up. And I need to understand it. Joe Rourke can fill in some of the gaps, I'm sure of it. I have to see him. Do you have an address?"

She shook her head. "He could be anywhere."

"Where should I start looking? What about his family, his friends?"

"His parents are dead. Joe didn't have many mates, with his temper. Them he had are mostly in the nick."

"There must be some address you can give me, a place where I can go and look."

Next door the baby was spluttering. "I've got to go," she said, but something in Harry's face made her pause. "You could try the place we used to go every Friday and Saturday. Before Wayne came along, that is. Joe always liked it. Yeah, try the Ferry Club."

Chapter Sixteen

"Froggy!"

The man with the bulging eyes had been opening the side door to the Ferry Club when Harry hissed his name. Instinctively, he pivoted, right arm raised to ward off an assault. Scowling into the unlit gloom of the alleyway, he called out, "Who's that?" He sounded nervous.

Harry moved out of the shadows. After a fifty-minute wait in the freezing night with only two dustbins full of decaying debris for company, his mind was as numb as his hands and feet. Since speaking to Jane Brogan, he had been fired only by the belief that answers to some of his questions might be found here. If Rourke was a regular, the people from the Ferry might know how to trace him.

"We crossed paths last Thursday evening. You spilled beer over me."

Froggy stared at him with, Harry thought, relief rather than fear. Had he been expecting to be waylaid by someone else?

"What do you want?"

"To talk."

"I don't know you," said Froggy belligerently.

"We've never been introduced, that's true. My name is Devlin."

Froggy screwed his face into a frown. He hesitated for a moment before making a defiant gesture with his left hand and saying, "So what?"

"Can we go inside?"

"I've got work to do."

The man was enveloped in a navy blue anorak a couple of sizes too big for him. Harry seized the anorak's loosely flapping belt and hauled Froggy's face up to his. At close quarters he was again conscious of the unpleasant smell he had noticed during their last encounter.

"I won't keep you long. Now let's have a chat in the warm."

If Froggy had contemplated further protest, a second glance at the set of Harry's jaw caused him to think better of it. "Five minutes, that's all I can manage," he said, striving for dignity. "The boss - "

Harry shoved him in the direction of the door. "Lead the way."

Once inside, Froggy pressed an internal light switch and pulled open a door marked staff only. Harry followed him into a tiny room containing two ancient wooden stools, cleaning materials and the wherewithal for making tea and coffee. A few dried-up biscuits were scattered over a dusty formica worktop. In the harsh light given out by a shadeless bulb, Harry noticed an earwig sliding away into a crack by the skirting board. Froggy tossed the anorak over the biscuits and waved him towards one of the stools.

"Take the weight off your feet."

"I'm not stopping." Harry took a photograph out of his jacket pocket. "Recognise her?"

He had taken the snap of Liz on holiday in Malta four years ago. She was sitting on a stone wall overlooking the Grand Harbour at Valletta. Her skin had a Mediterranean tan and she was wearing a skimpy tee-shirt, very short shorts and sandals. He hadn't been able to find a picture that gave a better likeness when rummaging through his flat after returning from Aneurin Bevan Heights.

Froggy's nostrils twitched as he calculated pros and cons. "Nice-looking chick," he temporised.

"You know who she is?"

A throaty, man-of-the-world chuckle. "Don't reckon I'd forget her in a hurry. Customer here, is she?"

"Was, Froggy. She's dead."

As the man went through a pantomime of non-comprehension, Harry said steadily, "She was stabbed last Thursday, the night you jostled me at the bar here. You'll have read about it in the papers. Her name was Liz Devlin."

"So you're the solicitor," said Froggy slowly. He tried to convey the image of a man upon whom realisation is beginning to dawn, but Harry didn't doubt that he had recognised the photograph straight away.

"You've got it. Now, do you know her?"

A gleam of cunning appeared in the protuberant eyes, belying the innocent uncertainty of his words. "I don't get it. She was mugged, wasn't she? Why are you asking all these questions?"

Harry laid a hand on Froggy's shoulder. "She used to meet someone here, isn't that right?"

Froggy made as if to resist but, catching sight of Harry's expression, again changed his mind. "Okay, I may have seen the lady here once or twice," he admitted, "but I never spotted her with anyone special. 'Course, I'm rushed off my feet most nights."

"Do me a favour," Harry said. "You know Mick Coghlan?"

Froggy gave this as much consideration as a judge called upon to deliver a verdict, but all he said was, "Doesn't he run the gym up Brunner Street?"

From outside the door came the sound of light footsteps - a woman's heels clicking towards them. Harry released his grip on the other man.

"Don't waste time."

"Haven't seen Coghlan in this place," said Froggy, shaking his head.

The footsteps paused. "Okay," said Harry softly, "what about a feller by the name of Rourke."

"Froggy!"

A woman's voice, smokily distinctive, saved the man from having to reply. Even so, Harry noted the flash of alarm in the prominent, red-veined eyes at the mention of Rourke, and the grateful way in which Froggy turned as the door of the room creaked open. "Herself," he whispered with a gap-toothed grin.

A tall, sinuous figure in a close-fitting sweat shirt and jeans was framed in the doorway. Auburn hair spilled on to her shoulders and her curved fingernails shone scarlet under the glow of the naked bulb. A subtle, expensive fragrance accompanied her into the room as she regarded the two men from under long lashes. "Sorry," she said huskily, "am I interrupting something?"

"No problem," said Froggy. "I'm just on my way to check the cellar. This is Mr. Devlin. He's - he's my solicitor."

Even as the woman's pencilled eyebrows rose, the man said in a tone of finality, "Okay, then?" to Harry and bustled out.

Angie O'Hare's features relaxed into a smile as she settled her gaze on Harry. She wouldn't see forty again and, without the camouflage of stage make-up, the wrinkles around her eyes and mouth were plainly visible. Yet there was something hypnotic about the look on her face. Harry had sensed the strength in her when listening to her sing last Thursday night and now he felt the force of her personality catching hold of him, much as a torch beam might transfix a moth. He felt his interest in Froggy melting away.

"Have you taken to visiting club-land in search of clients, Mr. Devlin?" she said at last. "Or is our Froggy such a valued customer that he has you at his beck and call twenty-four hours a day?"

Harry said, "I have a little unfinished business with Mr. . . . do you know, I've forgotten his second name."

The eyebrows lifted again, but she said, "Evison, I believe."

"Ah, yes."

"Don't tell me he really is a client of yours."

"No." Harry was suddenly conscious of the incongruity of his dress: the casual jacket, open-necked shirt and moth-eaten scarf. "But I'm glad you're prepared to believe that I'm a solicitor."

Angie smiled again. "The solicitors I've come across haven't been as conventional as you might expect. But then, I haven't known many."

"Count your blessings."

"You're too defensive, Mr. Devlin. The lawyer I use is a very good man. Quentin Pike."

"I know him." Yes, and Quentin could never be accused of cultivating tedious respectability. According to local gossip, he spent most of his time seducing pretty trainee lawyers whom he picked up at week-end Law Society advocacy conferences at which he discoursed on the technique of persuasion.

Angie leaned against the work surface, resting her elbows on the dirty heap of Froggy's anorak. She didn't seem anxious to leave, or for Harry to go. For some reason that pleased him. In the claustrophobic atmosphere of the tiny room, the aroma of her perfume was almost over-powering; like a truth drug, it made him want to unburden himself to her. He found himself saying, "I heard you sing on Thursday night. *Eleanor Rigby* and all the rest."

"The old favourites," she said lazily. "Have to keep the customers satisfied."

The rich colour of her hair and the provocative jut of the well-formed breasts beneath the shirt would have done justice to a woman fifteen years younger. He hadn't wanted to succumb to her charm and flirt with her, but she was hard to resist. He broke the eye contact and said, "I lost touch with your career."

Angie grimaced. "Most people did. I had some hard times. Tastes change. Female vocalists went out of fashion."

"I was glad to hear you again."

"Thank you." She moved her face nearer to his and *Ma Griffe* assailed Harry's senses. "Tell me, though, what really brings you here?"

With this woman, he felt no need to prevaricate. He wanted to tell her about Liz. Quickly, and without either emphasis or embarrassment, he ran through the chain of events that had brought him to the Ferry the previous week and said that he wanted to trace the man whom his wife had, he guessed, planned to meet here that fatal night. The singer listened gravely. She didn't indulge in easy exclamations of shock or sympathy and Harry was grateful for that. As he talked, he saw the sparkle fade from her eyes, to be replaced by an awed, almost haunted look.

"Do you know who he was, this missing boyfriend?"

"Maybe the man she used to live with, Mick Coghlan. Or someone she'd apparently once had a fling with, by the name of Rourke. Though she'd mentioned someone else to me and some of our friends - a rich businessman called Tony."

Angie breathed out and brushed his hand with the tips of her scarlet nails. Softly, she said, "You must be hurting badly, Mr. Devlin, but is this going to achieve anything? Chasing around after all your wife's lovers?" She sighed. "What are you trying to prove?"

"How can I rest while the man who killed her is free?" He didn't say anything about his thirst for a direct, physical revenge. That was still taboo, a secret whose existence he scarcely dared to acknowledge, even to himself.

Her tone gentle but decisive, she said, "Don't you think you ought to ask yourself - is she worth it?"

"What do you mean?"

The auburn head dipped. "I never met her, Mr. Devlin. And yet - the picture you paint makes me think I wouldn't have taken to her if I did. Faithless, selfish, greedy . . . isn't that the truth about your wife?" He stared at her, galled by the scathing words after the way in which she had seemed to understand him. Seeing the bitterness of his reaction, she continued earnestly, "I'm sorry, that must sound callous after everything you've been through. But wouldn't you be better putting the past behind you? Think it over. Surely it makes sense."

He drummed his fingers on the formica table, scattering the dust, but said nothing. After a short pause the nails touched his icy flesh again and she said, "Mr. Devlin?"

"Call me Harry," he said.

"Harry, you've got to understand - there's no going back. You seem to reproach yourself for something, God knows why. If she was the type who played around, she never would have changed. Once a marriage cracks at the seams, you can't ever put it back together again."

For a minute or more, neither of them spoke. Then Harry said, "You may be right. Probably are. Makes no difference, I'm afraid."

Someone knocked and a fair, tousled head appeared round the door. Harry recognised Angie's keyboard player. In a thick Scouse accent he enquired, "You ready, gorgeous?"

The singer nodded. "With you in a second, honey." She cast a final glance at Harry. "Coming to see the show?"

He said no, but thanks all the same. At the door of the little room, Angie O'Hare turned to face him. He moved towards her so that their cheeks were no more than six inches apart. "I'm sorry about your wife, Harry, truly I am," she said, "but you must get over it. For your own sake. That's the sad thing about life, isn't it? If you don't look after yourself, nobody else will."

No point in arguing. "I was glad to meet you," he said, "I liked hearing you sing about all the lonely people."

They stood there for a moment or two. Then the auburn hair bobbed and Angie said, "Goodbye, Harry." She followed the blond man towards the rising tide of disco music from the dance floor beyond the far end of the passageway. Harry gazed after her, relishing her proud, upright carriage and the sway of her buttocks in the tight jeans. He hadn't fallen in love with Angie O'Hare, but he could imagine what it would be to love her.

Left to his own devices, he wondered whether to pursue Froggy for further interrogation. The other staff, too, perhaps. But his conversation with the singer had unsettled him and after a few seconds reflection he swung on his heel and walked out by the way he had entered. Outside, he pushed through a group of drunken early evening revellers, oblivious to their jeers and invitations to a fight. He was trying to rid himself of the ghost of Liz that Angie O'Hare had conjured up, the ghost of a woman faithless, selfish and greedy, a woman not worth yearning to avenge.

Chapter Seventeen

Fuzzy after two hours' drinking, Harry sat at the bar of the Dock Brief, trying to remember what is was like to be capable of logical analysis and rational thought. A Victorian pub mirror hung on the wall and he gazed at his reflection: at the dark-ringed eyes and the features blurred by doubt as well as alcohol. Unbidden, a line from Shakespeare studied long ago rose in his mind. Where are your quiddits now, he asked the haggard image, your quillets, your cases, your tricks?

Pushing his glass across the counter, he nodded a goodnight to the barmaid. She was coping with a flirtatious drunk who was trying to tempt her into a shared week-end in Paris. Catching Harry's eye, she bustled over.

"Friend of yours was in here earlier on. Sorry, I forgot to mention it."

"Yeah?" The people he drank with in the Dock were better described as acquaintances.

"Dark-haired lady." The barmaid threw out a quizzical look. "Attractive."

For a fleeting, insane moment, he thought: It's Liz. Her ghost. Conquering that immediate reaction with an effort, he said carefully, "Did she leave a name?"

The woman searched in her memory, ruffling a hand through her tight brunette perm. At last she said, "Maggie, that was it."

Harry was startled. His sister-in-law and her husband frequented wine bars from time to time, but neither of them would normally contemplate calling in a place like this. What did she want? Christ, another question. He shambled out, buttoning his thin jacket in an inadequate effort to resist the razor edge of the wind from the sea. Someone in the pub had said that this was going to be the coldest night of the winter so far. At least it might help to clear his head.

He reached the Strand, lost in contemplation as he crossed the six-lane highway, almost walking beneath the wheels of a tanker that he hadn't even seen or heard. Why care about whether the murderer was found? Liz was dead and nothing that he could do would bring back her carefree laughter or tantalising mockery. Yet the spell that she had first cast over him at the Albert Dock firework celebrations, no more than a couple of hundred yards from this very spot, remained unbroken. Her leaving had not lessened her power over him and in death the spell had become a curse.

He took a short cut via the main car park that served the residents of Empire Dock. The solid bulk of the converted warehouse loomed ahead of him. Lights shone behind curtained windows, forming a chequer board of hidden lives, but the place was still, with just the rumble of the traffic in the background and the footsteps of Harry and another man fracturing the silence. Harry paused when he reached his M.G. Might as well check that the alarm was on, he'd been absent-minded about it lately. One day someone would make him pay for that.

The alarm was set, after all. He had been worrying about nothing. You're becoming neurotic, he told himself. At that moment, he noticed that the other man's footfalls had stopped. He couldn't help glancing over his shoulder. There was no one else to be seen.

Joining the path that led to the flat development, he heard the clip-clop of steel-tipped shoes again. Another look round. Nothing. He began to move faster.

Resurrected period lampstands ran along the edge of the path, casting cones of illumination down into the darkness. One of the lamps was out. Straining his eyes, Harry sensed rather than saw the movement of a figure a dozen yards ahead of him. It might have been a beer drinker's imagination. It might not. Harry calculated that if he spurted, the safe haven of the lit-up doorway of the Empire Dock was no more than forty seconds away. Yet that barely perceived figure could cut him off with time to spare. If he wanted to. Was the risk worth taking? Was there any risk at all or was he simply cracking up?

A sudden lateral movement by the other man decided him. The way home was being closed down. Time to change direction. Harry veered off the path, clattering along the cobbled area that led to the river, lengthening his stride, breathing in and out in short draughts. He caught the sound of the other man, hurrying by the wall of the building. No option now but to chance it. Harry broke into a run.

The man in front of him began to run as well. Harry gained the impression of an athlete's fluid, easy rhythm. His pursuer was driving him away from the lee of the Empire Dock and back towards the open road. Harry cursed. Already the exertion was making him gasp, one more reminder of his lack of condition. A whiplash of panic caught him. The other man was gaining ground.

One of Harry's feet caught a cobblestone that was raised a little above the others. He stumbled, fought to regain his balance. An arm stretched around his waist from behind, toppling him again. As he struggled free, a gloved hand caught at his shoulder. Staggering, Harry glimpsed a balaclava mask. This wasn't a teenage mugger, jumping a passer-by for a few quid. The man was only a fraction taller than himself, but steamroller-solid and as his muscular frame loomed against the night sky, whilst he steadied himself for the onslaught, Harry could only shield his eyes and wait for the first blow to descend.

The man hit him in the stomach with a fist that felt like a lump of steel. Harry crumpled.

There was no respite as he sank towards the ground. Harry shut his eyes and a ribbed glove sliced across his face, a cruel strike that left his cheeks singing and his nose feeling as though it had been buried in the back of his head. Retching violently, he wanted to weep as well, but the tears had been smashed out of him. Sticky blood oozed over his mouth and chin. He could taste its sour flavour. Somewhere in the distance a dog began to bark.

Harry thought: It would be quicker if the hound was set on me to finish the job.

His assailant stood back for a moment, like an artist admiring a canvas. Through a slit in the balaclava, he said, "You should've stayed out of it." The intonation was back-street Toxteth. He took another step back and launched himself into a steel toe-capped kick that crashed against the side of Harry's body. Had he not telegraphed that his attack was aimed at the temple, allowing Harry the time to twist away, that might have ended it all. Even the mis-hit filled Harry's mind, his whole being, with pain. For an instant, he could think of nothing else but the agony. Yet in the background the barking had grown louder and the racket broke into his consciousness.

"Shit!" said his attacker. The single syllable was crammed with violence, but also with fear.

In a moment he was gone. Harry heard his boots thudding away into the night. Now the barking was frantic. Harry forced his eyes open and saw a huge Alsatian bounding towards him. From a distance, the animal had a furious look. Even in his battered state, Harry thought how ironic it would be to escape from being pulped by the thug only to finish up as supper for man's best friend.

Panting noisily, the dog reached him. It surveyed his prostrate body with what might have been hungry relish. Harry tried to move, but failed. Groggily, he heard approaching footsteps from the direction of Empire Dock.

"You all right?" someone asked.

Fine, Harry thought, I bleed and vomit for fun. He managed to bend his neck sufficiently to see the owner of the voice. His saviour was a young man in the navy blue uniform of the security firm which patrolled Empire Dock after dark. He was fresh-faced and anxious and his "peaked cap was too big for him.

"Down, Sabre. Stay."

Harry uttered a low moan.

"You don't look too healthy. Let me give you a hand."

The guard bent down and patiently attempted to help Harry, if not to his feet, at least to a crouching posture.

It was a slow process, with a couple of false starts. Every bone in Harry's body ached. He felt like a trodden grape.

Wiping the blood from Harry's face with a handkerchief, the youthful guard said, "The guy sure took a dislike to you. You'll look a picture tomorrow and no mistake. Black eye, the lot." He gazed towards the Strand. "The bugger will be far enough by now. I'll call the police."

"No." It was Harry's first coherent syllable for some time, but he invested it with as much finality as he could muster.

The guard appraised him. "Do you know who he was?"

Harry didn't answer. Instead he probed his teeth with his tongue. None of them seemed loose.

"What was it all about?" When no reply was forthcoming, the guard said, "Suit yourself. Main thing is to get you home. You're a resident, aren't you? Third floor, am I right?"

The lad was observant. Harry contrived a painful nod of the head.

"You fit enough to make a move? All right, easy now. Take my arm."

They made excruciating progress to the entrance of the Empire Dock, Sabre trotting patiently at their side. Sitting behind the desk was Griff, the senior night porter, a square-shouldered, bushy-eyebrowed man in his fifties who was as Welsh as Cardiff Arms Park.

"Bloody hell, sir," he said, "you look as though you've had an exciting night."

Harry managed a wan smile. His rescuer described the incident briefly and again Harry declined an offer to call the police. He

145

thought twice when Griff suggested medical treatment, but he was reluctant to attract attention by turning up at Casualty and although every part of him was aching, there didn't seem to be any bones broken, nor any need for more than rudimentary patching up. Time would heal the cuts and fade his bruises.

"Up to you, sir," Griff shrugged. "Very well, Colin. Take over here for five minutes while I take -Mr. Devlin up."

Harry thanked the young guard. He would see him again later. Without his intervention, and the ferocious assistance of Sabre, Harry would have been a hospital case at the very least. Most probably, he would have been making a quick return visit to the mortuary.

As the lift took them upwards, Griff talked away. "Lot of dangerous people about in this city, sir. But if you don't mind my saying so, you need to watch your step. I don't know what all that was about and I don't want to know. You've had a rough time lately, but you want to be careful about who you get involved with. You'll be aware from your profession, sir, some of these hooligans are none too fussy who they hurt. Or kill. You may not be so lucky next time."

They arrived at Harry's flat. Griff took him into the lounge, helping him to ease off his jacket and shoes so as to rest on the sofa, before excusing himself and leaving the flat.

Harry shut his eyes again. Straightening out his thoughts and feelings immediately was difficult, but still he raged against the thug who had beaten him and the man who, Harry was convinced, had sent him. So Mick Coghlan was intent upon seeing him off. Harry's stubborn refusal to heed Ruby Fingall's velvet glove warning must have caused Coghlan to resort to direct violence.

Harry heard Griff talking to someone. A woman's voice. Brenda Rixton. He looked up as the two of them walked into the flat together. Brenda exclaimed in dismay as she saw him, then walked over to the sofa and bent over him, as solicitous as a doctor inspecting a patient in intensive care. He felt her fair hair brush against his cheek.

"Just look at you!" She winced. "What a mess. Wait a minute."

She fussed and bustled, ordering Griff to assist in handing her first aid supplies from the bathroom medicine cabinet as though he were a trainee nurse. Harry felt her cool hands checking his rib cage. A wet cloth was applied to his sore eye and cheeks. Painkillers were administered. He bit his lip and assured her that he would soon be all right, but she took no notice. Eventually Griff, satisfied that the recovery process was underway, returned downstairs.

Brenda squatted beside the sofa and took Harry's right hand in both of hers. "You don't look after yourself,

that's your trouble. You need someone to hold your hand."

Harry was too weary to argue. Besides, she might be right. He closed his eyes again. As consciousness slipped away, his last thought was that if Coghlan wished to shake him off, the man could scarcely have made a worse misjudgment. Briefly that evening, Harry's determination had started to crumble. But now he would never give up, no matter what the cost.

Chapter Eighteen

"How's the invalid?"

Brenda's voice, reassuring as the dawn chorus, wafted in from the hall. Harry lifted his face from a pillow which she must have slipped beneath his head after he had fallen asleep on the sofa. The slight movement sent a flash of pain tearing down the side of his face with the sudden force of an electric shock. Unable to stifle a groan, he gritted his teeth and checked the clock. Ten to eight.

She appeared in the doorway, slim and business-like in a grey suit. "I thought I would pop in before I went to work."

"Thanks." Harry hated the grudging note that he heard in his voice, but at present he felt like an animal wanting to lick its wounds; he would rather have been left alone. Knowing her kindness and concern was genuine and that he ought to be experiencing gratitude simply burdened him with an extra weight of guilt.

"Let's have a look at you." As she walked up to the sofa, Harry levered himself into a sitting position, moving as cautiously as a vertigo sufferer on a high wire. The effort was rewarded by a burning sensation that travelled from shoulder to waist and a renewed throbbing within his chest.

"You're still in pain," she said.

Confirmation was superfluous and heroic denials were not in his line, so he kept quiet and steeled himself to ignore the aching of his ribs. But his face must have betrayed him with a give-away grimace, for Brenda looked at him for a moment and then compressed her mouth in a determined manner.

"I'm going to call the doctor."

"No!" The firmness of his reply surprised even him.

"But you may have a fracture. There might be some internal damage."

"I played soccer for years, Brenda, I'm used to knocks. There's bad bruising, a few cuts and bumps, but not much more."

"You look as though you've done fifteen rounds in a heavyweight bout."

"I'll live."

She leaned over him, gazing down earnestly. "Aren't you going to tell me what it was all about?"

"Nothing to tell. A common or garden mugging. Happens every day. And night."

Exasperation flickered over her lightly powdered face. "Oh no, you don't convince me like that. You really think I'm naive, Harry, don't you? Griff said . . ."

"Never mind what Griff said."

"That young guard, Colin, may have saved your life. Griff told me that you could have been killed if he hadn't come upon the scene. You must call the police, Harry, don't you understand?"

"And tell them what? That I was jumped by a man in a balaclava, someone I couldn't recognise again if he walked into my office and asked for help with his social security claim? No, Brenda, there's nothing to be gained from involving the police. They'll never catch him."

"Certainly not if you don't give them a chance," she said. For the first time in their acquaintance, he detected signs of temper in her. He found that oddly satisfying, as if at last he had broken through the surface layers of good neighbourliness and struck the real woman underneath. With new interest, he looked at her as she said, "There's some other reason why you are so reluctant, isn't there? Connected with the murder of your wife. Am I right?"

She was more perceptive than he had guessed. He said, "I don't know what you mean."

A vexed sigh. "You don't fool me. But you won't let anyone help, will you? You're obstinate, Harry Devlin, you're one of the most pig-headed men I've ever met."

He had to smile. "I couldn't disagree with that."

More gently, she said, "It's not always a bad fault. I'm stubborn myself at times. When I make up my mind about something, I don't let go without a battle." Her gaze dwelt on him for a little while. Finally, she said, "I won't nag you any more. At least, not yet. I have to go now. Duty calls. Is there anything I can get you? No? Well, think again about seeing a doctor. And the police."

"You've been very good to me."

Unexpectedly, she coloured. "That's my pleasure," she said.

After she had gone, he dozed for a while. Later, he rang the office to break the news of his latest absence, carefully making sure that he spoke to Suzanne rather than to Lucy or Jim, who might have added their words of wisdom about medical attention and calling the police. One well-meant harangue was enough for this morning.

Getting up, he inspected the damage in the mirror, reminding himself that ugliness was only skin deep. Anyway, he had never been a Jeremy Irons. The facial damage looked mostly superficial. His left eye had darkened, as Colin had predicted, and his cheeks were red and chafed. Yet it had almost been so much worse. Thanks to Sabre, the masked assailant had left the job half done.

He saw no reason to shift from his instant decision of the previous night not to contact the police. Had his injuries been more serious, he would have had no choice but to seek medical help and, no doubt, to involve Skinner and company. But a doctor or policeman would want to make sure he took no active part in the pursuit of Liz's murderer and he was not ready to give up the chase. Was he risking another, life-threatening attack? He couldn't dismiss the possibility out of hand, yet he had no doubt that he was doing the right thing. The memory of Liz saying, "I'm frightened, Harry," surfaced in his mind and he told himself that he was doing the only thing.

The telephone rang. Before he could speak, Maggie's breathless voice asked, "Are you all right?"

"Still in one piece, yes."

"I rang your office. They told me you'd been involved in an accident. What happened?"

He gave her an edited account of the previous night's events, not implying that the incident amounted to more than a street mugging, but she saw through his clumsy subterfuge at once.

"Harry, I'm worried about you. Mick Coghlan killed Liz, he must have. Now he wants you dead."

Her vehemence took him aback. Before he could frame a reply, she added, "I wanted to see you, anyway. I called at the Dock Brief yesterday evening, and at your flat, but you weren't there."

He remembered what the barmaid at the pub had said. Subsequent events had driven it out of his mind. "What is it, Maggie?"

"Liz was being followed shortly before she was killed."

For the first time that morning, he became fully alert. "How do you know?"

"I went to see Matt Barley. Talking to you the other day made me want to find out more. He told me you'd been to see him. He'd been mulling things over too. I could tell he was holding something back. That was it. Liz had confided in him, said she was worried sick."

And, Harry suddenly recalled, she had told him as well on that Wednesday night. All at once he could hear, as distinctly as if she were standing beside him, her breathless tone: "He's even had me followed. I'm scared, Harry, I swear it. I believe - I believe he wants to kill me." He was bitter with self-reproach, realising it hadn't sunk in because he'd thought she was embroidering. Lying in bed in the early hours of Thursday morning, he had had a hazy recollection of the question he had meant to put to her: "Exactly who has been following you?" But again the thought had drifted from his mind.

Maggie said, "Are you still there? Liz told Matt she'd seen the man follow her about the city centre. At first she reckoned nothing to it, but when he kept turning up she started to get worried. All she could think of was that Coghlan had discovered she was playing fast and loose and had set someone to check what she was up to. Don't you agree the police ought to know this, could it . . ."

Piercing as a banshee wail, the doorbell interrupted her.

"Look, I must go," said Harry. "I'll talk to Matt. Thanks for telling me."

"Harry - " his sister-in-law's voice was edged with emotion " - it must have been Michael Coghlan, it must have been! If this wasn't an ordinary street crime, there's no other possible explanation, is there?"

It was as if she were seeking reassurance, rather as though she did not actually believe it herself. There was a strange, desperate quality in her conversation that he couldn't fathom.

"I can't imagine why anyone else . . ." he began. The bell persisted in its summons. "Sorry, Maggie, must answer the door. Talk to you again soon."

He hurried to the door. His visitor was Jim Crusoe. The grizzly bear's face gaped at the sight of him. "Dragged you out of bed, have I? My God, look at you. Someone's taken a dislike to you, old son, to inflict that kind of damage."

They sat down in the lounge and Harry told his partner what had happened. As he explained, Jim's natural calm dissolved into concern. "I don't like to say I told you so, but . . ."

Harry made an impatient gesture with his hand. "All right, all right."

Crusoe threw a look of despair at the ailing cheese plant, as if in search or moral support. "This isn't *Boy's Own*. You'll get more than your fingers burned if you keep playing with fire. Leave it while you have the chance."

Not for the first time during the past few days, Harry said simply, "She was my wife. I can't leave it."

"Liz could never belong to any one man."

Goaded, Harry said, "What did you know about her?"

"Plenty."

After a long pause Harry said, "Meaning what, exactly?"

"She tried it on with me, old son, believe it or not. Even me, conventional-to-the-core Crusoe. The happily married man. I think she saw me as a challenge. She had that in common with you, Harry - she could never resist a skirmish, however long the odds against. That night the four of us went to the Philharmonic, remember? She tried to set up an assignation then, when she and I went up to the bar . . ."

"I see," said Harry.

"Doubtful. Anyway, I turned her down. I won't pretend it was the simplest decision I've ever made or had to carry out, but it wasn't the hardest either. And I wasn't only thinking about Heather and the kids. I may not be Robert Redford, and she was a gorgeous woman, but anyone could see Liz was trouble. And this happened eighteen months before she left you, mind, long before she got her hooks into Mick Coghlan. Don't get me wrong, I don't want to sound pious. Fact is, Liz couldn't help herself any more than you could help idolising her. She was your blind spot, Harry, from start to finish."

Harry stared at his partner's implacable expression. It was the longest speech he had ever heard Jim Crusoe make. A wave of fury swept through him, carrying with it a suspicion born of bitterness, not logic. He almost asked: Did you really go to that football game on Thursday night - or did you kill Liz in Leeming Street instead? But he choked the question back. No one in his senses would cast Jim as a murderer.

Presently, he said, "I'll be back in the office soon. Maybe tomorrow if I get the chance."

"Forget it. We can cope. I want you fit, not acting like a clapped-out Rumpole."

Harry's ribs were beginning to hurt again. He said, "Thanks for coming over."

"No trouble. I'll see myself out. You stay there. Do the crossword, get better. Everything else - put it out of your mind."

Alone again, Harry slumped back in his armchair. Dwelling on what Jim had said was pointless. Whatever her faults, Liz hadn't deserved to die. At least now he understood Jim's hostility towards her. It was easy to imagine his partner's scorn for her unfaithfulness and his unease at being tempted. But Jim was no fool and he was the only incorruptible man Harry had ever met.

Rubbing his eyes, he forced himself to concentrate on what Maggie had said. She, at least, had dropped her opposition to his own investigations into the murder, although he didn't know why. Surely she was right in thinking that Coghlan must be responsible for the killing? The man who had pursued Liz might have been a hanger-on from the gym, perhaps Harry's own balaclava-masked assailant from the previous night, or some other hired hand. And, as Harry pondered, the identity of another candidate occurred to him: the man with the bulging eyes, the man who had arrived late at the Ferry Club on Thursday night. Froggy Evison.

Chapter Nineteen

"Shirelle, isn't it?"

The barmaid lifted her blonde head from bored scrutiny of the pump that was pouring out a pint of bitter. Tonight her earrings were magenta spheroids which danced at the sudden movement. Hostility flashed in her eyes as she said, "What's it to you?"

The Ferry Club was quiet as yet, with just a handful of women in short skirts and a couple of spotty youths perched on stools adjacent to the bar. The fair-haired keyboard player was slaughtering an old Coffin and King number while the drummer leafed through an old copy of *Melody Maker* and surreptitiously picked his nose. Harry said, "Where's Froggy this evening?"

She pushed the glass across the bar. "His night off, innit?"

"Any idea where I can find him?"

Suspicion gave way to unvarnished hostility. "You a busy?"

"Not me. Just a paying customer. I was in here last Thursday night, remember? Froggy spilt beer over me. That isn't why I'm looking for him, though. Our last conversation was interrupted. I'd like to finish it."

Weighing up his battered face, the barmaid said, "Someone wanted to finish you, by the look of things."

"Where's he likely to be?"

"Haven't a clue."

Harry stifled a yawn. He'd spent most of the day either asleep or resting and still he felt kitten-weak. There was work to be done, though. In the past few hours he had convinced himself that the man called Froggy could lead him to Liz's murderer. Passing the woman a ten-pound note, he said, "Keep the change. Where does he live?"

Tucking the note under her sleeve, she glanced quickly to right and left. Nobody was watching; the prostitutes were arguing amongst themselves and the young men were pretending not to be listening. Nevertheless, Shirelle spoke out of the side of her mouth, a habit perhaps picked up from watching too many black and white thriller movies on late night television. "Baden Powell Street. By the Municipal Baths." Unable to contain her curiosity, she murmured, "Why are you after Froggy if you're not a busy? Most people are glad to steer clear of him."

Harry ignored the question. A second tenner materialised in the palm of his hand, peeping at her from between his fingers. "Tell me, Mick Coghlan - is he a customer here? Does Froggy do any work for him?"

Shirelle considered the banknote. He could tell that she was torn between an instinctive desire to tell a stranger nothing and the timeless attraction of easy money. Even her earrings seemed to flutter with uncertainty. In the end, she opted for compromise. "Coghlan? The name rings a bell. But I don't think he comes here."

The tenner inched towards her. "How does Froggy spend the rest of his time? Where might I bump into him?"

The barmaid sniffed. "Haven't the faintest. The less I have to do with that feller the better. He loiters in bed till dinner-time as far as I know. After that, you're as likely to find him in the bookies' as anywhere."

"What number Baden Powell Street?"

"How would I know, sunshine? I'm not the rent collector or the bailiff." A mascara-masked woman at the far end of the bar leaned over and muttered something unintelligible. "Look, I've got a job to do, okay?" Shirelle held out her hand and the moment Harry slipped the note into it she swept away to serve the thirsty tart.

He sipped his drink slowly, keeping the entrance in view. More customers drifted in, the usual mixture of navvies, sales reps, divorcees and teenage kids out to spend their dolemoney. Another girl arrived on duty behind the bar. The keyboard player began to mangle the hits of Stevie Wonder. The suave manager whom Harry had seen on Thursday night put in an appearance, marching around with an easy air of authority and self-regard, not neglecting to loop an arm around the barmaids' shoulders when he exchanged a word with them.

Harry finished his beer. It was ten o'clock. His damaged arm and ribs were reminding him that without the timely intervention of the security guard's Alsatian, he would have been in intensive care rather than back on the booze. There was nothing to detain him here. He had had enough for one day.

He wandered out of the club and back to the Empire Dock. The anti-climax of failing to pick up Froggy, coupled with the aching of his body, had wearied him. Tonight no masked thug barred the way to the brightly lit entrance hall of the old warehouse, although anxiety knotted his stomach as he crossed the Strand and he was glad to nod at Griff and say with casual affability, "Unscathed for once, see? Goodnight."

Moving quietly along the thick-pile carpet of the third floor corridor, he tip-toed past Brenda Rixton's room and was about to enter the sanctuary of his own home when he became aware of footsteps approaching from the far end of the passage. Looking up, he saw Brenda walking towards him.

She smiled readily at him, although he sensed at once that her mood was one of strained patience. "I spent the evening with Joyce Mahoney at three-oh-nine," she said. The name meant nothing to Harry; he was unacquainted except by sight with the rest of his neighbours. "How are you feeling? Have you been to the hospital this evening?"

"Afraid not," he said.

As she drew up by his side he could tell that she was smelling the alcohol on his breath. The lines of her face hardened, not so much with disapproval as with sadness. "I might have known."

157

"I decided to go out for a meal," he said. True enough as far as it went. He'd eaten a mixed grill in one of those dependable, boring steak restaurants with uniform decor and waitresses chosen for shapeliness rather than speed of service. After sinking a bladderful of coffee he'd strolled to the Ferry in search of the man with the bulging eyes.

Plaintively, Brenda said, "I brought something back for the two of us. I didn't think you would be fit enough to go gadding around. Roast chicken and a salad. But even at half-seven you weren't here." No, he'd been in the mood for a couple of drinks before eating. "In the end I shared with Joyce instead."

So Brenda possessed in abundance that female knack of imposing guilt, thought Harry. With some women, it seemed as natural as breathing. Conscious of the constricting pressure of unnecessary remorse, he said defensively, "Sorry, I didn't realise. It was kind of you."

"No, it doesn't matter." Thus neatly was the point scored.

In the ensuing lull in the conversation, he felt awkward as well as ungrateful, scratching around for something placatory to say. "I was just going to have a nightcap. I suppose you wouldn't . . ."

"Thank you, I'd like that."

Once inside his flat, she quizzed him about his injuries. He tried to be dismissive without conveying the impression of nobly suffering in silence. After pouring them each a glass of Grand Marnier, he settled back in his armchair. Brenda was on the sofa, her shoes kicked off, legs tucked beneath her. Good legs in sheer tights, he noticed. Her fine hair shimmered in the glow cast by the wall-lights.

Raising her glass, she said, "To a rapid recovery."

The rich taste of the liqueur kept the two of them quiet for a minute or so. The central heating had been programmed to come on four hours earlier and the air in the room was warm and dry.

The floods of pain that had washed through his body all day were beginning to subside.

"Tired?" Brenda asked.

"Mmm."

"You shouldn't have gone gallivanting," she said, but not unkindly. "You really should take more care of yourself."

He didn't reply, but presently sensed a movement in front of him and looked out through narrowed eyelids. Brenda was kneeling in front of him. She eased off his shoes and socks and began to rub his feet. Smiling, she said, "You don't have to wake up. Relax for once. That feels nice, doesn't it?"

"Yes."

How long she carried on, he didn't know. His mind was emptying, like a jug tipped upon its side. All the grieving and the hating and the riddles of the past few days had started to drain away. The policemen's questions, the squalor of the Nye, his brief, foolish yearning for Angie O'Hare - none were more than faint memories. For him, the world had shrunk to this warm room and the tender touch of Brenda's fingers running rhythmically up and down his soles.

He heard her say, "It's late."

Unable to camouflage a yawn, he prised open his eyes. She was leaning over him now, her delicate perfume noticeable for the first time that evening. Her jersey-clad breasts rested against his chest.

"I've been left in the lurch too," she said. "I think I can guess how you feel about losing your wife. I've imagined being with Les each day since he walked out. For long enough I dreamed he'd come back one day, though I've more or less learned not to delude myself any more. God only knows, it takes an age to adjust. I suppose something died in my life, too, that dreadful day."

She was sliding her fingers through the tangle of his hair. "I don't believe in moaning about bad luck. Perhaps it's true that life is what you make it. I ought to grab what I can whilst there's still time. I thought you . . ."

Her voice trailed away and he mumbled, "Go on."

"No," she said with a new briskness. "How stupid I am. I can tell the agony that you've been through these past few days and I mustn't add to it. It's time for me to go, before - well, never mind."

She kissed him gently on the cheek. His eyes closed and he felt the tip of her tongue touch his skin, her body pressing against his. Then she withdrew.

"Goodnight, Harry."

And as the door closed behind her, he was conscious of a sense of loss.

Chapter Twenty

He slept badly, the battered arm and rib-cage protesting each time he tried to turn over in his bed. Liz's face kept appearing in his ruptured dreams. Not smiling, for once, but downcast with reproach.

It was a relief when early morning sun began to lighten the room through a chink in the curtains. His body was stiff and getting up was a slow and painful business, made no easier by the sense of guilt which hung around his neck like a weight.

He hated feeling that she was on his conscience. That if he had done more, she would not have died. And that he'd betrayed her by wanting to respond to the touch of Brenda's lips. How bloody typical of Liz, he thought, at least she's consistent. Unreasonable in death just as in life.

Stepping under the shower, he turned his thoughts to the woman from next door. What if he had asked her to stay? He didn't doubt that she would have said yes. He didn't love her, she could hardly love him, but did that matter? The jet of hot water stung him, but not as much as his anger with himself. Why shouldn't he want a woman again?

Since Liz had left him, he had usually slept alone. His occasional affairs had offered no fulfilment. There had been a sociology student, doing a stint as a barmaid at the Dock Brief, who said she was in search of experience. A copper-haired solicitor called Sinead whom he had met at a seminar about developments in divorce law. A couple of drunken one-night stands with girls whose names he couldn't even remember, picked up at parties thrown by people he hardly knew. None of them compared with Liz, none held for him more than a fleeting appeal.

Brenda Rixton was fifteen years older than any of them. A week ago the thought of her as a lover would never have crossed his mind. Yet Angie the singer, at much the same age, exuded sexuality. If he could fancy her, why not his neighbour? Brenda wasn't a bad-looking woman.

As he dressed he gave his reflection in the mirror a grin. Perhaps that birthday last Wednesday had marked a change in his taste. He was getting on. Jim would say he was starting to grow up.

The doorbell summoned him. Brenda. He said hello, feeling faintly ridiculous. Minutes earlier he'd contemplated making love to this respectable lady. Now, seeing her neat, trim and middle-aged in her business suit, he was ready to let the fantasy fade.

"I thought I'd just see how you are before going in to work."

"That's kind of you, but I'm okay, thanks. A bit stiff, but nothing to make a fuss about. Er - won't you come in for a moment?"

She stepped into the room. Was it his imagination, or did her hips swing more jauntily than he'd noticed in the past?

"At least it's a fine start today. Though the forecast is bad." She perched on the sofa's arm, seemed to have difficulty in choosing her words. "Look, about last night, I hope you didn't think . . ."

"Brenda, don't worry. I was glad to see you. You've been very good to me. I'm an ungrateful-seeming sod, but I do appreciate it. Really."

She smiled and shook her head. "No, you're a kind man, though you try to pretend otherwise. I'm sorry about your wife. It takes time to get over something like that. But, remember, you can't mourn forever. Eventually you need to make a fresh start."

"Easier said than done."

She stood up. "I won't try to argue. Besides, I wouldn't win. Look after yourself, though. Please."

"I will," he said. "Depend upon it."

At the door she turned. "Harry, I *am* depending on it." After her footsteps had died away down the corridor outside, he washed and dressed. Between mouthfuls of coffee, he dialled the Ensenada, his favourite restaurant in the city. Taking Brenda out for a meal tonight was the least he could do. Just a meal, though. Nothing else.

At such an early hour, he got straight through to Pino. The Ensenada's proprietor was a voluble extrovert, one of the biggest gossips in town. As a source of hot news, he rivalled the *Echo* and he often said he loved good conversation (by which he meant talking to an appreciative audience) as much as *haute cuisine*. His florid condolences and exclamations about Liz's death lasted for several minutes without a pause.

"And to think," he announced in melodramatic style as Harry tried to speak, "that I was talking to her less than two - yes! - hours before the tragedy occurred."

In the theatrical pause that followed, Harry demanded in a voice suddenly hoarse, "What do you mean?"

"Ah, you did not know?" Pino could scarcely conceal his pleasure at breaking an exclusive to the victim's husband. "But she was dining with Mr. Edge. Your brother-in-law, is that not correct?"

Derek, of all people? Trying to conceal his amazement, Harry said, "When was this?"

Shorn of frills and flourishes, the answer was that Liz and Derek had been among Pino's first customers on Thursday evening, arriving at half-six and leaving just before eight.

"And within hours - no, minutes even! - this terrible thing . . ." Pino's shock-horror vocabulary temporarily failed him.

"Do the police know about this?"

It had somehow come to their attention, Pino admitted. Despite the fact that he had scarcely mentioned the matter, they had deemed it worthy of enquiry. But there was so little to tell. He had exchanged a few pleasantries with Mrs. Devlin. As always, she was in high spirits. Mr. Edge was perhaps a little more subdued, but then who would not be content to sit and listen to such a charming and delightful woman? It was an infamy, this crime, an outrage.

Harry eventually brought him down to earth and pressed for more information. But Pino had little more to tell. Amidst further expressions of sympathy, Harry booked a table for two for eight o'clock. Eventually, he managed to ring off and after a moment's thought called the local office of Krikken and Company, the firm in which Derek was a partner.

"Mr. Edge is in a meeting, I'm afraid." The switchboard operator chanted the phrase in ritual fashion. Harry recognised office code for "Piss off unless it's an emergency" and persisted, hinting that a mega-buck deal hung on his being able to consult with Derek immediately. Money talked and after a flurry of resistance, he was put through to a secretary and finally the voice of the man himself came on to the line.

"Harry." Derek Edge communicated in the two syllables a blend of obligatory sympathy for the recently bereaved and the tetchiness of an important professional man disturbed in the midst of complicated work.

"I need to see you straight away, Derek. It's about Liz."

His brother-in-law responded with a lot of dignified nonsense about having to consult his diary. Harry interrupted.

"I won't waste your time, I promise. I'll be there in fifteen minutes."

He rang off without waiting for a reply. He had always wanted to bully Derek, as a semi-civilised alternative to throttling the smugness out of him. But now he had to put aside petty dislikes and concentrate on learning why Maggie had never told him about her husband's dinner with Liz.

He walked over to Krikken's. The exercise might help ease the stiffness in his body that was a constant reminder of the brief ferocity of Monday night's attack. The accountants occupied a building at the corner of Drury Lane which looked like an upturned egg box. In an entrance lobby big enough to hold a circus, a stainless steel plaque recorded that Krikken House was the registered office for a hundred or more companies. Most of the names included-words like "Investment", "Offshore" and "Holdings".

A uniformed commissionaire gave him a security pass flatteringly labelled authorised visitor and directed him tot he seventh floor. The lift whirred upwards without asound and when the doors opened, he was greeted by a sleek secretary whose startling resemblance to Kim Basinger would have guaranteed her a job even had she been unable to type her own name. She ushered him into Derek's presence and then withdrew.

Immaculate in a dark grey three-piece, his brother-in-law came from behind his desk, right hand outstretched.

"My dear fellow. Take a seat."

Harry sat. The chair was low and squelchy. Like all the furniture in the room it was black: some designer's concept of chic, heedless of comfort. A picture window behind the desk commanded a view of the Liver Building and the Mersey. Harry saw the Seacombe ferry was chugging towards the Pier Head.

He brought the conversational preliminaries to an end. "I gather you dined with Liz on the night that she was murdered?"

Derek's pallid face invariably yielded as many clues as a sheet of blank paper. Coolly, he said, "It's rapidly becoming common knowledge."

"I've talked to Maggie more than once. She's never mentioned this to me. Haven't you told her?"

"Yes, I have. There was no particular concealment on my part. The police came to see me, as a matter of fact. I made a statement. Unfortunately, I wasn't able to do any more than sketch in Liz's movements during a part of the day in question."

Harry stared at him curiously. "And why exactly were you out on the town with my wife? I hadn't realised you were such bosom buddies."

Derek Edge shrugged. "Frankly, it was a spur of the moment thing. Liz was my sister-in-law, after all. I offered her a meal for old time's sake."

In common with most of the affluent people whom Harry knew, his brother-in-law was not noted for generosity. He said, "Was she more to you that just a sister-in-law, Derek? Did you fancy her?"

"For heaven's sake!"

"Or ever sleep with her?"

That evoked a facial reaction. Derek pressed his thin lips so closely together that they almost vanished from sight. Harshly, he said, "I realise you're upset, and I'm making allowances, but if you're going to be gratuitously offensive, I shall have to ask you to leave."

Harry banged his fist on the desk, scattering the assortment of pens and paper clips that lay beside Derek's leather-trimmed blotter. "I want the truth, Derek. Don't forget, I'm a lawyer. I'm familiar with prevarication. More so even than an accountant discussing a client's tax return. The glib stuff won't work with me."

Edge toyed with his wedding ring. "Liz was right about you," he said. "She said you'd never be more than a poor man's brief. Too many "B" movies in youth, she suspected. They made you irredeemably second-rate."

It was a rabbit's punch: Liz had teased Harry to his face, saying much the same. Calmly, he said, "She was right about many things, Derek. Including her estimate of you. I'll spare you the details. Let's just say I'm not convinced by this beloved sister-in-law crap, whether the police fell for it or not."

The accountant hesitated. He was still playing with the wedding band; it was as near to a neurotic gesture as Harry had ever seen in him. "This doesn't go beyond these four walls?"

"No promises, Derek, but you know I'm not a blabbermouth. You should concede that, however second-rate I am."

Edge twisted in his chair. "I didn't mean to - well . . ." He essayed a flickering smile. "I suppose all our nerves must be a little taut in the circumstances."

"Go on."

Taking in a gulp of air, Edge said, "If you must know the gory details, then you could say that I was besotted with Liz. Like a schoolboy, though you may find it hard to credit."

Harry studied his brother-in-law. Derek gave the impression of having been born middle-aged. He still wasn't forty, but with that neatly parted, thinning brown hair, uninflected voice, and fondness for bridge and the *Financial Times,* it was a feat of imagination to believe he had ever been young.

Harry would have though him no more susceptible to Liz'swiles than an inanimate piece of computer hardware.

"Maggie guessed, of course. My wife's no fool. She kept Liz well away from me until we'd tied the knot. I gather she'd lost a string of boyfriends to her sister over the years and she wasn't inclined to take any more chances. But Liz had a way of looking at you so that, whatever she said, however trivial or joking, you felt that she was longing to be alone with you."

Harry knew what the man meant. His mind switched back to courtship days; he saw them like sepia stills from an old silent movie, with Liz as the heroine; himself as the Chaplinesque simpleton who had fallen for her.

The story dribbled out. Derek had resisted temptation for a time before succumbing. There had followed a game of cat and mouse: when he expressed an interest in Liz, however obliquely, she backed away. When he pretended indifference, she would take advantage of any moments alone together to flirt with him before reverting to more orthodox teasing as soon as anyone else entered the room. This had been the way of it before, during and even after her years with Harry. After she had started living with Coghlan, Derek had seen much less of her. But six months ago he had bumped into her in the Cavern Walks and she had responded eagerly to his invitation for a drink. He sensed her discontent with her new life and, hoping to play upon it, arranged to take her out from time to time. Again her interest had faded, but by now Derek was caught like a mouse in a trap.

"I would ring her up," he said, "but always there was some excuse why she wasn't able to see me. I couldn't understand it. Coghlan would never change his ways, I told her so a thousand times. She'd never be happy with him."

"By then she'd found herself another playmate."

Edge stood up and looked at the view through the window. The ferry was now out of sight. When at last he spoke again, his tone was heavy with despair. "Who could read her mind? Not me. But on Thursday I was just stepping out of India Buildings when I spotted her on the other side of the street. I was on my way to lunch with a client. She waved and seemed glad to talk. She told me she'd walked out on Coghlan and was staying with you. Not that you were getting back together, she said you had more sense, but you'd offered her a roof over her head while she sorted one or two things out. I was excited, I thought I had a chance. So I asked her out to dinner that night and she said yes."

"And?"

A hollow laugh. "And nothing. We ate together, and I was rebuffed, naturally. Oh, in a good-humoured way, of course. As you say, she had someone else waiting in the wings. Some wealthy businessman. I didn't ask for details. I pressed her, but there was nothing doing. I was just a one-night meal ticket. She seemed happy and glad to be rid of Coghlan, so I paid the bill and left. I had a formal dinner to attend at the Adelphi, I was late as it was. I crept in and didn't bother with the main course. Concentrated on the brandies. End of story."

"Where did she go?"

Edge fiddled nervously with his fingernail. "The police harped on about that. Frankly, I have no idea. I think she was going to meet her fancy man, but I couldn't swear to it. By that stage, I wasn't taking in much of what she said." He risked a glance at Harry. "I have to say, I didn't tell the detectives all about - my feelings for Liz. I thought it would only complicate matters. Maggie had to know, but no one else."

No wonder Maggie had been behaving so oddly during the past few days, had been so anxious that Harry should not ferret around, had been so willing to seize on Coghlan as a suitable scapegoat. She must have been nursing a secret fear that her husband had been provoked by Liz into murder. But was she, in her distress, over-reacting? Or did she believe that beneath Derek's unemotional exterior lurked a violent man of impulse?

Roughly, Harry said, "You realise that this puts you in the frame, so far as Liz's death is concerned?"

"Do you think that hasn't crossed my mind? I may have been the last person to see her alive - other than the murderer, that is. But I've made one or two discreet enquiries and it's apparent that the police have checked my arrival time at the hotel. Plenty of people can vouch for that. It's hardly a perfect alibi, but it's the best I can do." Suddenly, Edge began to tremble. Harry sensed that he was about to cry. The incongruity of it seemed shocking: it was like expecting an adding machine to burst into tears.

Harry had seen and heard enough; he rose and walked swiftly through the door. Soon he was back at the Empire Dock, where he picked up the M.O. and in less than ten minutes was in the heart of unreclaimed Liverpool, threading his way through a maze of back-to-backs. As he drew to a halt, a grimy urchin approached.

"Mind yer car, mister?" The lad was carrying half a brick in his hand, a clue to the fate which might befall a vehicle whose owner omitted to invest in local security. Harry said, "You know where Mr. Evison lives?"

"Yer mean Froggy?"

"Yes."

The small rat-like face assumed a cunning expression. "Might do."

Harry extracted his wallet and, when satisfied with the display of cash on offer, the juvenile hoodlum said, "Number eleven."

Harry handed over the money and, waving a hand at the M.G., said, "Guard it with your life." But the lad vanished even as Harry walked up the front door to which he had been directed. Froggy's home wasn't one of those terraced gems with gleaming window panes and a freshly scrubbed doorstep. Torn and dirty netting curtained the windows and cobwebs canopied the door. Harry pressed the bell three times before realising that it didn't work. He rapped instead, until his knuckles hurt.

A prune-faced woman, laden with shopping, passed by. He called to ask if she knew where Evison might be. She scowled and asked, "You the man from the credit company?"

"No. But I need to speak to Froggy right away."

She sniffed. "His missus will be out at the shops, spending money they haven't got, as usual. As for him . . ."

"Yes?"

"Probably down at the tip. Some folk have no pride."

"Which tip, love?"

"Pasture Moss, of course. Where people dump their rubbish. He'll be on the root, if I know anything."

One small mystery resolved itself in Harry's mind as he thanked her. So Froggy Evison was a totter, one of those who skulked around refuse heaps, scavenging. That explained the smell that always seemed to cling to him. It was the stink of rotten debris.

Chapter Twenty One

Hunched figures were spread across the uneven slopes of the waste heap. They wore ancient anoraks or duffel coats, bending double as they sifted through the rubbish that other people had no use for. Most of them wore hoods, one or two had donned balaclavas. They were not merely, Harry realised, seeking protection against the February wind, but also aiming to avoid recognition if a social security snooper came here to check on those claiming benefits from the state. Through the high wire fence, Harry watched the totters at work. He might have been observing a scene from the Third World on the television screen. But this was his home town.

Overhead, seagulls whirled, wings flapping as if in contempt for human degradation. For Harry, the sight of the filthy surface of Pasture Moss being slowly stripped held an almost pornographic fascination. He had heard of those who lived literally on and off the scrap heap, of course, but had never before seen their activities at close hand.

He walked slowly along the perimeter between the fence and the electric railway line. A teenager had died here twelve months back, he recalled, making a false move and touching the live wire. Scavenging had its risks. Soon he discovered a beaten track which led in the direction of a hole in the fence evidently made by wire cutters. Treading carefully, he crossed the line. Glad that he had taken the precaution of changing into his car-repairing gear in the hope of blending in with the landscape, he crawled through the muddy hole.

Scrambling up the side of the tip was harder than it looked.

Harry slithered in all directions, the rubber soles of his shoes unequal to the sogginess of the terrain. He was soon up to his ankles in cardboard and old newspapers, shrivelled apple cores and potato peelings. The stench made him gasp for breath, draining him more than the physical effort of keeping his foothold on the slime beneath his shoes. One or two of the rooters already had their eyes on him, assessing his progress, noting his unfamiliarity with the geography of the place. Others, busy with their work, ignored him. Finally, he made it to the brow of the heap and, putting one foot gingerly before the other, waded towards the nearest of the hooded men.

He called out, "Seen Froggy Evison today?"

"No names here, pal." The speaker had a lidless electric kettle in his hand. He wielded it like a weapon.

Harry opened his mouth again, but before he could utter another word, he was interrupted by the noise of a vehicle engine and the incoherent shouts of several of the scavengers. A council waste lorry was drawing near. He stood back as it approached and then turned in a circle fifteen or twenty yards away. As its back lifted, preparatory to dumping, a dozen men converged upon it, as if acting out a pagan ritual. The driver ignored them.

Rubbish poured from the rear end of the lorry. The wind caught fragments of it. Some landed on the eager rooters as they ran forward to claim their trophies. Bits of old food, slivers of plastic, were brushed off heads and shoulders as the hunt continued for better pickings: copper wire, transistor radios, trinkets of jewellery perhaps.

The lorry rumbled off into the distance and Harry stumbled towards the hooded men. He decided to try again. "Know where Froggy is?"

"What's it to you?" asked a freckled youth on the fringe of the group. He had been examining the intestines of a de-gutted settee. At first sight he seemed the youngest of the scavengers; perhaps he should have been at school.

Honesty wouldn't be the best policy here. Harry made a quick guess about the kind of lie that might achieve results.

"His missus has been took ill," he said in a congested Scouse accent, shamelessly stealing Froggy's own lie to the barmaid at the Ferry.

"Myra?" scoffed the lad. "She's built like an ox. He probably poisoned her with that tin of salmon he found here yesterday." He addressed a grizzled older man beside him, whose smoker's cough rasped incessantly. "Wasn't Froggy here earlier on?"

"Search me, kid."

"Reckon I saw him an hour or more ago. Before dinner."

Harry didn't ask what dinner on the tip consisted of. "Where was he?"

The freckled youth jerked a thumb. "Down by the skips." He gazed for a moment at a couple of soggy paperbacks that he had retrieved from the mess deposited by the lorry. Novels by Harold Robbins and Mickey Spillane, their gaudy covers smeared with what might have been excrement. Wrinkling his nose, he threw them back into the mire. "What use are books? Come on. I'm headed down there now meself."

Harry followed as his guide traced a path through the tin cans and the slush of wet paper. "Glad to gerraway, actually" confided the lad. "That cough. Honest, it makes me want to puke."

Harry couldn't ignore the fetid smell all around. "Doesn't everything here?"

The lad glanced back over his shoulder, grinning. "Got to you, has it? Yer first time?" When Harry nodded, he went on, "It's not so bad after a while. You stop noticing it. Me name's Geoff, by the way."

"Harry."

"Pleased to meet you. Won't shake hands, mine are a bit mussed up, know what I mean? Can't be too fussy about what you touch round here."

By now they were within fifty yards of a row of yellow-painted skips, each marked domestic only. "Keep yer eyes skinned," advised Geoff. He seemed to be relishing his veteran's role, giving the benefit of his experience to a newcomer. "The fellers on the compactors are all right, but you have to watch that foreman, he's a tight-arse."

With a quick look to right and left, Geoff approached the skips and clambered up to inspect their contents. Harry gazed round. The place was quiet. A handful of the men who worked at the site were having a cup of tea in a Portakabin. The rest of the totters were back on the waste mound, scrabbling through heavy duty debris which bore a disconcerting resemblance to stuff Harry had seen exhibited at the Tate. He wandered towards the corrugated iron sheds which stood below the iron bulk of the incinerator and the crusher.

Geoff called him back. "You won't find Froggy that way. Nothing for the likes of us there. Too close to the buildings. And will you look at this? Criminal, what some folk throw out." He held aloft a man's double breasted jacket in a bilious shade of green.

Spots of rain began to fall. "No sign of Froggy here," said Harry. "I'd best be off."

"What's he done?" asked Geoff.

"I told you," said Harry, "it's his wife."

"Gerraway. I'm not soft."

Harry dropped the accent, which had already been wearing thin. "I need some information from him, that's all."

Geoff grinned. "It'll cost you then, if I know Froggy. Always on the make, that feller. No self-respect."

Harry gazed back at the tip and the thin dark line of scavengers, strung out along the horizon. Some of them had started a fire, perhaps to burn the plastic casing off a worthwhile haul of copper wire. The smoke drifted up into the sky and the wind took it in the direction of the distant rows of council housing.

"Thanks anyway."

"No sweat. When you find him, tell him about this. He'll be sick as a pig, will Froggy. Been on the look out for a decent jacket for ages, he has."

Harry returned to the main road via the public entrance. Nothing would induce him to endure that stink again today at such close quarters. He had to skirt round a diversion caused by a gang of labourers working lethargically on the repair of sewers that lay beneath the road and by the time he reached the M.G., the drizzle had become a downpour. But on Pasture Moss, the rooters' work went on.

He drove straight back to Baden Powell Street. The brick-carrying infant was nowhere to be seen and he reached the door of number eleven unmolested. He banged on the cracked wooden panels and heard a woman bellow, "Wait yer hurry." After half a minute she answered the door, a large woman with short brown hair and an air of truculence. Geoff's comparison hadn't flattered the ox.

"Froggy in?"

"And who might you be?"

Acting the well-intentioned simpleton, Harry invented a story about a bet placed at the Ferry Club; he owed Froggy a tenner and now he was in a position to pay. Trying to find this man was beginning to strain his imagination, but however implausible the line, big Myra was sufficiently impressed to offer to take the cash and hand it over to her bloke when he came in. Harry explained that this wasn't enough; he wanted to have a private word with Froggy.

Losing interest, she shrugged. "Can't help you, mister. You say he's not down at Pasture Moss? The bookies' then, or the boozer. But don't ask me which one. I'm past caring."

"When he comes back, can you ask him to give me a ring? My name's Harry Devlin. From Empire Dock. The number's in the book."

"If I remember," she said and banged the door shut.

As he drove back to the city centre, he attempted to gather together in his mind the various scraps of the puzzle. Liz claimed to have been involved with a wealthy, married businessman, but there was no proof that the man had ever existed. She was trying to disentangle herself from Coghlan, but had found time for some sort of fling with a roughneck called Joe Rourke. Rourke might be connected with Coghlan; then again, he might have been the father of the unborn child. She had spurned Derek and never taken Matt seriously. Froggy knew something about Liz's link with one of her lovers, or else about the circumstances of her death. He might have been the man who had followed her, though Harry was sure that his had not been the voice of the masked assailant outside Empire Dock. More and more, it seemed that Evison held the key. In his absence, it might be worth having a further word with Matt.

He parked in the multi-storey by the Moat House Hotel and walked over to the Freak Shop. An old man with bloodshot eyes was taking a close interest in the exotic lingerie. Behind the counter, Matt Barley raised his eyebrows at Harry's expression.

"Can we talk in private, Matt?"

He summoned a purple-haired girl called Tracey to take over and led the way through the bead curtain into his inner sanctum. Shifting a pile of sex aids supposed to help the incapable to achieve the physically improbable, he squatted on a chair and said, "And what can I do for you?"

"Maggie told me that you'd mentioned Liz was being followed. Or believed she was, at least. It rang a bell in my mind, because she did say something of the sort last Wednesday night, only I was too preoccupied to pay much attention."

Matt nodded. "Whether it was true or not, I dunno, but she certainly said it. I thought if there was someone hanging about, he might have been one of Coghlan's runners. Or even a private detective of some kind if he was wanting to check up on whether she was playing away from home."

"The details, the description - did she say anything more?"

"Can't recall. Your first instinct was probably right. If she was killed on purpose, Coghlan must have been behind it. There's no one else."

Harry scratched his nose. "Do you know someone by the name of Joe Rourke? I think he was involved with Liz recently."

The little man stared. "Never heard of him. And how do you mean "involved"?"

Harry told him about his visit to Aneurin Bevan Heights. Matt didn't hide his disgust. "Yet another stud?" He pointed a finger at Harry. "Now will you admit the truth and take her off that pedestal?"

"Never mind about that. The truth about her death is what I'm looking for."

"Christ! Why don't you open your eyes? She was a whore, Harry, a gorgeous whore, and we all knew it." The roundface blazed with rage. "Admit it! She made a laughing stock out of us all."

Harry said quietly, "I hadn't appreciated that you felt so strongly, Matt. Did you hate her so much?"

The little man was shouting now. "I loved her, you oaf! Worshipped her. From the time she was the kid who lived next door, wearing a sensible school skirt and knee-length socks. She was fun, she was generous to a fault. She could wrap me around her little finger and I'd have done anything to make her care for me a tenth as much as I did for her. But she was a whore all the same, that was her nature. We are what we are, and that's what killed her. It's the truth."

They glared at each other for a moment. In the space of a few hours, Harry thought, both Derek and Matt have told me that they were crazy about her. She teased them and, as if that were not enough, tried to tempt Jim from the straight and narrow. When she fancied a bit of rough, she picked up Rourke in the Ferry Club. Couldn't she leave any man alone?

He bit his lip. This was the wrong time to row with an old friend. Aloud, he said, "I'll be making tracks, Matt. See you around."

He strode out without another word. So far his enquiries had yielded a battering and a sick realisation of the extent of Liz's wantonness. Once again, he had half a mind to abandon the hunt to the professionals who knew what they were doing. He wouldn't give up, of course, to do so was not in his nature, but as he paced Mathew Street he realised he needed a break from his self-imposed task. Forget about her for a few hours, he urged himself, come back to it fresh tomorrow morning.

Calling in on the office, he skipped round Lucy's well-intentioned questions about his accident on Monday night and exchanged a few gruff words with Jim. At five he pushed the non-urgent mail to one side and headed back to the Empire Dock.

Brenda popped round as soon as she arrived home and didn't conceal her delight at the invitation to dine at the Ensenada. "That's marvellous," she said. "Of course I'd love to, but what shall I wear?"

Harry laughed. A normal, foolish conversation with a woman. That kind of thing had been in short supply for too long. They chatted for a while about matters of no consequence. Brenda seemed more relaxed in his company than ever before, less fussily anxious to please.

After leaving her to get ready, he shaved and changed into the only suit he possessed which was unlikely to make Pino sniff with dismay. He was adjusting his tie in front of the mirror when the doorbell rang. Brenda was there, wearing a body-hugging black velvet dress beneath a long red cape. Pearls glinted at her neck. She looked ten years younger.

"Will I let you down?"

He laughed. "No danger. Come inside for a minute. Table's booked for eight."

As he was offering her a seat in the lounge, the bell summoned him for the second time. He groaned and hurried to answer the door. Outside were Skinner and Macbeth. Immediately, he was transported back to the nightmare of the previous Friday morning, but he swallowed and managed to say calmly enough, "Evening, gentlemen. What can I do for you?"

In his customary sorrowful way, Skinner said, "I believe that you are acquainted with a Mr. Stanley Evison."

The unfamiliarity of the forename baffled Harry momentarily before he said, "You mean Froggy? I've come across him, yes. I've been trying to make contact with him today."

"And why might that be?"

Harry noticed that Skinner was no longer calling him "sir".

"Let's just say that I want to ask him one or two questions."

"I hope you're not waiting on the answers," said Skinner softly.

"What do you mean?"

"Mr. Evison's body was found earlier today. He had been murdered."

"Where?" It was the first thought that occurred to him.

Looking straight at him, Skinner said, "At the Pasture Moss Waste Disposal Site, off Pasture Road."

It was a nightmare, like something out of a *film noir* scripted by Cornell Woolrich. "But I was there earlier today."

Unblinking, the Detective Chief Inspector said, "So we understand. And I have reason to believe that you can help us with our enquiries."

The clichéd phrase, and the manner of its delivery, stung him. "Surely you don't . . .?"

Both policemen were motionless. Just as in his first encounter with them on that terrible Friday, Harry felt as if he were being measured and found wanting. He looked from one to the other and said, "This is absurd."

Skinner sniffed, evidently still struggling with his cold. He said, "Would you mind accompanying us to the station now?"

"What if I refuse?"

The set of the mournful face hardened. "In that case we would simply take the necessary steps. You know the score."

Harry knew what that meant. They considered there was a prima facie case against him on a charge of murder, perhaps of a double crime. They had enough evidence to justify arresting him, though not enough - surely? - to want yet to proceed with a trial. He could choose between resistance and co-operation. Over the years he had seen too many of his own clients make the wrong choice. He nodded at Skinner and looked around for his raincoat.

The sound of voices had brought Brenda to the doorway of the lounge. He saw her made-up face crumple with dismay and the policemen stare at her with grim curiosity. Their minds were easy to read: His wife's not buried yet and already he's knocking a slice off the next-door neighbour.

Quietly, he said, "Please would you ring Pino at the Ensenada, Brenda? I won't be able to make it tonight."

Chapter Twenty-Two

"Why did you lie to the boy?"

Macbeth's sardonic tone and the sly sidelong glance he shot at Harry gave the impression that he scarcely expected an honest answer. He had taken off his tie and the sleeves of his white shirt were rolled up to reveal brawny arms thick with dark hair. His hands lay flat upon the scratched top of the round table that stood between them, his palms down as though he were trying to crush the wood. For the last ten minutes he had been chewing something. The need for common courtesy had gone.

Harry let his eyes roam around the mustard-coloured walls of the interview room. The furniture comprised the table and three chairs; the walls were bare. In one corner sat the constable with the pitted face, ballpoint pen raised. A fresh page in his notebook awaited something new: a breakdown and confession, perhaps. All evening, the drip-drip-drip of the inquisition, repetitive but seemingly endless, had stretched Harry's nerves to snapping point. He had to keep biting his tongue to remind himself of the need to take all this seriously and to concentrate. The police were not treating the interrogation as a game.

"Why did you lie?" Macbeth repeated.

"I've already explained a thousand times."

"Try again."

At first, two or three hours ago, Harry had down-played his activities after Liz's death, had not acknowledged the strength of his determination to identify her murderer. But he hadn't lied outright - why should he? -and under Skinner's patient, probing cross-examination he had been forced to admit the full extent of his quest for Coghlan and the attack upon him outside Empire Dock. When Skinner left the room, the sergeant took over, not bothering to hide his contempt. Macbeth concentrated on the death of Froggy Evison, yielding no information, nagging for the reason why Harry had visited Pasture Moss that day.

"You couldn't even fool Pensby," he said derisively.

Pensby, it turned out, was Geoff, the freckled youth from the tip. Harry gathered that the lad himself had found Froggy's body, not long after his own departure from the scene. The cause of death had not been mentioned and Harry knew he was being tested. There was always the chance that a killer might make the mistake of revealing knowledge of more facts about the crime than the police had disclosed. Harry had seen the strategem work too many times with his own clients to disparage its effectiveness. There was no danger of his falling into that particular trap, but Geoff had evidently regaled the police with a detailed account of Harry's arrival at the tip in search of Evison, not omitting to mention the initial cock-and-bull story about Myra's illness. Macbeth had fastened on to the silly subterfuge and would not let it go.

"All I wanted was to talk to Evison," said Harry. Wearily, he went back over the old ground. "I was sure he'd been holding back on me when I spoke to him at the Ferry. The first time I'd seen him, on the night that Liz was stabbed, he'd come in to work late and seemed agitated about something. When I challenged him at the club, I was sure he knew more than he was prepared to admit. Might have been bravado, a desire to impress, but I didn't think so. I had to speak to him again to have any hope of getting to the truth. At the rubbish tip, I had to spin some kind of line to get even the kid to talk to me."

"A regular Sherlock, aren't you?"

"Listen, Evison's dead. He may have been killed by a Keep Britain Clean campaigner, but more likely he had a clue to this mess and that's why he had to die. Whoever did this," Harry gestured at his own bruised eye " - would hardly scruple at eliminating Froggy if he was a threat."

"Wasn't Evison a threat to you?"

Mustering every last ounce of self-possession at his command, Harry said, "You're on the wrong track, Sergeant. While we sit here wasting time a killer is on the loose."

"To believe all this, we have to accept you were devoted to your late wife, despite the fact she treated you like dirt. That you have no pride, that you will let a woman walk all over you, turn you into a laughing stock, and still shed a tear when she gets her just desserts."

The calculated provocation made Harry flinch, but all he said was, "Accept what you like."

"And yet with the inquest not yet over, with the woman still not decently buried, you're carrying on with your next-door neighbour. Your period of mourning didn't last long." Macbeth relaxed in his chair, almost smiling, daring Harry to lose his temper.

He could recall countless occasions such as this. Sitting in on an interview, sometimes in this very room, and feeling impotent whilst his clients protested, pretended, evaded, elaborated, before in the end deciding to confess to their crimes. Over the years he had seen everything from the remorseless grilling of a teenage yobbo already black-and-blue as a result of injuries sustained whilst allegedly resisting arrest before his lawyer arrived, to the careful wearing down of a conman or petty blackmailer. The occasional breaks that paved the way for a change of tactics towards a tricky customer. Switches in mood and personnel, from the gentle let's-get-it-off-our-chest approach to the bluff that there was already enough evidence to lock the suspect up and throw away the key. All conducted in an environment that might have been designed to reproduce the claustrophobia of the waiting prison cell. Harry had seen clients succumb through fear, fatigue and ignorance, as well as guilt.

Returning Macbeth's gaze, he realised just how easy it is to confess. Here and now, even he had the momentary urge to put an end to all this hassle. How tempting it would be to tell the man what he wanted to hear, making it up as you went along. Was it any wonder that people claimed responsibility for crimes they hadn't committed, simply groping for the illusion of respite from those endless questions that wore you down like water slowly eroding stone?

Suddenly Macbeth asked, "How old is she, Mrs. Rixton? Forty? Forty-five?" When Harry shrugged in reply, he continued, "Very different from your late wife, that's for sure. Not exactly a dolly bird."

Don't be provoked, Harry told himself, break the spell. As lightly as he could, he said, "Maybe I ought to have a solicitor present."

"Losing your bottle?" jeered Macbeth. "You people are all the same. Bent as a corkscrew and less guts. Call for Fingall, why don't you? Or Hendrickson, perhaps. They know all the dirty tricks of your trade."

"Or," said Harry, "I could simply walk out. I'm not under arrest."

Macbeth's arched eyebrows said: Not yet. Harry rose to his feet. "Face it, Sergeant, you don't believe I killed either Liz or Evison. You're pissing in the wind."

The policeman stood too. "Don't you see, Mister Solicitor? There's only one link between the two deaths. You." He drew a deep breath and then spoke more deliberately. "Was she carrying your child? Did you beg her to leave Coghlan? Or was Coghlan the father and did you blow a fuse when you found that out? Either way, Evison must have known too much or at least have put two and two together. You traced him to the rubbish tip, had an argument - and killed him. Pensby turned up before you could get clean away, so you panicked into feeding him a load of bullshit."

"Go back to the drawing board. Coghlan's your man." Harry wiped a hand across his brow. The sweat was sticky to the touch. Decision time had come. "If you're not going to arrest me, Sergeant,

I think I'll be going." He took a couple of paces in the direction of the exit.

Macbeth was saved from the need to reply by the opening of the door. Skinner looked in and said coolly, "Spare me a minute, Sergeant." The younger man strode out into the corridor, where the two detectives held a muttered colloquy. In his corner, the constable began to chew his biro. Presently, Harry heard approaching footsteps and the Chief Inspector saying, "Okay, Dave, it's over to you." In response, a face appeared round the door, weather-beaten and welcome.

"Christ," said Harry, "the cavalry's arrived."

Detective Constable David Moulden grinned in his lopsided way and said to his note-taking colleague, "Scarper, son, this master-criminal and me are going to have a quiet chat."

The young constable scuttled out and Moulden settled his burly frame into the chair that Macbeth had recently vacated. Clicking his tongue, he said, "Well, Harry lad, another fine mess you got yourself into."

"Dave, will you speak to that bugger Macbeth and his bloody boss and convince them I'm not a double murderer?"

Soberly, the older man said, "Convince me first."

Irritated by the reply, and reminded by his empty stomach and parched throat how long it was since he had last eaten or had a drink, Harry said, "They must be desperate if they've sent you to prise out a cough, mate."

Moulden didn't smile. "You're in a tricky situation, don't misunderstand that. So what's been going on?"

Harry gave him a precis of events. When he had finished, he said, "Skinner put me through the wringer. Macbeth too, though with less finesse. They almost had me thinking I was guilty."

"They're good jacks, Harry. It's a tough case. But Skinner's determined - reminds me of you in a funny sort of way. Once he gets into an investigation, he's like a bloody limpet. And Wes

Macbeth . . ." Moulden sucked in his cheeks. "Well, he doesn't like lawyers."

"I'd noticed. But who does?"

Lowering his voice, Moulden said, "He has his reasons. His kid sister was raped when he was a teenager in Kirkby. The feller who did it lived in the same deck-access block. He took his time, didn't spare her anything. Some sharp defence brief from Manchester spent hours cross-examining her about her sex life, driving her to hysteria in order to get his client off. You know the drill. He argued that she led the creep on. Worked a treat. The jury fell for it hook, line and bloody sinker. A month later the girl gassed herself. A kitchen oven job. Wes found her body when he got home from school."

He gave Harry a considering look. "It could have turned Wes crazy, but he decided to fight back from the inside and joined up with us. Got his promotion in record time, and not just because he's a token black. He's a hard bastard, Harry, but he follows the rules and he's good at his job. You can be sure he won't let any lawyer stand in the way of getting a conviction. He regards your lot as worse than the thugs and thieves you represent. I've told him myself that's as daft as judging us by the odd ones who put their hands in the till or rough up a youngster on sus. All the same, if I'd been through what he's been through, I don't suppose I'd chum up with any defence brief who came my way."

Harry said, "The lawyer was only doing his job."

"So is Wes, so stop bleating."

Neither of them spoke for a minute. Harry shifted his thoughts back to the central problem of the murders. Two deaths now - three if you included the unborn child. With Evison gone, he was as far away as ever from being able to prove that Liz's lover had murdered her. To his dismay, he became aware of tears of frustration pricking at his eyelids.

"It must be Coghlan, Dave. No one else fits the bill."

186

Moulden said, "I know you hate the man, and I don't blame you for that. But we need more to go on than a gut feeling. Face it, if that wasn't the case, you'd have been locked up by now."

Obstinate as a chastised child, Harry said, "He had the motive and the temperament."

"Not the opportunity, though. When your wife was killed he was two hundred miles away. That's for certain."

"His alibi checks out?"

A curious expression flitted across Dave Moulden's face. Was it veiled amusement? "We're satisfied about his movements, yes."

"These things can be set up from a distance, have you thought about that? Coghlan has plenty of hired hands available, I suppose it was one of them that attended to me the other night."

"You think that hasn't been considered? Give us credit for knowing our own business best." He hesitated. "All I can say is that in the light of our inquiries we have reason to doubt whether Coghlan was connected with the death of your wife."

"What makes you so sure?"

"Sorry, mate, can't say anything more."

"Was Coghlan aware Liz was pregnant?"

"We don't think so. At least, not until we told him. Unless he's a bloody good actor."

Harry thought for a few seconds, then said, "Who else did your people tell about the baby?"

"The sister-in-law. No one else as far as I'm aware. We were interested to find out who your wife had confided in, but it seemed she was a lady who liked to keep these things close to her chest."

"Have you traced the businessman she was involved with? This Tony?"

Moulden shook his head. "So far we've drawn a complete blank. Which is interesting. Your wife was a talker, said everything but her prayers, by all accounts. Yet we hadn't even been able to put a name to the man until you told Skinhead an hour ago. She obviously said more to your mud-wrestling friend than anyone else, and even with her she didn't let much slip, did she? Makes you wonder if he might have been a figment of her imagination, doesn't it?"

"Remember, the man was married."

"That may explain it." Moulden winked. "Matter of fact, though I don't officially approve, it's true that you've picked up one or two snippets that had escaped us. This feller Rourke, for instance. None of the people we've talked to have let on about her seeing him."

"They may have met at the club," said Harry. "Could that be significant?"

The policeman heaved large shoulders. "I'm not paid to do much thinking, but obviously we need to interview the man. Trouble with this case is, all the leads take us nowhere. Take an example - your brother-in-law's farewell meal with her had us interested. Of course, we sniffed around. Very embarrassing for a pillar of the community like Mr. Edge, I'm sure. The upshot being, we found he did arrive at the Adelphi precisely when he claimed. No one there had the impression that he'd just left his sister-in-law's corpse lying in an alley. No forensic links whatsoever and the timing would have been too tight for comfort anyway. And as far as we can tell so far, he was working in his spick-and-span office in Water Street when Evison was killed."

Moulden scratched his nose reflectively. "This second murder, it's hard to explain away, you see. Unless there's been a hell of a coincidence, it wipes out any chance that your wife was simply the victim of a random street crime, Yet if we're right, and Coghlan and Edge are clean, who does that leave?" He gazed solemnly at Harry. "You see why you've been subjected to a touch of the third degree? No alibi for the first murder, on the scene of the second at just the right time. Motive and opportunity . . . it doesn't look good."

"What about means? How was Froggy killed?" Dave Moulden smiled, but his eyes were watchful. "That's what we can't tie in with you. I suppose you've realised that already? The boys reckon they went over your flat with a fine toothcomb. Perhaps you'd hidden it somewhere else or picked it up for the sole purpose of wiping little Evison out."

"Stop talking in riddles. Tell me how he was killed." Moulden said softly, "Pensby's been blabbing to the Press, despite our words of warning, so there's no point in my holding back, I suppose. Evison was shot with a sawn-off shotgun, probably fired when the din of the dumper trucks provided a cover. So far we haven't been able either to find the weapon or to link you with it. Until we do," he said, unsmiling now, "no copper, not even Wes Macbeth, is likely to risk an arrest. You may as well be on your way. No more third degree for the time being. But Harry, mate, if there is a link, you're finished. And not all the legal loopholes in Liverpool will be enough to save your skin."

Chapter Twenty-Three

Brenda was waiting for him when he arrived home on the stroke of midnight. She must have been listening for his footsteps down the corridor, since she emerged from her flat at the moment he began unlocking the front door of his. Barefoot, she seemed much smaller than usual, unvarnished and defenceless. Looking down at her, he could see more clearly than before the traces of grey in her hair as it spilled on to the shoulders of a kimono patterned in black and gold.

"You look wrecked," she said.

"I'm all right."

"Come in for a minute."

Inside her flat, he realised that his whole body was aching. In half a dozen fractured sentences he told her what had happened. Released from the need to control his temper with the police, he felt a sudden fury at all the violence and death and at the sickening knowledge that the killer still walked free.

She poured him a generous measure of whisky. "Here, have this."

He gulped the drink down and banged the empty tumbler down on a table. He was breathing hard.

Softly, she said, "Hey, you're having a bad time."

She leaned over to pat his arm. Without thinking about it, he grasped her wrist and pulled her towards him, pressing his mouth on hers. He could feel her tremble and then respond. Their tongues met. Touching her made him want her. They didn't stop kissing for a long time.

Eventually, she took his hand and led him to her bedroom, a tranquil place decorated in pink and blue, with the image of a double bed reflected in the doors of the mirror wardrobes that lined one wall.

"Will you stay with me tonight?" she asked.

When he nodded, she smiled and slipped the kimono off, letting it slide on to the floor. As he kissed her breasts, she undressed him, her nimble fingers unfastening buttons, belt and zip whilst all the time she made little moans of pleasure.

Their flesh merged to shut out the world in a joint rejection of all its misery and viciousness. When he looked down, he saw her face shining and at last the thought of satisfying her blotted out his anger and sorrow. Deep into the night she cried out with joy, but he remained mute, lost in her and in the unexpected Tightness of their coming together.

Next morning she was awake before him, smiling as he made a sleepy effort to prise stubborn eyelids open. Running fingers through the tousle of his hair, she asked, "And how do you feel today, Mr. Devlin?"

"Fine, Mrs. Rixton, fine."

"You were . . ." She flushed and broke off, embarrassed. "No, I always say too much. Anyway, I - God, is that the time?"

Half eight already. He had slept through the alarm. "I must rush," she said. "Though I would love to stay."

Over breakfast, he confined himself to monosyllables, not grumpily but content to listen to Brenda talk about the day ahead of her in the office. She had cooked a meal of bacon, tomato and fried egg with toast and marmalade to follow and he ate hungrily, unable to remember when last he had consumed so much at such an early hour.

Suddenly, Brenda exclaimed with irritation and clapped a hand to her brow. "Oh God, I forgot! One of your lady friends called to see you last night."

"Yes?"

Brenda smiled slyly. "Inquisitive of me, I know. Poking my nose in. But I heard someone ringing your bell so I took a peek. Your - er - friend was on the point of giving up. She was all dressed up in a kaftan, said she was going to a party and had wondered if you wanted to go along."

It could only be Dame. "Did she leave any message?"

"Only that you weren't to worry about missing her. She had remembered something you might like to know, but it probably wasn't important. And she wouldn't give her name, just said she was a fellow art lover."

"My friend has a peculiar sense of humour." He grinned. "She's called Dame. By profession she's a mud wrestler and I've known her for years. Not a romantic entanglement. She's a sweet lady."

Brenda gave him an earnest look. "Even if there was a romance, it's none of my business. Don't worry, Harry, I won't start thinking I own you on account of our having spent a little time in bed together."

He touched her arm. "Tonight we may make it to the Ensenada."

Her slim hand reached across the oak breakfast bar. "No need for promises, Harry. Let's just make the most of this while we can. It's been - well, you know how it's been. Whilst you were gone yesterday evening, I was thinking things over. I'm not looking for commitments, truly I'm not. Here and now is sufficient for me."

"Brenda, I . . ."

"No, no, there's no need for us to say any more at present. Though I'd be glad to come over for lunch today, if you're free."

"I'll be free," he said, "provided I'm not beaten up or accused of killing my own wife. Life hasn't been predictable lately."

She fetched her coat and bag and then kissed him gently on the cheek. "Mind how you go, Harry. Next time I see you, I don't want it to be in prison or a casualty ward."

Five minutes later he followed her downstairs to the car park. Flecks of rain swirled about in gusts of wind that came in from the Irish Sea. He climbed into the M.G. and, turning right out of the main gates, headed away from the city centre towards Aigburth Road. Reaching the area where many of the university students lived, he entered a maze of side streets, finally pulling up in front of a dilapidated Victorian villa with an overgrown front garden. This was where he had dropped Dame off after their Sunday meal together.

Her name was inked on a dog-eared card next to a bell labelled flat 5b. Harry had noticed that none of the curtains at the windows were drawn; this wasn't the home of early risers. He rang half a dozen times and at long last saw through the multi-coloured glass panes of the front door a bulky silhouette stomping down the hallway. Dame's muttered imprecations were plainly audible.

Throwing the door open, she was already launching into a tirade of abuse when Harry said quickly, "Mind if I come in?"

She stared. "What brings you here at this God-awful hour?"

"Dame," he said, "it's quarter to nine. All over the city kids are arriving at school, people are working. Besides, I got a message that you wanted to tell me something."

She grunted. "You know I'm a creature of the night, darling. And you haven't picked the ideal moment. Anyone else and I'd tell them where to go. Never mind, follow me."

Leading him upstairs, she said, "Been in the wars, have you? You look the worse for wear."

"Who isn't?"

"Ouch," she replied as they reached the landing, "I know I'm not at my best right now, but you don't need to rub it in. This way."

The sitting room of her flat was large, high-ceilinged and furnished out of a second-hand shop. A dark red Indian rug, which Harry recognised from Dame's previous digs, was draped over one wall. In the middle of a faded settee was another old friend, a moth-eaten teddy bear unoriginally named Aloysius, whose amber eyes were fixed in a permanent, disapproving squint. There was a faint aroma of incense in the air. One of the internal doors opened into Dame's bedroom and Harry could see a young man there, hastily sliding into corduroy trousers.

"Don't worry, Rupert," she called, "it's not an angry husband or the man who comes to collect the rent." She winked at Harry. "As you can tell, I've turned to cradle-snatching. Rupert's at the Uni. We met last night at a party, wasn't I lucky? He studies Economics and wants to become amerchant banker." With a disgraceful leer, she added, "I hope he values my assets."

Rupert came into the room, buttoning his shirt with clumsy movements. He was tall and willowy and around eighteen years old. In an accent picked up in some public school a couple of hundred miles away, he said, "Actually, I think I ought to be going, Dame. There's a lecture at eleven, I really ought . . ."

"Suit yourself," she said with a tired wave of the hand. "This is my solicitor, by the way. Harry, Rupert. Rupert, Harry."

Harry nodded gravely as the student shot him a bewildered glance from under dark, feminine lashes. The boy said, "Hello. Right. Well. I'd better be off, then."

"Cheeribye," said Dame, yawning.

Rupert wavered in the doorway. "I - I'll give you a call sometime."

Dame arched her eyebrows, causing his pale features to redden. "I doubt it, darling, but I am in the book, should you ever want to continue our fascinating conversation about John Maynard Whatsisname."

Rupert blushed again and was gone, one of his shoelaces still flapping wildly as he hastened down the stairs. Sitting herself down beside Aloysius, whom she gave a comradely punch in the stomach, Dame sighed and said, "You must forgive me, Harry, I picked him up at a party last night. Never could resist a pretty face."

"Sorry to interrupt."

She shook her head. "Think nothing of it. Your arrival provided an opportunity for him to slip away without commitment. The alternative would only have been pretence and promises that wouldn't be kept. I know the score, all right." She contrived a grin.

"I regard myself almost as a social service these days, passing on all my experience to a younger generation, more or less anyone who has a spot of energy and is willing to learn. Price is reasonable, too. A few drinks, a meal. Any road - you didn't come here to listen to me sermonise on the subject of men."

"My neighbour told me you'd remembered something."

"Your neighbour, yes." Dame regarded him thoughtfully. "A lady who seems very solicitous about your welfare."

He didn't want to get involved in a discussion with Dame about Brenda, or to embark on up-dating her about the death of Froggy Evison and his interrogation by the police. Firmly, he said, "What came to mind?"

"After I saw you on Sunday, I went round to see Matt the next morning. To have a bite of lunch, talk things over. He said that he'd been talking to Maggie and to you. And he told me there was something he'd forgotten to mention, about this character who was following Liz. She told him that she'd tried to play it craftily when she was trying to work out whether he was really after her. He used to be hanging around in the city centre when she left the Freak Shop at lunchtime and in the afternoon. One time, she told Matt, she waited round a corner in the Cavern Walks and the guy almost cannoned into her. Then he mumbled something and went on his way. But she managed to see that his face was battered. Scratched, you know, as though he'd been in a fight. That made her all the more certain he was one of Coghlan's roughs from the gym, according to Matt."

Slowly, Harry said, "Now that is interesting."

Dame ran a hand through her hair. "I told him you would want to know. It's only a little thing, I realise, but you'd look on it as another link in the chain. Matt was doubtful. He reckons the last thing you need is to get embroiled any deeper in this whole bloody mess. I see what he means, but . . ."

He nodded. "Yes, thanks. You're right. Dead right. And, Dame, there's another thing - did you tell anyone at any time that Liz was pregnant?"

With a puzzled frown, she considered. "No, I don't think so."

"Sure you didn't mention it to Matt, for instance? Before your last conversation with him, I mean."

"No, I'm fairly certain of that. Why do you ask?"

Harry made a dismissive gesture with one hand. "Something's been nagging at me, that's all."

Dame tickled Aloysius under his chin and confided in him, "Harry doesn't change, does he, Al? Loves to be enigmatic." Turning back to Harry, she said, "Can I offer you anything? Coffee, booze, and illicit substance? You can bolster my ego, tell me that Rupert can't recognise a good woman worth cherishing when he sees one."

"I have to go," said Harry, "but you already know that you can do better for yourself than some scrawny undergraduate who isn't even ambitious enough to want to change the world."

"Yes, darling, but so few worthwhile members of your sex realise what they are missing where I am concerned. A good man is hard to find, as well as vice versa."

He grinned. "Okay, Dame, keep in touch. I'll be seeing you."

She blew him a kiss and he climbed back down the stairs. He felt infused with a new vigour, as though Brenda's love-making had the restorative properties of a patent cure for his hangover of grief and guilt. He drove back to the city centre fast, but not recklessly, alive again with a mental checklist of people to see and questions to ask.

At the Freak Shop, the exotically-coiffed Tracey was wrapping up a wad of Swedish magazines for a middle-aged man with a caught-in-the-act expression. When Harry approached the counter she nodded in the direction of the bead curtain. "If it's the boss you want, he's in the back."

Parting the beads, Harry found Matt poring over a pile of invoices; his pen was poised and his mouth pursed in disapproval. John Lennon looked down from the wall with the cool superiority of one who had made a fortune without ever having to fret about who paid the bills. The short man glanced up briefly and waved Harry towards the rickety chair.

"Becoming a regular visitor, aren't you, mate? With you in a minute."

Harry reversed the chair and perched on it, legs astride. "How did you know that Liz was pregnant?"

Matt jabbed the point of his pen so sharply into the document he was studying that the paper tore. Jerking his head to look at his visitor, he said brusquely, "What do you mean?"

"Don't try to fob me off, Matt. You and I should have too much respect for each other to piss about."

"I'm not. . ."

"You knew she was pregnant. You told me so yourself last Sunday. The police deny telling you. So does Dame. No one else was aware of it. So how did you find out?"

In the pause that followed, Matt avoided Harry's eyes, instead looking blindly at the sheaf of papers in front of him. When at last he spoke, his voice was subdued. "Liz told me."

"Yes?"

The round face grimaced as Matt made an evident effort to keep himself under control. That surprises you, doesn't it, mate? That she let me into her secret, but not you."

Harry shrugged. "You were an old friend. When did you learn the news?"

Matt hesitated. He seemed to be trying to frame his reply with care. This kind of moment often cropped up in cross-examination, when a witness's story was about to crack. Harry decided to bluff. "She hadn't worked for you the week she was killed, yet she was only two months gone. Odds were, she'd not long found out herself."

Licking his lips, Matt said, "Okay. She told me on the day she was murdered. I hadn't known before."

"Go on."

"She came here that day. Around one. She explained about staying at your place, said you'd been chivalrous and surrendered your bed. Apparently, she'd tried to call you on the phone that day, but you always seemed to be busy." Harry groaned at Liz's characteristic exaggeration there. "She had meant to have lunch with you, but she thought as you were tied up, she'd wander over and apologise for not coming in to work that week. Tracey was off sick and Liz should have been on duty, so I decided to shut the shop and take her to Mama Reilly's for a bite to eat. That was when she told me about having made up her mind to break off with Coghlan and move in with her new boyfriend."

"Did she say anything about him?"

"Only the usual dreamy stuff you would expect from Liz. That he was rich and handsome and had finally agreed to dump his undeserving wife. I asked her if she was certain and that was when she told me about expecting a baby. The idea seemed to delight her. She said she could hardly believe that it was all happening to her at last. The man she wanted and a kid as well. It's time for me to settle down, she said."

Matt's face had darkened as he spoke. Something in his tone, a thinly veiled anger, made Harry say, "And were you happy for her?"

"Happy? I was sick with rage and envy. There she was, prattling away about this bloke who'd stepped out of the pages of a woman's magazine, and all I wanted to find out was who was the father of the baby."

Startled by Matt's outburst, Harry demanded, "Why did it matter so much to you?"

The little man lifted his head defiantly. "If you must know, I wanted to find out if the child was mine."

Chapter Twenty-Four

Harry stared at Matt in bewilderment. "What do you mean?"

"What I say." The words were blurred and indistinct, as though they were all that remained after tears had been choked away. "Liz and I slept together. Yes, that shocks you, doesn't it? Yet it's true. I say "slept", but we made love for a couple of hours and then she said she had to go. It was last Christmas Eve. You remember, when the snow fell? The shop had closed, the takings were good and we'd been celebrating, with too much to drink. Liz was on the Bacardis. Suddenly she put her arm round me and asked if by any chance I wanted her. I was lost for words, but she simply laughed and told me to hail a cab for a hotel at the other end of town. We had a room the size of a shoebox and a bed that screeched each time we moved, but none of it mattered to me. I had her and it was the moment I'd been waiting for half my life."

He took a deep breath and continued, "I don't need to describe how I felt. Let's just say that all through Christmas I was in a daze. I suppose I'd loved Liz since the day I met her. Even as a kid, her smile could melt an icecap. And she was good to me, too. Teased me about my height, yeah, but never in a cruel way, just as an old mate would do. And she always kept in touch. But I never thought I'd have a chance with her, not when I was only half a man and she was able to pick and choose. On Christmas Day I woke up though and asked myself if I could make it happen after all. Could I offer her enough to make her mine? Stupid, eh? Behaving like a moonstruck teenager.

"Of course, it didn't last. When she came back to work after New Year, it was as if we'd simply kissed and wished each other goodnight, as if nothing had occurred to change the way we were. I couldn't fathom it at first. Then one day she said something about my Christmas present and treated me to a grin that ran from ear to ear. I realised that she'd just been doing me a kindness, that was all. To Liz it meant no more than helping a man with a white stick across the road."

"No need to be bitter, Matt."

The little man's face was a fiery red. "When she told me about the baby, I couldn't help myself. I asked if she was sure it belonged to her latest beau. She curled her lip and said that it certainly wasn't Coghlan's. And then, as plainly as if I could read her mind, I saw it dawn on her that I thought I might be the child's father."

He made a low moaning noise, like an animal in pain. For a short while neither of them spoke. Eventually he looked up and said, "God help her, she laughed. Not intentionally heartless, that might have been easier to bear. It was the sheer - I dunno - unexpectedness to her of the idea that a dwarf could ever sire a child of hers. She tried to keep her face straight and I realised that for all our times together over the years, the fun we'd had, not just in the shop and going out on the town every now and then, but back in the days when old Ma Wieczarek was alive, she'd never regarded me as a proper man. She'd been able to behave more naturally with me than with any other feller, you included, simply because she didn't think of me as one of them. I was a midget, a member of a race apart. Then she solemnly said that she was sure I wasn't the one responsible for putting her in the family way and wasn't I glad that I wouldn't have to do the decent thing and marry her? Christ, if only she knew.

"I walked out on her. There was no other option. If I'd stayed a moment longer I would have hurt her. The old red mist had descended, you understand. Believe me, right at that instant I *could* have murdered her and not have turned a hair." He barked with mirthless amusement at Harry's reaction. "Oh, yes, I know what you're thinking. But I didn't creep up behind her in Leeming Street. I wouldn't have killed her in a hole-and-corner way and then slunk off to save my own neck. No, I didn't re-open the shop that afternoon, but it wasn't for any nefarious reason. I simply needed to try to flush her out of my system. So I went on the piss. I toured round the pubs - can't even remember all the ones I supped in. Some kind soul chucked me into a taxi and I spent most of Friday drying out. No, Harry, you'll have to look elsewhere for your culprit."

"Why not tell me all this to begin with?" To his dismay he heard himself posing the same question as D.S. Macbeth. "Why did you lie?"

"Would you believe I was ashamed? And scared, but mostly ashamed. People had seen me with her in Mama Reilly's. I must have caused a bit of a stir when I walked out, though I was fighting back the tears and didn't take any notice. When it seemed the police hadn't latched on to the fact that we'd been together, I made up my mind to keep stumm. I couldn't help them, offer any clues. She was murdered hours later and I had no idea where she went afterwards. No, all I would get for mouthing off would be the third degree from tired scuffers desperate for an arrest. Funny how the mind works, builds up defences. I even convinced myself I was helping by not distracting the cops with my squalid little tale that didn't have any bearing on Liz's murder."

"I wish you'd told me."

Matt looked sheepish. "Truth is, I felt guilty as far as you were concerned. After all, you were her husband." He sighed. "I always envied you your time with her. Still do, as a matter of fact. At least it's there, it happened. All I have is the memory of two stolen hours. It's more than I ever dreamed of, but it isn't enough."

Tracey's purple head bobbed round the door. "It's gone time for me break," she said.

"With you in a minute." Matt stood up. "Sorry. I should have been franker. I remember you once told me that Crusoe and Devlin make more money out of their clients' lies than from the times when they forget themselves and tell the truth. But we don't always do what we should, do we?"

Harry joined him at the door. "You can say that again."

"Look. It must have been Coghlan. There's no other explanation."

"I don't think it's as simple as that."

A fierce look crossed the small man's face. "Why not? He drove her to despair and then he lost her. He's not the sort to take that lying down."

"Maybe not. I'll see you, Matt."

Harry walked through the shop and out into the morning drizzle. His head was buzzing and the sense of well-being that his night with Brenda had engendered had ebbed away. Matt's story had rocked him; he felt more hurt by Liz's ignorance of the little man's secret hopes than by the news of her latest adultery.

He picked up a newspaper. Froggy's death hadn't even made the front page, which was devoted to ructions within the city council. He found a half-column headed riddle of tip death under Ken Cafferty's by-line, but there was no hint to link the murder with that of Liz. Ken was too shrewd not to have sniffed out the connection once he learned that the same police team was handling the Evison case, but he had obviously been asked to keep it quiet and the report concentrated on the location of the body. A local politician had already suggested that it was all the fault of cuts in security and manning levels at the Pasture Moss site. Soon someone would be blaming the Government.

He tipped the paper into a litter bin and turned his thoughts to his next move. Now, at least, the pattern of Liz's last day alive was emerging. She had risen late, tried to call him at the office, been too lazy to keep ringing and, to amuse herself, wandered into town to spend some time with Matt. When he had left her, she must have paid up at Mama Reilly's and headed back through town. She had been in Water Street at the time of meeting Derek. More than likely, with time on her hands, she was en route for Fenwick Court. When Derek had offered her a meal at the up-market Ensenada, she must have decided to indulge in a little shopping to celebrate, and taken her haul back to Empire Dock. There she had exchanged a few words with Brenda outside the door of the flat before getting ready for the date with her brother-in-law. For the third time in less than twenty-four hours she had in her carefree way demoralised a man who had dared to believe that her leaving Coghlan opened the way for him. Might either Matt or Derek, unlike himself, have translated anger and humiliation into murderous action? Harry thrust the thought aside. Matt was right. Forget the police's reluctance to arrest the obvious suspect. Concentrate on Coghlan.

Time to pay that gentleman another visit, Harry told himself. Make him understand that no amount of beating would throw him off the track. Force him out into the open. Pressure him into making a mistake. Confront him at the gym.

He picked up the car and drove to Brunner Street. From the outside the Fitness Centre seemed strangely lifeless. As Harry walked over from the opposite side of the road, he realised that yellow blinds had been drawn at the windows. Reaching the door he saw that the closed sign was up. Beneath it someone had scrawled in black felt tip until

FURTHER NOTICE - WE APOLOGISE FOR ANY INCONVENIENCE.

Baffled, he pulled at the steel handle and banged on the opaque glass pane.

He heard footsteps from inside, followed by the drawing-back of bolts and a chain. A clean-cut young man in a tweed suit that seemed a size too big and a generation too old for him finally broke his way through the security and smiled regretfully.

"The Centre's closed today, I'm afraid."

"So I see." Harry craned his neck to look beyond the young man. There was no sign of the gum-chewing assistant or Paula or

Arthur. On the floor of the shop front were several large cardboard boxes and a girl in a smart jacket and tight black skirt was kneeling beside them and inspecting their contents, a clipboard in her hand. "Is Mr. Coghlan around?"

The young man said, "Sorry, he isn't. Are you a member here?"

"No, but I do need to see Coghlan. What's going on?"

His cheeks pink, the young man said, "I'm afraid there has been a slight hiccup. My colleague and I are from the office of the joint receivers, Bowler, Goldsmith and O'Gorman. We . . ."

"Receivers? You mean the place has gone bust?"

"Oh no, I wouldn't go so far as to . . ."

"Spare me the professional niceties, Bowler's are my firm's accountants." Harry extracted an old business card from his wallet. "Don't worry, I don't act for Coghlan, I just need to find him. Fast."

The girl had joined her colleague at the door. Her manner was as crisp as the cut of her short fair hair. After scrutinising the card, she said, "The bank called us in this morning. Michael Coghlan has defaulted on his loan repayments and they decided to pull the plug. Where he is, no one seems to know. The staff are upstairs, helping our people to fathom how the business works. There's an idea it might be sellable as a going concern. Trouble is, it's closely identified with Coghlan and there's an unconfirmed rumour that he's been arrested."

"Arrested? Why?"

The girl shrugged. "No idea. Hand in the till, I suppose. That's the usual in these situations, isn't it?"

Harry stared at her, thinking on his feet. An arrest. Was the long search over at last? He must speak to Skinner. Or Fingall. "Can I use your phone?"

"Be my guest. Or rather, the bank's guest."

She stepped aside and he dialled the number of the Canning Place headquarters. Skinner and Macbeth were out, as was Dave Moulden, and the junior detective on the murder inquiry team to whom he was put through deflected his questions in a more-than-my-job's-worth manner. Harry rang off. He would have to go there in person. On his way out, he thanked the fair girl, who had resumed the tedious chore of stock-taking.

"No trouble. Any of your clients wants to buy a gym, let George Harvey-Walker know."

"If he believed any of my clients was rich enough to buy a business from a bank," said Harry, "George would put up my audit fees! See you in the office some time, perhaps."

He smiled at the girl and left. In the space of five minutes his spirits had soared. Arrested? Rumours like that didn't spring out of nothing. Evidence must have come to light connecting Coghlan with the crime - perhaps both of them. As he crossed the road to the car he smacked the air with his fist in celebration. Now let the bastard sweat.

Before calling at Canning Place he decided to visit Coghlan's solicitor. The reception area at Fingall's office was crammed with a family of gypsies whose members were all trying to talk at once to the hapless secretary who had been sent out to deal with their complaint about a delay in handling some legal work on their behalf. Harry fought his way to the front and asked the small, mousy-haired girl behind the desk to tell her boss Harry Devlin wanted to see him right now.

Experienced in resisting such demands, the girl said that Mr. Fingall was down in London on an important case and wasn't expected back that day.

"What is he . . .?"

The bleeping of the switchboard distracted the girl. She picked up the phone and said, "Fingall and Company . . . oh, yes . . . not till tomorrow afternoon? Certainly. I'll ask Veronica to check your diary."

Struck by the note of deference that had entered her voice, Harry leaned forward. "Is that your boss?"

Irritated at his interruption, the mousy girl nodded. "Excuse me, love." Harry laid a hand on the receiver and pulled it from her, ignoring a shriek of protest that for a moment silenced even the grumbling gypsies in the background. "Ruby? This is Harry Devlin."

Even at a distance in excess of two hundred miles, Ruby's anger was unmistakable. "Devlin? What the hell are you doing butting into my conversation with a member of my own staff? You've - "

"Is it true Coghlan is under arrest?"

"Still waging your crusade? You're a fool, Devlin, I said you were wasting your time trying to pin your wife's killing on my client."

A sick sense of defeat engulfed Harry. Was the rumour untrue after all? The switchboard girl tried to retrieve the receiver, but he brushed her tiny hand away as if swatting a fly. "So he hasn't been arrested?"

In a tone evasive yet indignant, Fingall said, "Mind your own business. Put me back to my receptionist."

"Tell me one thing . . ."

The phone went dead. Harry swore and banged the receiver down on the desk. The girl glared at him and said, "Satisfied?" He grimaced and strode back through the melee to the door. One of the gypsies was apparently about to commit an act of criminal damage on the property of Fingall and Company in the hope of grabbing attention and Harry barely resisted the temptation to shout encouragement.

Outside again, he quickly decided on what to do next. He hurried over to the Magistrates' Court round the corner and used the payphone to call Ken Cafferty. Whilst he waited he watched the scurrying of barristers and solicitors, the frantic conferences with clients, the striking of deals with the prosecution. Normally he would be in the thick of it all himself, but today the concerns of his professional colleagues seemed as remote as those of a race of extra-terrestrials in a bad S.F. movie. He was wondering if Coghlan would ever be brought to trial, when the reporter's breeezy voice came onto the line.

"What can I do for you, pal?"

"Can you spare me a few minutes?" Harry consulted his watch. "Look, my throat's as dry as a bone and it's almost opening time. We could talk in the Dock Brief in five minutes, perhaps?"

"This is about your bete noir, Mister Michael Coghlan, I suppose?"

"Right. I'm hoping you'll be able to shine some light in the darkness."

"Doubtful. After all, I'm a journalist. But the Dock in five minutes is all right by me. Mine's a pint."

"I'll have it waiting for you," Harry promised.

He arrived at the pub as the doors were opening and had collected the drinks when Cafferty arrived. The reporter's cherubic face was pinker than ever and he was breathless from hurrying through the town.

"Glad to see you're still out of jail, Harry."

"So far." He raised his glass. "Now tell me what's going on. Have they arrested Coghlan for the murders or not?"

Ken Cafferty took a couple of sips and then said, "As you legal chaps like to say, on the one hand yes and on the other hand no. That is to say, he has been arrested. The Met issued a statement an hour ago."

"The Met?" So that was why Ruby was in the capital. Harry was still mystified. "What's it got to do with London police?"

"Everything. You see he's been arrested on counts of attempted murder and conspiracy to steal four million quid from a security outfit in Leytonstone. The big bullion raid last Wednesday."

Of course. Harry had read about it casually in the Bridewell.

"Apparently he was big mates from way back with some bloke who ran a heavy mob down the East End." Cafferty sniggered, unable to resist a dig at the soft South. "Stupid bugger, he should've known that a gang of Cockneys couldn't organise a piss-up in a brewery! Anyway, he was in the car and he took a pot shot at a have-a-go guard who was brave or daft enough to try to stop the gang. The man's still on a life support in intensive care." Unable to conceal his pleasure in announcing a scoop, Ken paused to finish his pint whilst Harry stared at him.

After half a minute the reporter put his glass down and said reflectively, "But you see what it means? It's hardly likely that even an ambitious member of the criminal fraternity such as Michael Coghlan would arrange to bump his girlfriend off at the same time that he was up to his neck in a robbery that's probably going to earn him twenty years in Parkhurst. There are limits, even to the criminal imagination."

Chapter Twenty-Five

"Gold," said Dave Moulden. He made a lip-smacking noise of satisfaction. "Lots of it. Okay, maybe small change by Brink's Mat standards, but still enough to keep the likes of you and me in Woodbines till the end of our natural." He added grudgingly, "Got to hand it to the Sweeney. They've wrapped this one up good and proper."

"Liz's murder must have been very convenient for the police," said Harry grimly. He was twisting his fingers round the handle of a plastic mug filled with tepid tea. They were in a small room in the same corridor as the one in which he had been interrogated the previous night. Harry had come back here as soon as Ken Cafferty had left him to follow up a rumour about corruption and councillors' expenses.

"Even if Coghlan twigged he was being watched," he said, almost to himself, "he wouldn't necessarily fear that his part in the raid was known to the police. I suppose his first hope was to weather the storm. When I found him at the West Liverpool I could tell that he was bending under the weight of guilt. I should have guessed he might have something else to be guilty about."

"Coghlan must feel as sick as a pig," said the policeman with relish. "Look at it from his point of view - the murder enquiry was another piece of bad luck. Along with the inside man at the warehouse losing his nerve and naming names when he decided to cough, and that guard trying to be a hero when Coghlan had a sawn-off in his hand and an itchy trigger finger. Not the same gun as killed Evison, by the way, to stop you wondering. Apparently, our friend was meant to be away from Liverpool for less than forty-eight hours. In the normal course of events no one would have missed him. He never dreamed he'd become a centre of attention through his lady friend getting herself murdered."

Noticing Harry flinch at that, Moulden rubbed his nose and continued more soberly, "The ringleaders of the gang are East Enders who live in the posh parts of Essex these days. Their names wouldn't mean anything to you, though they're well known in their own patch. Now the bastards must be kicking themselves. Coghlan was supposed to be an asset to the team, a nail-hard Scouser with a track record of successful robberies and a mate in the jewellery trade who happened to have a smelter that they could use to melt down the gold."

"Killory?"

"You've got it. I'm glad that little worm has been locked up, we've been chasing him for years without any joy. The two of them were under surveillance at the request of our friends from the Smoke. Anyway, last night word came through that the big boys had been lifted. Two of them were en route for warmer climes, I gather. Matter of fact, Coghlan was picked up at roughly the same time that we were letting you go from here."

"Thanks for confiding in me."

"Be reasonable. SOS - that's the Flying Squad to you and me - told us the minimum possible. That was fair enough, it was a delicate operation. Handled on a "need to know" basis. And we did tip you the wink that you were making a mistake in pursuing Coghlan. I understand Skinhead dropped a hint on day one. But would you listen? Any road, justice should be done. The man'll be inside for years and skint when he comes out. You heard his gym business is on the rocks? The gee-gees are to blame, so people are saying. He's gambled all his money away. No wonder your old lady's interest in him waned. No disrespect, but she did have an eye for the wallet, didn't she? "Course, this bullion job was designed to set him back up in the manner to which he was accustomed."

As the policeman sat back, content, Harry gestured to the fading bruise around his own eye. "And this?"

Moulden frowned. "Truth is, we're not sure about the attack on you, Harry. In fact, Skinhead's bet is that Coghlan wasn't responsible. Okay, so he did get Ruby to have a word with you after you caught him in his panic stations conference with Killory. So what? Isn't that what lawyers are for, to protect their clients' interests? Doesn't mean to say the bugger had you roughed up a few hours later before he was certain you wouldn't be heeding the friendly words of advice. Innocent till proved guilty, Harry, as you solicitors would say."

"If not Coghlan, who?"

"You've got enemies, Harry, must have. At your end of the legal market, it's only to be expected. That beating may have had nothing to do with your wife's death."

"I told you before, the man who attacked me wanted me to take my nose out of other people's business. Who else could have set that up but Coghlan?"

Moulden looked unconvinced. "Obviously we've put the lads from London in the picture about your wife's death. Nobody's taking anything for granted, even though we don't think he's involved. They'll be questioning Mister Coghlan intensively about it over the next few days. Mind you, he's not feeling too grand at the moment. Got hurt whilst resisting arrest, it seems." He allowed himself a smile. "You won't be sorry to hear that in the circumstances, I suppose."

"All I want now is to find the man who killed Liz. Despite everything, it's hard to accept that Coghlan had nothing to do with it. But assuming that's right, a murder remains to be solved."

"You think we've overlooked that?"

"No, I realise the wheels keep turning. But not fast enough for me. What's the latest?"

"I shouldn't tell you this," said Dave Moulden slowly, "but we got word this morning that she spent some time with your pal Barley at lunchtime on the day she was murdered. They were spotted at Mama Reilly's. Story is, he walked out in a paddy. He didn't let on when we interviewed him originally. Intriguing, eh? Skinhead set off in person half an hour back to have another chat with him."

"Look, Matt's got nothing to do with it. I know about that lunch, I was with him this morning." He avoided going into detail. Let Skinner ferret out the sad story for himself. "Besides, I don't think for a minute that he could have brought himself to stab Liz to death."

Choosing his words with more care than a man on oath, Moulden said, "Not personally, perhaps."

"Then how - oh, Christ, you don't think he hired someone to kill her just because they had a tiff?"

"Anything's possible, Harry. "Course, the same might be said of your brother-in-law."

"Derek? Are you kidding? The only contract he'd recognise is one for long-term car parking beneath the Atlantic Tower."

Poker-faced, Moulden said, "Still waters run deep."

"Spare me your words of wisdom, Dave. Not even you can really believe Derek Edge is responsible for wiping out his sister-in-law and that grubby parasite Evison."

"Much as I think accountants are parasites too, mate - to say nothing of your lot - I'm inclined to agree with you. If only because he lacks the bottle. Barley, on the other hand, is a volatile character by all accounts. He might snap. Like a man who flips when some tart taunts him about his virility. Say your wife made some nasty remark about his height and he reacted violently? You're going to tell me she wouldn't, they went back years together, and that anyway he'd never wait cold-bloodedly for hours before taking his revenge. But who knows? I'll be interested to learn what the Skinhead comes up with."

Harry glanced sharply at the detective, aware of the shrewdness concealed by his ponderous manner. Plenty of criminals, including some of Harry's own clients, had over the years betrayed themselves by underestimating Dave Moulden. The police hadn't given up on Liz's stabbing, however many gaps might still exist in their picture of the background to the case. Improbable as was the thought of Matt's guilt, Harry felt glad that he hadn't mentioned the idea -was it so unlikely? - that his old friend might have been the father of Liz's unborn child.

"What about the Evison murder?"

"Whilst you remain the obvious suspect." said Moulden slyly, "you'll have noticed that we still haven't arrested you as yet. Otherwise, we're asking around in the usual way. Looking into the Ferry Club side of things, naturally. Turns out one of the barmaids was on a social security fiddle. Wes is with her now. Pike's representing her. A bail job, probably, but we may turn up something worthwhile."

Harry put his cup down and stood up. "So it goes on. Thanks for your time, Dave. And for the tea, though your vending machine's due for an overhaul, I think. Did you check Rourke out, by the way?"

"What do you take us for? The young man is known to us, I can tell you that, though we've not been able to lay our hands on him so far. Joseph Malachy Rourke. Twenty-two years of age. Never knew his father, spent his formative years in care. Used to go shoplifting as a kid. Committed an assault outside the Ferry Club - where else? - twelve months back. But the complaint was withdrawn. Frighteners were put on the kid he duffed up, I expect. Happens all the time, doesn't it?"

Moulden shook his head sadly. "There's a smack possession charge that dates back a couple of years, though he's a user rather than a dealer by all accounts. Plus a wounding that dates back to his teens, and a taking and driving away without the owner's consent. But he's spent more time in remand centres than in jail. A run-of-the-mill ruffian rather than a master-criminal, by the sound of him.

214

Not a pleasant chap for your wife to have been consorting with. At least you could say that Mick Coghlan was your better class of crook. Four million quids worth of bullion isn't to be sneezed at."

"Fool's gold," said Harry. "All right, keep me posted."

"Will do. And Harry?"

"Yes?"

"Obstructing the course of justice is part of your job, okay. But don't let it spill over into your private life. Leave the detecting to us."

Harry returned to the foyer where he spotted two figures disappearing together out of the main door. A short tubby man in a dark suit and a blonde wearing a black PVC macintosh and huge circular earrings. Quentin Pike and his client. Harry hurried to join them on the step outside.

"Afternoon, Quentin." he said breathlessly to the solicitor. With his sparse curling hair and steel-rimmed glasses, the man's resemblance to a middle-aged Owl of the Remove was belied only by his reputation for charming the ladies. "And Shirelle. Sorry, I don't know your second name."

The barmaid stared angrily at him and said, "It's Lafferty, Shirelle Lafferty."

Pike tapped him on the shoulder. "What's this, Harry, trying to poach my clients?"

"Perish the thought. This is a private matter." Out of Shirelle's range of vision, Harry winked at Pike in a man-of-the-world way. "The lady and I are previously acquainted." He turned back to her. "Can I have a quick word with you, love?"

The barmaid looked doubtfully at her solicitor, but he simply shrugged and said, "Don't worry, I'm sure you can handle Mr. Devlin. In any case, there's nothing more for us to discuss at present. I'll be in touch." With a vague wave of the hand, he was gone.

She turned to Harry and said, "So what's all this in aid of? I've worked out who you are - that brief whose wife got killed the other day. And last time I saw you, you wanted to speak to Froggy. Now he's dead and all. You ought to carry a Government health warning."

"Did you know my wife? She used to spend time in the Ferry, or so I believe."

"Look, I've only been working there a few weeks, haven't I? And now the busies have taken an interest, it looks as though I'm all washed up. Mr. Pike reckons they won't send me down, but it's not nice, is it? I was only trying to make ends meet, wasn't I? Anyway, what was I saying? No, I never came across her. I've just been telling that black bugger the same. No matter how much he kept on at me, I couldn't help him. All right, I saw her picture in the paper, but it didn't mean anything to me."

"There was a boyfriend of hers - you may recall him. A man called Rourke. He spends a lot of time at the Ferry."

Clicking her tongue impatiently she said, "I've already told the police I can't help them. I've only been there a short time, hardly got to know the regulars even."

Harry felt the first spots of a renewed shower of rain fall upon his shoulders. While Shirelle fished in her capacious handbag for a pink folding umbrella, he cursed the inadequacy of Jane's description. Only one bit of it stood in his mind. "Another thing," he said, "I think he's been in a fight lately. Someone made a mess of his face."

"A fight?" Her brows knitted in concentration. "You don't mean Joe, do you?"

A shiver of excitement ran down Harry's spine. For once he had guessed correctly. "You've got him. Joe Rourke."

"Used to see a lot of Joe." She sniggered. "He was certainly smitten."

Harry grasped her by the hand. "Now can you remember him being with my wife?"

"Sorry. When he wasn't hanging around the stage, he'd be with Marilyn."

"Marilyn?"

"It's not her real name," said Shirelle bitchily. "Reckons she looks like Marilyn Monroe just because she's got that same kind of hair and tits the size of pumpkins."

"Any idea where I can find her?"

She shot him a quizzical glance. "You want to meet Marilyn?"

"Yes. She might be able to help me."

Shaking her head, Shirelle said, "Mister, you don't want her kind of help. Or maybe you do. Anyway, you'll be able to find her easy enough. Even if she isn't in the Ferry tonight, she'll as like as not be around and about up Toxteth way." Seeing light begin to dawn in Harry's expression, she added maliciously, "But be sure to take a few quid with you. They say Marilyn's one of the greediest whores in Falkner Square."

Chapter Twenty-Six

Hurrying round the corner into Fenwick Court, Harry collided with a woman walking in the opposite direction. He was about to mutter an apology when he recognised her.

"Brenda!" A thought hit him. "Oh, shit! We were going to have lunch together."

She brushed some hair out of her eyes. Her face was puffy with frustration and disappointment. She looked her age.

"A couple of hours ago, yes. Never mind. Your secretary was very kind. Stuck up for you and even offered to share her sandwiches. I waited till it was time for tea!"

"Christ, what can I say? I'm sorry. Look, don't leave right now. Come back to the office for a minute."

"I've got a job to do, remember? And I'm very late. It may not seem important to you, but I've already had to ring my friend and ask her to cover up for me."

"Brenda, please, I've said I'm sorry. Listen, I've been all over the city today. I think I've got a lead on the murders."

She sighed. "Yes, that's what matters most to you, isn't it? Finding the man who stabbed your wife. Despite the way she treated you - flaunting her infidelities. Perhaps that's what we have in common, Harry. We're both gluttons for punishment."

He swallowed hard. She was preaching at him, as Angie O'Hare had done. And, as before, his flesh prickled as he realised he couldn't deny the truth in the sermon. The Liz he'd loved had treated him like dirt.

Brenda was still talking, as much to herself as to him. "I suppose the world's full of those who take and those who give. You're unusual; mainly it's women who do the giving. And for what? Just a name. I'm still a Rixton, although he dumped me so long ago. I never went back to my maiden name, yet why should women always be called after their husbands, anyway? It seems so bloody unfair."

She was on the brink of tears. He put a hand on her shoulder but she shrugged it away.

"I'll leave you to it," she said. "I hope you find what you're looking for."

"Brenda, I'll see you tonight," he began to say, but she had gone.

He swore under his breath. This morning she'd not been looking for commitments. Hours later he was already in the wrong. All the same, he hated the thought of letting Brenda down. Whether it was Liz's fault or his didn't matter. He'd vowed to find her killer and he couldn't give up now. It was no longer a question of simple vengeance. He hungered for the truth, had to discover it, whatever the cost. Until he did, he'd never be able to get on with the rest of his life.

Back in the office, Lucy greeted him. "Your - er, neighbour just left. She seemed upset."

"I bumped into her on my way here."

"Oh dear. Recriminations? I did my best for you, told her that if you'd been called away, it must be urgent, said you always put your clients first."

He couldn't help grinning. "The perfect secretary. You lie so convincingly, there must be a future for you in the legal profession."

At the reception desk Suzanne was talking to Jim Crusoe. His partner swivelled at the sound of voices and assumed an expression of mock amazement. "Mr. Devlin, I presume? Word in the city is that you've been helping the police with their enquiries."

"The report of my arrest has been exaggerated," said Harry.

Jim walked down the corridor with him to his office. Sitting down on the edge of the desk, the big man asked, "What news?"

Harry took a deep breath. "Coghlan's been charged with attempted murder and conspiracy to steal four millions' worth of bullion. There's been another killing - a man who knew something about Liz's death has been found shot to death on the rubbish heap at Pasture Moss. Turns out neither my brother-in-law nor one of my old friends was as impervious to my wife's charms as you, and shortly before she was killed she was being followed around Liverpool by a two-bit hoodlum who may have been an ex-boyfriend bent on revenge. Oh, and I spent last night at Canning Place trying to convince the scuffers I'm not a double murderer. Other than that - nothing much to report."

Jim's craggy face puckered with bewilderment. "Are you having me on?"

"Would I?" Harry leafed through the telephone pad tear-offs tucked underneath the desk calendar. Nothing that Lucy couldn't cope with. "I want to check a file, it'll only take a moment. Then I'll be off again."

Jim contrived a wry smile and hoisted himself down off the desk. At the door he said, "Don't rely on me for bail, that's all."

"Trust me, I know what I'm doing."

"Famous last words." With a shake of the head, Jim wandered off to his room.

Delving into the top drawer of his second filing cabinet, Harry located a buff folder marked TRISHA SLEIGHTHOLME-SOLICITING CHARGE and rifled through the sheaf of papers secured by a green treasury tag. The first page of his handwritten notes confirmed that Trisha wasn't on the phone, but gave the address of the Toxteth flat in which Peanuts Benjamin had set her up to ply her trade. He jotted it down on a scrap of paper which he thrust into his inside pocket. Having a contact amongst the street girls might help him to find Marilyn and thus, he hoped, Rourke more quickly. Today's calendar motto, he noticed, was: *It is possible that blondes also prefer gentlemen.*

After a quick parting word with Lucy, he picked up the M.G. and set off up Duke Street. The February night was falling now and the sodium lights cast their eerie glow on the darkening city streets. Graffiti on the walls of a disused bacon factory angrily proclaimed that the I.R.A. would win. He passed the austere bulk of the Anglican Cathedral, not two hundred yards away from the gym which Coghlan was never going to see again. Turning on to Upper Parliament Street, he slowed down, starting to squint into doorways, searching in vain for a prostitute who bore a resemblance to Marilyn Monroe. At the traffic lights opposite the mosque, a police Escort pulled alongside him; Harry sensed its occupants giving him the once-over. He accelerated away. The idea of having to explain a kerb-crawling charge to Skinner and Macbeth did not appeal. At the next lights he turned into Grove Street and managed to shake off the police car. Another left brought him into Falkner Square, notorious as the favourite outdoor haunt of the city's prostitutes. No one was in sight, there were just a couple of black cabs cruising hopefully. Perhaps it was too early yet.

A minute later he was in Castlereagh Avenue, one of half a dozen broad, lamp-lined streets in the vicinity built in the days when Toxteth was where Liverpool's prosperous merchants lived in splendour. He pulled up outside the tall terraced building numbered thirteen and said a silent prayer that the M.G. would still be there when he returned. Stone steps led up to a front door which stood ajar. There were half a dozen doorbells but only two had accompanying name cards. Harry checked the piece of paper in his pocket. Flat F, that was it.

Keeping his fingers crossed that he wasn't interrupting Trisha in the middle of a professional engagement, he pushed the door open and climbed the flight of stairs that led from the scruffy hallway. On the first landing were Flats C and D. He climbed again and found himself outside a door marked F. Sellotaped to it was a card marked TRISHA and decorated by little heart shapes in mauve felt tip letters.

His loud knock brought an immediate response. Trisha's voice, challenging yet with an undertow of anxiety. "Who is it?" The question of a woman who is not certain that her next customer will not be the last. A rapist, perhaps, a psychopath, a murderer . . .

"Harry Devlin."

After a moment's scrutiny via the spyhole, she admitted him. Crossing the threshold, he absorbed at a glance the rush matting in lieu of carpet, the cracked mirror hanging from the old-fashioned picture rail, the dripping *I Love Ibiza* tee shirt draped across the clothes maiden in the hall. Curry smells wafted in from the adjacent kitchenette.

"You had me flummoxed there. It's a bit soon for punters. Besides, only me regulars call at the house first, and then they're likely to give me a ring first." Her eyebrows lifted a fraction as a thought occurred to her. "Changed your mind?"

"I'm here to beg a favour."

Mischievously, she breathed, "Nothing - out of the ordinary?"

"Behave, Trisha. All I need is your help."

"Last solicitor who asked me for that, I charged him double."

Harry refused to be diverted. "I'm looking for a girl known as Marilyn. She works round here. I'd like to find her fast."

"Is she another of your clients?" A faint grin. "Or the other way around? Don't make me jealous."

Patiently, he said, "I simply want to talk to her."

"You wouldn't be wanting to cause bother for her? The law's the law. You're either inside it or not. You're in. Marilyn and me, we're out."

"This is personal." He leaned back against the wall, arms folded. "You'll have read about my wife in the papers, yes?"

"More than that, Harry. The busies came round to check your alibi. Remember us meeting in the Ferry last Thursday? They wanted to know all about it."

Harry had forgotten telling the police about his casual meeting with Trisha, had overlooked the diligence with which they checked and counter-checked.

"Sorry, I didn't mean to . . ."

She waved away his apology. "No problem. I wasn't entertaining when they arrived. What's this all about, anyway?"

"It's possible that Marilyn knows someone who knows something about who killed Liz."

Trisha scanned his face for a moment, then said, "Wait here. I'll get my coat."

She darted into the living room and re-emerged a minute later wearing a knee-length fake fur coat. "A present from Peanuts," she said with a trace of pride. "He's not as bad as people make out."

Her legs were bare and she was still wearing her fluffy indoor slippers. He gestured towards them. "Don't you want to put some shoes on?"

"We're not going far."

She led him back down the stairs and into the street. The sharpness of the evening breeze made him wince, but Trisha didn't seem to care. She traced a path through the streets. A couple of cars passed, moving slowly. The drivers peered furtively at Harry and his companion before continuing on their way. At the bottom of Falkner Square, Trisha halted at the pavement's edge. Up ahead a taxi had pulled up alongside a telephone kiosk. A thin figure in a leather jacket and mini skirt skipped out from behind the red box and spoke to a man on the passenger side of the cab. Then she opened the rear door and clambered in.

"That's not her," said Trisha authoritatively as the taxi sped off in the direction of Myrtle Street. "Young Carla, she's only fourteen. Wrong, innit?"

Harry waved towards the Square. "This is Marilyn's patch?"

"If she's working tonight, she won't be more than a hundred yards from here. Goes round in ever decreasing circles, she does. Course, you've got to keep on the move, otherwise it's an easy lock-up for some lousy scuffer with nothing better to do."

Harry said nothing. He had spotted a woman moving out from the shadows on the other side of the road at the sound of another approaching vehicle. As a scrap metal truck lumbered by, she retreated again into the blackness, but for a moment a nearby street lamp had shed its cone of light upon a thatch of blonde hair. The woman was vaguely familiar. He realised that he had seen her for a brief moment in the Ferry. Of course, it struck him now. He had actually seen her interrupting a man - Rourke? - who was talking to Evison.

He tensed with excitement. At last it was all beginning to come together. He had been right to link Liz's vague report of the man with the battered face who, she had claimed, had been following her, with the ex-boyfriend whom Jane Brogan had attacked in the Nye. Shirelle had confirmed that. And now he knew there was a connection with Froggy. But there was still much that Harry did not understand.

"Seen her?" asked Trisha.

"I think so."

"Leave the talking to me. She can be a rough cow. Moody, too. But she's all right, Marilyn, just had a hard time, see?"

In little, mincing steps Trisha went on ahead of him. Harry held back. The familiar knot of tension was grinding away in his stomach again. Instinctively, he sensed that he was on the verge of a breakthrough, that the truth about the deaths of Liz, her child and Froggy Evison was about to come within arm's reach.

The two women came into view. Trisha had her hand on the arm of the blonde, as if to prevent her making a bolt for it. Marilyn was well nick-named. At first glance on a February night her hair and curving figure might remind anyone of the screen goddess. The illusion didn't last long, even in semi-darkness. Her eyes lacked sparkle and the red mouth was stretched in an ungenerous line.

Trisha took charge. "Marilyn, this is a mate of mine. Harry Devlin."

"Yeah?" There was no sign in the dull eyes that she was acquainted with his name.

"He just wants a word with you, that's all."

Suspiciously, the woman said, "I'm working, Trish, can't you see?"

"This won't take a minute. And he'll make it worth your while."

"Yeah?"

"That's right," he assured her. "I'll pay you for your time. Easy money, better than working."

"You want to talk here? It's freezing, I have to keep moving to keep warm, never mind the bleeding busies."

"Use my place if you like," offered Trisha.

"Thanks," said Harry. "All right with you, Marilyn?"

"Suppose so."

The three of them started back towards Castlereagh Avenue. Out of Marilyn's range of vision, Trisha looked meaningfully at Harry and mouthed the words: "Smack head." Harry nodded. He acted for enough drug addicts to be able to recognise the signs of their weakness. Heroin was cheap these days and freely available. His thoughts turned back to Rourke. Two women more different from Liz than Jane and this Marilyn would be hard to imagine. Perhaps the man had eclectic tastes. Or was there another explanation for his interest in Harry's wife?

Peanuts was waiting for them inside the flat. He was stretched out in an armchair like an eastern sultan, taking his ease. Reggae music filled the room. As Harry and the two prostitutes walked through the door, Peanuts grinned and said, "Shit, man, I never knew you were kinky. Two beautiful ladies. For anyone else, this would cost real money, you know what I mean?"

Harry left the explaining to Trisha. As she talked, he whispered to Marilyn, "Joe Rourke, your feller, I need to talk to him right now. Where is he?"

She yawned. "Who cares?"

"I care, Marilyn. Tell me."

"No idea. I'm finished with him anyhow. We was only together for a couple of weeks. Got other protection now. Me old boyfriend's come out of the nick last Monday."

The stomach knot was tightening again. "Give me an address. Anything."

"Can't help you, mister. He stayed at my place till I threw him out. What do I want with him now? Besides, the money's all gone."

"The money?"

"Yeah, yeah, he had a few quid. All spent, like I said. It doesn't last long."

Harry gripped her bony arm hard, his fingers digging into the flesh. Marilyn cried out, as much in surprise as in pain.

Peanuts said, "Hey, man, that isn't nice," and made as if to get out of his chair.

In a warning voice, Trisha said, "Harry, be careful."

He released the blonde, but the suddenness of his action seemed to have loosened the woman's tongue. She said, "He'll be out on the razz as usual. Fancies himself, does Joe. You'll find him easy enough."

"Where, Marilyn?"

Pouting, she said, "Try the Ferry Club. He likes the scenery."

Harry groaned. "That place, yet again. All right, I'll try it."

Trisha gave him a make-the-best-of-a-bad-job smile. "Might see you there later on, then. You're getting to be a regular. Better watch it, else Tony'll fix you up with a job."

Harry spun round. "Tony?"

"You must know Tony," said Trisha.

The stomach ache had become agony. "No," he said. "Who is he?"

She gazed to the heavens. "He's only the boss man. The feller who runs the Ferry."

Chapter Twenty-Seven

The city centre streets had an uneasy early evening calm as Harry walked towards the Ferry Club. From a basement bar came the sound of the drunken singing of "Danny Boy". A loiter of kids aged twelve or thirteen hung around a hamburger stall nearby, loudly re-telling old jokes about the Pope. A police van cruised towards Dale Street, the men inside scanning the pavements in search of the first signs of trouble. Harry nursed closer to his chest the heavy object that he was carrying wrapped up in a chamois cloth inside his jacket. He was aware of the rapid beating of his heart. He arrived at the Ferry to find its entrance bolted and barred. The doors would not open for another two hours. He paused outside, looked up and asked himself how he could have been so blind. The realisation of his own stupidity hurt him as much as the drubbing he had taken outside the Empire Dock the other night. Tony - Anthony. Anthony - Tony. He had noticed the name of the boss of the club above the main door on the night of the first murder. Reginald Anthony Gallimore, licensed pursuant to Act of Parliament, et cetera et cetera. That unthinking failure to make the obvious connection when Dame had mentioned the name of Liz's lover was wormwood and gall to him. He understood now why his wife had suggested that they meet at the club on that dreadful Thursday night. Not, after all, in order to see Rourke. She had planned an assignation with the man in charge that night and had meant to accompany him back to the Ferry, so as not to miss the chance of a minute in his company before they split up for the night.

So it was Gallimore of whom she entertained such high hopes. Moneyed and handsome, the man she hoped to marry. What had gone wrong and why had he not come forward in response to the news of her death? And was it mere coincidence that Rourke, the man who kept her picture, who followed her around the city, also frequented the Ferry? Slowly, the fog within Harry's mind was beginning to clear. At last he could identify the shadowy outlines of the truth.

He turned down the alleyway where forty-eight hours earlier he had lain in wait for Froggy Evison. It was deserted. Lined up against the wall were half a dozen black bin liners from which old ring-pull lager cans and torn crisp packets spilled. The side door was shut. He tested it. Locked.

For half a minute he beat on the metal panel until his knuckles were raw. Nothing. Impossible to make anyone hear inside. He had taken a step back towards the front of the building when he heard a key turn in the lock. The door swung open and the fair-haired keyboard player whom he had encountered on his previous visit stepped out into the night.

Glancing back over his shoulder, the man was saying, "Maybe the agent will come up with someone. The kid from Wrexham might be free. The one who sings like Randy Crawford."

The reply was too low for Harry to hear. As the door began to close, Harry moved swiftly. Grabbing the door's edge, he held it fast for a moment and stepped inside. He was looking straight at a tall black-haired man in a slim-fitting designer suit, the man whom on previous visits Harry had assumed was the manager, without appreciating that he must actually own the place. In the intervening week the tan seemed to have faded and his moustache to have drooped. Wrinkles had crept around dark eyes that no longer smiled with complacent authority. At the sight of Harry he stared as if coming face-to-face with a poltergeist.

He knows who I am, thought Harry. He's been afraid that I would turn up.

"Tony. Tony Gallimore." The words came out harshly; for Harry, it was like listening to someone else talk. During the past few days he had spoken to more than one man who had slept with his wife. But this was the one whom she had thought she loved.

"You're Devlin." A statement rather than a question, spoken in smoothed-down mid-Atlantic tones which bore not a trace of the Scouser's catarrhal whine.

The keyboard player joined them in the doorway. "Problems, boss?"

"Nothing I can't handle, Neil. I'll see you later."

"If you're sure . . ."

"Yes, Neil. No sweat. There's no need for you to stay."

With a last dubious look at Harry, the keyboard player zipped his white blouson and was gone. Gallimore said, "What do you want here? We have nothing to say to each other." That charming smile reserved for the punters and his ladyfriends was nowhere to be seen.

"Wrong." Harry jerked his thumb. "Let's talk indoors."

Gallimore hesitated, but another glance at Harry's face helped to make up his mind. "As you wish."

He led Harry to a room at the far end of the passageway. Its door was marked manager - strictly private. The office was palatial in comparison to the cubby-holes which Harry had seen on his previous visit. Comfortable chairs, a paper-laden desk, swish cordless phone and a year planner festooned with coloured oblongs and triangles. Two walls were covered with photographs of club acts. Perhaps half of them showed Gallimore with his arm round skimpily clad singers and dancers. Most of the pictures were adorned with trite messages and autographs: *All the best from the Stimson Sisters, Luv to Tony from Cara xxx.* Gallimore sat behind the desk and waved Harry into the other chair.

"You didn't answer me, Mr. Devlin. What do you want?"

"To talk."

"Talking won't help any of us. Elizabeth is dead."

Elizabeth. Harry would never associate the full name with the woman he had married. To him, she had always been Liz. Perhaps that had been her problem: she was a Liz who yearned to become an Elizabeth. He said, "It's about her death that I wanted to see you."

"I can't tell you anything."

"I think you can," said Harry.

Tony Gallimore laughed sourly. "Elizabeth used to talk about you. She said you were sharp enough on the surface, but that crazy obsessions would take hold of you, then you became unreasonable. I hope I'm not going to be one of those obsessions."

"She seems to have spent most of her time discussing me with her fancy men," said Harry wearily.

Gallimore started to rise from his chair. "I don't mean anything to you, Mr. Devlin. The one link between us has gone. Now why don't you go home and start putting your life back together again? That's something we all need to do."

"Sit down."

Harry took the gun from his jacket. It was a 9mm Mauser automatic, short-barrelled but, Peanuts confirmed, effective enough at short range. Harry had pressured the pimp first to admit that he still kept an unlicensed firearm as a souvenir of his days as a hard man who handled tricky jobs for the proprietor of a Caribbean night spot, then to lend it to him for the night.

Peanuts had been reluctant. "Man, you don't know the damage this thing can do. Okay, people call it a ladies' gun, but you can bet it'll still cut a big man down. And if you open up some guy's stomach, I sure as hell ain't gonna help you beat the rap." But Harry had persisted, calling in all his owed favours, and at length his client had given in and handed over the gun. "You going to use this, man?" Peanuts asked after showing how to cock the pistol. Harry had said simply, "I need to be prepared."

So now he was prepared and Tony Gallimore sat down again, mesmerised by the Mauser. Slivers of sweat shone on his forehead.

"Okay, let's hear it. When did you first meet Liz?"

Gallimore kept the Mauser under an unwavering gaze. He was breath|ng rapidly. "Three months ago. She was here one night alone. Coghlan had disappeared somewhere, up to no good as usual. Some men were bothering her. I sorted the problem out, the lads on the door made sure their feet never touched the ground. We got talking. That's how it began."

"And you became lovers " Harry squeezed every last trace of emotion out of his voice. He might have been a newscaster on Radio 4.

That night. I simply couldn't get enough of her. She was beautiful, warm, vivacious. Not like some of the plastic dolls we get here. She was a real woman."

"And Coghlan?"

"He terrified her," said Gallimore, still watching the gun. "I told her not to worry - I had some connections. You don't survive in this business without knowing one or two rough people. But it wasn't a straightforward situation. There was my wife, too. She's a jealous woman. I told Elizabeth we had to be careful, for both our sakes. It was our secret. Elizabeth liked that, it seemed to add to the excitement for her. She took a job at the shop where she used to work in town, it was handy for lunchtimes and gave her an excuse to be out if Coghlan ever got nosey. We moved round the hotel circuit."

"When did you decide to make it permanent?"

"There were difficulties," said Gallimore. He twisted a little in his chair, as if to illustrate what he was saying. "I needed her, of course I did. But I didn't want to leave my wife, nor the club. I'm not a rich man, and Elizabeth had no money of her own. Coghlan had a tight grip on the purse-strings. She had found out that he was short of ready cash. The money that went on his gambling was criminal, she used to say."

He mustered a wry grin, his first attempt to try on Harry the charm-the-pants-off-you style that Trisha had said was his stock-in-trade. Harry tapped the Mauser impatiently on the surface of the desk. Running the tip of his tongue over his lips, Gallimore continued, "I asked her about divorcing you, but she said you couldn't afford heavy alimony. Besides," - again a hint of a winning smile- "whoever made money out of suing a solicitor? She said you weren't a fat cat, more like Robin Hood in an old suit from C & A. All the same, she kept pressing me to make something happen. That was how she came to cut her wrist."

Harry leaned forward. "Tell me."

"I'd arranged to meet her, we'd booked a room at the North Atlantic. She was just getting into the bath. She'd already sliced through one wrist, there was blood all over the carpet." He half-closed his eyes. "Fortunately, there wasn't much damage done. I got her to a doctor who was able to stitch her up without asking too many difficult questions. She spun some cock-and-bull story to Coghlan, although she said he was so bound up in his own affairs that he hardly noticed. She thought he had another woman. And she said she'd tried to kill herself because she couldn't see us ever getting together. Said she was depressed and couldn't carry on. She was trying to push me into a corner, force me to leave my wife. Oh, yes, I understood how her mind worked. But I didn't intend to lose her."

"No?" Harry didn't bother to hide his disbelief.

"No. Whatever you may think, Mr. Devlin, we cared deeply for each other. And in any case, we were overtaken by events."

"She announced her pregnancy?"

"Yes. At first, I wondered whether I should believe her. She might have been making it up, I wouldn't have put it past her. But she showed me the confirmation from the testing centre. Admitted she'd been careless, hadn't taken proper precautions. So, you see, I had to make up my mind and choose."

"And?"

"And I chose Elizabeth," said Gallimore. "She was wild, unreliable, at times untruthful - I don't have to tell you that. But she was everything a woman should be. God forgive me, I had to have her. Somehow I broke the news to my wife. It's the worst task I've ever had to undertake. If I hadn't loved Elizabeth so much, I could never have hardened my heart to resist the tears, the pleading in her voice." A remote look, another excerpt from his seductive repertoire, came over the tanned, blemish-free face. "You may think you loved your wife, Mr. Devlin, but I - I worshipped her."

What chilled Harry most was the memory of how heavily Liz had fallen for this man, with his soap opera rhetoric and over-rehearsed mannerisms. He skewered Gallimore with his gaze. "Did you know she was being followed?"

"You heard about that? Yes, she told me. I found it hard to understand. God forgive me, to begin with I thought she might have invented it, perhaps she hadn't believed me when I said we would soon be together and she would be free of Coghlan. She told me he'd put one of his men on to her, she was sure that he'd realised she was seeing someone else and was determined to get the proof. I tried to reassure her. If he had a new girlfriend of his own, why would he bother? It didn't make sense to me. Again I couldn't be sure she was telling the truth. But I knew she was afraid of him, said how ruthless he could be if someone got in his way."

A security guard in East London had discovered that to his cost, thought Harry. "Did she recognise the man who followed her?" he asked.

"No. He wasn't one of Coghlan's usual hangers-on, she said. Eventually she caught the man off guard and came close enough to see that he'd been in a fight recently. His cheek had been badly scratched. When I learned about that, I knew who the man was."

Gripping the Mauser tightly, Harry said, "Go on."

Gallimore waved at their surroundings. The happy faces of the artistes in the photographs beamed back at him. "One of the regular punters here. He was always hanging around backstage as well, though I'd noticed he took care to shift whenever I came anywhere near. A hard man. People called him Joe. I never heard his second name."

"Rourke."

"Is that it?"

"So what did you do?"

The reply was a non-commital movement of the shoulders. Gallimore was beginning to relax. Perhaps he had decided that Harry would never use the gun. "I told her not to worry. I didn't believe anything would come of it. It isn't unknown for men to follow attractive women around. Perhaps he had a thing for her, I didn't know. She thought he'd been sent by Mick Coghlan to spy on her, but I couldn't see that. What would have been the point? Coghlan wasn't short of female company by all accounts. I said she was working herself into a lather over nothing."

"What happened after that?"

"I had to go to Birmingham. We were negotiating a fresh loan from the brewery, re-financing this place. I had a couple of long meetings. All Wednesday and most of Thursday I was hammering out the deal. I promised Elizabeth that when I got back, I would sort everything out. We'd soon be together. She was panicking, Coghlan was down in London, also on some kind of business, but she didn't dare go back to their house. She was convinced he was going to harm her. God forgive me, I thought she was being childish."

"When were you due back in Liverpool?"

"She said she'd meet me at Lime Street. If the train was on time, we would have an hour or so together before I had to be back here. I'd booked a room for us at a place up in Mount Pleasant."

"Train?" asked Harry. "Why not drive? It isn't far."

"I'm banned from driving," said Gallimore. "One of the penalties of being in this trade, I suppose. They picked me up on the M62 last Easter, I was twice over the limit, got a twelve months' ban. My lawyer's Pike, you must know him, he said I got off lightly."

"So did you meet her at the station?"

"Of course not. The train was on time for once, but she wasn't there. I waited for twenty minutes until it was obvious that she wasn't going to show. I couldn't understand it. I called the hotel, but they hadn't seen her or taken a message. So I came back here."

Harry recalled the man's abstracted manner on the night of Liz's murder. His story explained that, but it was still worth digging deeper.

"Carry on."

Still looking at the gun, Gallimore said, "There's nothing much more I can add. Until I read the papers the following day, I had no idea about what had happened. I couldn't believe it. She was so alive, so . . ."

"You weren't sufficiently shocked to volunteer a statement to the police," interrupted Harry. "Why not?"

"What could I say? I was in a difficult position, I . . ."

The self-justifications went on for over a minute. Harry barely listened. Beneath the glossy looks and fluent line in chat was jelly. But might Gallimore yet prove to be a murderer? Now was the moment to find out.

Without warning, Harry raised the pistol and pointed it at Gallimore's forehead.

"Are you quite sure you don't know Joe Rourke, Tony? Wasn't he the man you hired to kill my wife? Didn't the pressure get too much for you?" He watched the dark eyes glaze over as Gallimore stared in mixed horror and fascination at the Mauser. "Liz pestered you, didn't she? You had a nice set-up, it suited you to have a mistress, but you weren't so keen on a change of wife and all that maintenance pay. Liz had threatened to kill herself, now she was expecting a kid. Where would it end? You had the idea of getting rid of her. What better idea than to pay a yobbo you'd met in the Ferry to do the necessary while you were nicely alibied, tucking into a sandwich on British Rail? I'm sure the train times will stand up, the story tripped so easily off your tongue. You've obviously been practising just in case the police got a whiff of your identity. But I'm not fooled, Tony."

Gallimore's hands shook as if he had Parkinson's disease. The temperature in the room seemed to have dropped below zero as Harry slowly rolled out the final question.

"How much did you pay Rourke?"

It was a credible theory, soundly reasoned. Harry had been building up towards it for several days now. So many of the pieces fitted if Joe Rourke was a hired killer, Tony Gallimore his paymaster. The motive was there, so too plenty of circumstantial evidence. Rourke's sudden access to liquid cash, the photograph to help him identify the victim, the clumsy attempts to keep Liz under surveillance whilst waiting for the right moment to strike. And afterwards, Rourke's conversation in the club with Froggy, who must have stumbled onto the truth on the very night of the murder, a conversation which Marilyn had interrupted in front of Harry's own eyes.

But even as he watched the man his wife had loved squirm at the sight of the gun poised to blow his good looks away for ever, Harry became conscious of an agonising wrench inside his stomach, more acute than ever before. At once he realised that it was a physical sign of how wrong he had been.

Fragments of conversation came back to mind. Put together, they pointed away from Gallimore's guilt and towards a different culprit. Liz herself had told him all he should have needed to understand; on the night he had found her in his flat in the Empire

Dock. And this very day a chance remark from Brenda Rixton should have helped him to work out what had really happened.

With infinite care, as Gallimore watched in bafflement and held his breath, Harry laid the Mauser down upon the desk. Now, at last, he knew the truth.

Chapter Twenty-Eight

At the other end of a crackling telephone line, Quentin Pike was saying, "You realise I shouldn't be telling you this?"

"Sure," said Harry. His thoughts were racing and the offhand way in which he spoke failed to convey his gratitude to the man who had helped to fill in most of the gaps in his knowledge. With little more than a mild grumble, Pike had answered questions which Harry had not dared to put to Tony Gallimore.

Time was short, Harry was certain of that. The murder of Froggy Evison had been a panic move. Before long, the police would be on the trail. Yet Harry still had the desperate urge to be there before them. He didn't know why confronting the murderer was so important to him. Did the primitive thirst for vengeance still rule him or was there buried within his heart and mind some subtler need, the nature of which he could not understand?

"Where is this place, Quentin?"

"Woolton. It's called Paradise Found, would you believe?" Pike clucked his tongue in deprecation of the nouveau riche and their lack of taste, then explained how to get there.

It was eight o'clock. Miracle of miracles, Harry had found a public phone box in working order in the city centre within five minutes of leaving Gallimore at the Ferry. The club manager - he was not after all, Pike confirmed, legally its owner - had appeared bemused by Harry's sudden change of manner and mood. Without waiting for a reply to his accusation of murder, Harry had asked another question to which Gallimore said at once: "Yes, of course, didn't you know? But what has that got *to do* with - what you were talking about?" Harry hadn't trusted himself to answer; instead he stuffed the Mauser into its protective chamois and cursed his own stupidity.

"I don't suppose," said Quentin Pike sadly, "that you are going to tell me what this is all about? But answer this - am I going to lose a client?"

"Don't worry," said Harry soberly, "clearing this mess up will probably keep you in business till retirement. Thanks anyway."

He hung up and strode to the M.G. Despite the purpose-fulness with which he moved, he had no clear idea of what he should or would do. All he knew was that there was no possibility this time that he might be mistaken. He understood why Liz had had to die. Strangely, he had felt a sudden spurt of pity on realising what had happened, but he had striven to banish any emotion which might cause him to waver at this late hour. One day, perhaps, he would feel differently, but tonight was not the time to sympathise with murder.

As he drove, an unbidden image of Liz leapt to the forefront of his mind. He remembered her in the flat at Empire Dock, saying: "I won't give you any hassle. I'll be out of your hair soon, I promise." Harry pressed down on the accelerator. Would he ever be free of her, ever be able to start again? Or would she continue to haunt him - would he be unable to recall the provocative twist of her lips as she smiled without this wrenching, futile sense of having abandoned her to death?

Headlights flashed at him in furious remonstrance as he overtook a slow-moving van on a bend, and a warning blast on the horn of a passing Sierra reminded him to concentrate oh the road. Rain was beginning to fall and his wipers scratched the windscreen noisily, blurring everything in sight. As urban sprawl gave way to suburban dwellings of increasing opulence, he eased his speed and peered around in search of the avenue that, according to Quentin, led to his destination in Freshfield Close. Eventually he spotted it and, braking sharply, he took two sharp turns, bringing him into the boulevard where

he meant to confront the creator of his past week's agonies.

Tall conifers obscured the house, but looking down the drive, Harry saw a lamp burning above the porch and another light behind a curtained first floor window. Outside a front gate which bore a slate sign inscribed paradise found, someone was parking a Citroen hatchback. Harry slowed, straining through the darkness to identify the figure clambering out from the driver's seat and slamming the car door. The figure moved beneath a street lamp: a man, black-haired and strongly built, wearing a navy's jacket and jeans.

Harry pulled up behind the Citroen. The man had been about to walk up the drive of the house; now he looked back over his shoulder. Harry opened the door of the M.G. and the man spun round. Harry took a couple of paces forward. The rear quarterlight of the Citroen was shattered and he caught sight of a dark shape on the back seat of the car. Easy to guess it was a shotgun from which the barrels had been sawn off and that the car had been stolen by the man at the house gates. From fifteen yards away, Harry could feel the violence in the stranger: it sparked in the air like electricity.

"Rourke?"

In the clear evening air Harry's voice sounded unnaturally loud. He was cold and tense and the Mauser was rubbing painfully against his chest.

"Who's that?" The tone was threatening, but perhaps it carried a hint of fear as well. The two syllables were all Harry needed to confirm that this was the man who had attacked him outside the Empire Dock. And, for sure, stabbed Liz to death in Leeming Street.

Harry advanced. Twelve yards between them now. Ten. Eight. Rourke's hand slipped inside his jacket, a reflex action. Harry wondered if the knife was there.

Five yards short of the man, Harry stopped, "I know you murdered my wife, Rourke. I've been looking for you."

"Yeah?" Joe Rourke stared at him defiantly. "Now you've found me. So what?"

Harry took a step forward. He felt no uree to rave or rant. His own restraint surprised him; seemed strange and unnatural. He said, "How much were you paid, Rourke? How little was my wife's life worth?"

A scornful laugh. "Five grand." The dark head tilted back; in the glow from the street light Harry could see the faint outlines of the scar tissue which Jane Brogan's attack had left under Rourke's right eye. "Two and a half up front. The rest after. It's all spent. Soon goes." He might have been talking about money won on a bet.

"And Evison?"

"Not a penny." Rourke spat on to the ground. "Had to clear him out, didn't I? He said he'd seen me follow her down Leeming Street while he was on his way to work at the club."

"And he put the squeeze on you?"

"Yeah, the silly fucker. All the same, it was worth something, killing him. I came here to collect."

Harry had guessed as much. "And?"

"And you're trying to fuck me about. I should've finished you off while I had the chance the other night. That fucking dog." Another laugh. "No Alsatians here, though. You won't be lucky twice."

As he finished speaking, Rourke whipped his hand out of the inside pocket. Harry saw steel glinting through the stubby fingers. There was a dark smear on the blade. Harry almost gagged at the sight of it. The man had not even bothered to clean the weapon that had killed Liz. Rourke took a step forward. This was their second encounter on a dark night and Harry knew it would be their last.

The Mauser. He remembered it just in time and with a single instinctive movement ripped the gun from its hiding place beside his chest. In his grasp it felt smooth and solid, it gave him courage. He pointed it straight at Rourke's marked face. For the first time,

241

he looked directly into the murderer's eyes. Something shone in them - was it fear?

Shoot him, said a voice inside his head. Shoot him while you have the chance. He would do the same to you. What mercy did he show to Liz or to the baby that she carried?

"Put the knife down," he said. Inwardly, he cursed his own weakness, the tremor that he heard in his voice.

Rourke did not reply. He threw himself forward like an animal intent upon the kill, clutching the knife at waist height. Harry swayed to one side as the blade came arching up in a savage blow aimed at his heart. It missed by inches and as Rourke followed through, the hard bulk of his body caught Harry's shoulder.

As they both went sprawling, Harry kicked out in desperation at his attacker's wrist. In the moment before the two men hit the ground less than a yard apart, Harry heard the knife fall too. As it clattered away just out of reach, Rourke let out a muffled cry. The impact of collapsing backwards on to the pavement knocked the breath from Harry's body and the cracking of the side of his head against the concrete slabs filled his eyes with tears. Yet it seemed as if he were too numb to feel pain and somehow he managed to cling on to the gun and, with it, the hope of staying alive.

Harry rolled over on to his side and saw Rourke stagger to his feet. The man seemed dazed; he took one look at the Mauser and stumbled on to the road, to the driver's door of the Citroen. Harry hauled himself up off the ground, first to a half-crouching position, then back to the vertical. As he did so, the Citroen revved furiously. Harry flattened himself against the fence edging the pavement, still gripping the gun so tightly that the metal bit into the flesh of his fingers, and watched as, with a squeal of brakes, the French car swept away and out of sight.

Harry hobbled back to the M.G. and started it up. Although Rourke had vanished, he had seen him turning at the end of the close. Back on the main road, he spotted the Citroen's sleek lines a hundred yards ahead. Harry put his foot down, oblivious of the aching of his head and the forty-mile-an-hour limit. Rourke must have realised he was being followed. He accelerated through changing traffic lights and hurtled off into the night. Harry held his breath, and with barely a sweep of his eyes from left to right drove straight through on the red.

Further on, the road narrowed into a single carriageway. Harry could, see Rourke manoeuvring the Citroen with dodgem skill around parked cars and slow movers, daring oncoming vehicles to bar his way. Harry kept on after him, spinning the steering wheel this way and that, offering a silent prayer of thanks for the lightness of the traffic. The M.G. might be rusty, but it responded like a racing horse to an Aintree jockey's whip. Harry's breath was coming in short gasps. He was closing on the killer's car.

I won't let him get away, thought Harry. If it's the last thing I do, he won't escape me now.

Twice at the last moment Rourke swerved off into side streets, but he couldn't lose the M.G. They were in South Liverpool now. The streets were built up with rows of terraced houses and there was a small shop on every corner. Few people were about, just one or two taking their dogs for a walk and the usual knots of teenagers shouting and jostling. The gap between the cars was down to twenty yards. Brakes screaming again in protest, Rourke took another tight corner at fifty, with Harry only seconds behind.

Down this way the buildings thinned and gave way to waste land. Harry recognised this place. They had chanced upon the road that circled the scrap heap of Pasture Moss. He glanced about him. Even under a starless sky he could make out the silhouette of the refuse tip. The scavengers had long gone home and the dark mound resembled a funeral pyre.

Harry pressed his foot down further. He was almost on Rourke's tail now. They were approaching another sharp curve in the road. Without warning, the Citroen veered crazily off course as it took the bend too fast. Skidding, it cut a swathe through a series of roadwork cones which cordoned off the sewer repairs which Harry had noticed on his visit here the previous day. A red warning sign went spinning into the darkness.

Seeing the danger, Harry stamped on the stop pedal just in time. As he lost speed, his attention Was split between the frantic effort of keeping the M.G. on the road and the horrific fascination of watching Rourke's desperate effort to regain control. The French car ploughed along the verge of grass and mud before slewing over the railway line that ran between the road and the tip. Finally the collision with the wire perimeter fence brought it to a shuddering halt.

From the other side of the-'road, Harry, heard the train before he saw it. He listened to the howl of the train's brakes as the driver realised what had happened and made a desperate attempt to achieve the impossible and avoid impact. Harry shut his eyes as the crash occurred and counted to twenty before opening them again. Over his shoulder, he could see that the train had at last pulled up. It had shoved the Citroen thirty yards down the track and the smooth lines of the front of the car were now mangled beyond recognition. As he watched, the engine of the wreck exploded and the first flames shot upwards, like orange fingers pointing to the sky.

Jesus Christ.

Only now did Harry become aware that his shirt was drenched with sweat. Panting, he gazed at the uniformed figures which dismounted from the train and hurried towards the burning car. The heat drove them back, but heroics were not called for in any case. Even if Rourke had withstood the neck-snapping jerk as the car flew off the road, he would have perished instantly in the blast that followed. The fire was merely destroying what was left of his lifeless carcase.

His eyes fixed on the blazing tomb, Harry felt again the sickness in his stomach. After his close encounter with the pavement during the struggle with Rourke, his head was throbbing. The whole of his body felt sore. But someone from the train was pointing in his direction and he could hear the sound of cars approaching in the distance. Groggily, he reached for the gear-stick. Time to go. This latest death was not the end of the nightmare for him. In the frenzy of his pursuit of Rourke, he had forgotten the woman who held the purse-strings. The woman who had priced his wife's life at five thousand pounds.

The woman who had paid Joe Rourke to murder Liz.

Chapter Twenty-Nine

The front door of the house called Paradise Found was unlocked. It opened to his touch. The first-floor light was still on. Not bothering with the bell, Harry walked into the reception hall. Ahead of him, an open-tread staircase led to a galleried landing. From upstairs, he could hear the sound of running water. However many baths she takes, he thought, nothing will cleanse her of the guilt.

He called out: "Angie!"

No reply.

"Angie, it's me. Harry Devlin."

Up above, the water was switched off. He waited for a few seconds and then heard soft footfalls. Angie O'Hare appeared from round the bend in the staircase. She wore a short crimson gown with sleeves rolled up and seemed unsteady on her bare feet. The auburn hair was uncombed and strands of it drooped over her face. Her unmade-up cheeks seemed sunken and old. For a moment Harry wondered why he had ever thought her attractive. Then he looked into her deep blue eyes and remembered.

As she reached the bottom step, he said, "It's over. Rourke's dead. He lost control of his car and came off the road on to the railway track. The Hunt's Cross train did the rest."

"My God." Her voice was hoarse. Then: "I'm glad."

Harry moistened his lips. "I know what happened."

"Yes." Her ruined face managed a mirthless smile. "When we talked, I realised how dogged you were, that you'd never give up. In a way, I'm thankful. So much went wrong. I never thought it would end like this." She motioned towards a door leading off from the hall. "Let's sit down for a minute."

He followed her into a spacious lounge built in the shape of an L. Above the gas fire, on the stone chimney breast, hung a framed photograph, a wedding picture taken outside a register office. He moved over to look at it. Angie was dressed in lemon crepe-de-chine with white handbag, hat and matching gloves. She was holding a bouquet of roses and looking into the complacent eyes of Tony Gallimore. It was an adoring look, and strictly proprietorial.

Harry thought of the man he had left in the Ferry Club, a man flimsy as tissue paper, and asked himself what the two women had seen in Tony Gallimore. Liz had died for him. Angie had killed for him. Neither woman was a fool. Why had they not been able to look beyond the sharp suits and glib chat?

Talking to Gallimore earlier that evening, threads of past conversations had linked in his mind, forming an unexpected pattern. Liz's casual mention of her lover's neurotic wife. Brenda talking about her maiden name. But of course, he had thought, some women never adopt their husbands' surnames because they are feminists, or perhaps for professional reasons. Like some women lawyers and - yes - entertainers.

As soon as the possibility that Angie O'Hare might be married to Gallimore had occurred to him, finding corroborative clues was easy. On the night of the murder, when dedicating that old Burt Bacharach song to her man, she had been gazing towards the back of the concert room where Tony Gallimore stood. At that time he had no doubt been thinking, not of his wife, but of his mistress's failure to keep their clandestine appointment. And, of course, there was Harry's own visit to the Ferry last Monday evening. Why had it not occurred to him that it was strange that a club singer should be walking around long before the show was due to start, treating the place as her own? No doubt she had eavesdropped on his conversation with Froggy, fearful of what Evison might say, interrupting as soon as it seemed Harry might persuade him to talk.

So, after putting down the Mauser, Harry had asked Gallimore the last question, trying to make it appear offhand. "Your wife is Angie O'Hare, isn't she?"

Gallimore had given the necessary confirmation. Baffled by Harry's abrupt change of mood, he had stared as if sure he was in the company of a dangerous lunatic. The relief on his face as Harry brusquely got up and left had been as plain as a notice to quit.

At different times, both Angie and her husband had said that their solicitors were Windaybanks. The phone call to Quentin Pike had filled in the background. And what the keyboard player had said to his boss at the door of the Ferry that evening implied that Angie O'Hare would not be performing at all that night. Harry had speculated that she might have arranged a crisis rendezvous with Rourke, something that could not be handled backstage. At last his guesses were getting nearer the mark.

Still looking at the wedding photograph, not facing her, he said, "The Ferry Club belongs to you, I found that out this evening." Windaybanks had handled the conveyancing, Quentin said. "Although that came as a surprise, it shouldn't have done. After all, most singers dream of owning their own club, isn't that right? You were never going to be a second Cilia Black, but you made a few bob in your day, all the same. When you finally gave up hope of hitting the charts again, you put the money into buying a place where you could always top the bill."

He turned round. "You were married to your manager in those days," he said, "and when he ran off with a dolly bird you had a nervous breakdown."

A terrible tragedy, Quentin had sighed, losing out on her career and her marriage within such a short time: she simply couldn't handle it.

"The Ferry had a succession of managers while you tried to pick yourself up again. No wonder the place went downhill, turned into such a dive. Finally you hired a pretty boy called Tony Gallimore.

No one would say he had the greatest business acumen in the world, he was simply an opportunist with a smooth smile. But you fell for him and that was that." Harry's tone roughened as he tried to provoke a response from the woman on the sofa. "I suppose he saw you as his meal ticket."

Tears glinted in the blue eyes, but she kept her voice under control as she answered, "You're wrong. He loved me. Then, he loved me."

Deliberately cruel, Harry said, "You were besotted with him."

"All I ever needed," she said, "was to be with Tony. You wouldn't understand."

"Wouldn't I? I was married too, don't forget."

"That woman." The words reverberated with Angie's contempt for his wife. "She wrecked everything for me. Tony and I, we were so right for each other. Our marriage worked. Oh, yes, I know he had other women. I wasn't born yesterday. But none of them meant anything to him. He'd take what he wanted, then kiss them goodbye."

"And you could live with that?"

She lifted her head in a gesture as defiant as that of a martyr going to the stake. "Yes, Mr. Devlin, I could live with that. But with your wife, it was different. She simply would not leave him be."

"Liz was certainly different," he said, almost to himself. "When an idea became fixed in her head, there was no dislodging it. At least until she grew bored and started searching for something new. I'll bet she swept him off his feet. So he spun her a line, told her he owned the club, gave the impression all the money was his. Relegated you to the status of a nagging nobody in the shadows and persuaded Liz to keep quiet so you wouldn't discover the affair too soon.

"She took a part-time job to be near at hand for their lunch-time adulteries. The two of them tried to be discreet, but it didn't work. Obviously you realised Tony was playing away from home again and tried to reel him back in as usual. Trouble was, when he began to back off, Liz put him under pressure. She wasn't some empty-headed bimbo who was happy to fade into the scenery." Harry opened his eyes again and asked, "Did you know that she attempted suicide?"

"Yes. He told me so." She picked at the seam of her gown. "What you say is right. I soon cottoned on that he was seeing someone. He denied it at first, but he still made the silly mistake of leaving a photograph of her in his wallet. I found it, of course. Eventually, I forced the story out of him. Poor Tony isn't strong. He admitted everything. I made him promise to get rid of her. He said he'd been intending to break it up anyway, but then she did that melodramatic thing. He said he'd caught her only just in time, though I don't believe for a minute that she meant to kill herself. It was just a ruse, and Tony fell for it."

Poor Tony? Harry's heart did not bleed. The man had been forced to choose between his wife and his mistress, yet the idea that he might have seen murder as a solution to his dilemma had always been far-fetched. Angie had married an easy option man. He must have fancied screwing a worthwhile settlement out of a divorce. The risks of serious crime were not, Harry was sure, in Tony Gallimore's line.

"And shortly afterwards, your husband told you that Liz was pregnant by him. That he'd made up his mind to go to her and bring your marriage to an end. Did you decide then that she must die? That for you to stay together, you'd have to murder the woman he wanted?"

The auburn head nodded, but Angie said nothing.

Harry persisted, "You'd met Rourke at the Ferry, I expect. How did you settle on him to do your dirty work?"

After a long pause, Angie said, "He used to hang around backstage. Full of big talk, you know the type. He said he was a dangerous man to cross. I think maybe he fancied me and that his idea of a chat-up line was to scare me with stories about how tough he was. So, you see, that was how it all began. It made me think - what if I could use him to put that woman out of the way? I'd have Tony again, we could get back to the way we were before." She looked towards the photograph hanging on the chimney breast. "I've had plenty of men, Mr. Devlin, over the years. Of course I have. And Tony has his faults. I'm not naive. But even so, he's the only man I've ever really needed. Do you understand?"

"For me, it was much the same with Liz."

She lowered her eyes. "I won't apologise, make excuses. Words are worthless. Only one thought drove me on: that if Liz Devlin died, I would keep my marriage alive. What I

didn't realise was how simple it would turn out to be. At first, that is. Joe Rourke didn't take much persuading. He wasn't shocked by the idea, far from it. I had the money, he didn't negotiate too hard. He was a cheap killer. I couldn't believe how easy it all was to set up. I even gave him the photograph that I'd taken from Tony. So that he could identify her."

The photograph. That much-travelled photograph. The one that Jane Brogan, too, had discovered: but she had leaped to the wrong conclusion about its significance. No longer, Harry reflected, was it a romantic keepsake. It had become part of the baggage of murder.

"I left everything to Rourke," she said wearily. "In a strange way, I trusted him. He might have taken the down payment and then laughed in my face, but somehow I never doubted he'd do as he promised. I felt - the idea of committing murder in cold blood excited him. I didn't have to tell him what to do - how could I have done? All I said was that I'd let him know the right time. It had to be when Tony had an alibi. I didn't want him under suspicion if the police found out about his affair with your wife." She groaned. "I wanted it to look like a random crime, didn't want to point the finger at anyone special. Just as long as Tony was in the clear."

"Rourke followed her. He was working out her movements, I suppose. Trying to judge the best opportunity."

"Yes. She'd seen him, he admitted that to me. I was getting edgy. I was afraid that any day, Tony would pack his things and leave. On the Thursday morning, Rourke rang me to say he'd lost track of her. She hadn't been home the previous night. I was desperate, told him he'd have to find her and do it quickly. Tony was down in Birmingham, the timing was perfect. I thought it might be the last chance. That evening, Rourke phoned again. He'd been hanging around the shop where she worked and had caught up with her again. He'd been following her ever since. She was having dinner with some other man - the whore! I told Rourke to go ahead and earn his money."

She broke off and wiped a palm across her face. Harry could see tear-stains on her cheeks. "Rourke saw me later at the club. All he said was, "Mission accomplished." Tony had almost made a mess of my plans by coming home early. I should have realised that he would arrange to meet her off the train. But I was happy. I believed I'd saved him for myself. Having her killed was just a means to an end. I didn't regret her death." She stared at him as if challenging him to doubt her word. "I still don't. Even though everything has fallen apart."

"Did Gallimore guess what you'd done?"

"I don't know." There was a haunted look on her face. "He's never said so. But there have been moments - I've caught him glancing at me strangely. Suspiciously. Perhaps it's only my conscience. I never dreamed it would ever occur to him that I . . ." Her voice trailed away.

"Whose idea was it to murder Froggy Evison?"

She bowed her head. "Rourke's, of course. I was getting desperate. I'd heard you talking to Froggy. I told Joe, and he wanted to put you out of the way for good. I said no, I wouldn't have that.

No more killing. He was just to warn you off. Rough you up a little if necessary."

Harry ran a hand over his injured ribs. "Yes, he did that."

"What can I say? It's too late for regrets. Everything was getting out of control. Froggy had already told Joe that he'd seen him kill that - I mean, your wife. We didn't believe it, Froggy wasn't the sort to hang around if danger was in the air. But obviously he'd seen something, put two and two together. He wanted money. I was willing to pay, but Rourke said we couldn't take a chance. Once you give in to blackmail, he said, you never stop. And the morning after you spoke to Froggy here, he got in touch with Joe and said that he'd decided to double his price. He reckoned you'd be willing to cross his palm with silver, even if we weren't. That settled it, as far as Rourke was concerned."

She looked up at him, hopelessly.

"Ridiculous, isn't it? A middle-aged woman in a suburban living room, talking about a contract killing. It isn't what I meant to happen. It's not what I meant at all."

"As you said, it's too late for regrets."

"I should have realised shooting Froggy wasn't going to bring it to an end. It's become a waking nightmare.

Things went from bad to worse between Tony and me. I must have been hell to live with. This morning he said maybe we should live apart for a little while. A trial separation, he called it. I begged him to give me another chance - I know I haven't been myself lately. I pleaded. I almost told him what I'd already done to try to keep him. But it was no good. For Christ's sake, he looked as though he was afraid of me. And then it dawned on me: murdering your wife hadn't altered a thing, he was still determined to go."

"And Rourke?"

"He spent his money soon enough. He's one of those men who could lose a million inside a month. Frittering it on women, booze and drugs. He rang today, said he wanted another five thousand for

Froggy. I said no, I'd paid what we agreed. Then the threats began. I put the phone down on him. He was vicious, I never deceived myself about that. But he didn't realise you can't frighten someone with nothing left to live for."

They looked into each other's eyes. For a moment, Harry was aware of a bond with her, as though her destructive invasion of his life had brought them together, sufferers in the common cause of misplaced love. It was like the sense of closeness to her which he had briefly experienced that Thursday night as she sang in the Ferry, that night when, unknown to him, she had arranged for Liz to die.

She nodded, as if reading his thoughts. "We've both fed off fantasies for too long, haven't we? Well, you have all your answers now. But there is one thing more. The phone is in the kitchen. Call the police. Let them take charge of this whole bloody mess."

"And you?"

"I'm dirty. All over. That's what murder does to you, Harry. I can still call you Harry, can't I? It seems as if we've known each other much longer than this little while. Well, Harry, I need to get clean. Though there are some things you can never scrub away."

She stood up and walked to the door, bare feet moving silently over the thick pile of carpet.

"Wait," he said, "one more question." He stopped for a moment, almost ashamed of this last, helpless naivete. Yet he had to ask. "You're - you're not an animal. Not like Rourke. Why did you have to kill to get your way?"

"I thought you understood, Harry. It's sharing this feeling that draws us together a little, isn't it? I've been alone before, I know what it's like, just as you do. I didn't want to be alone again. I was willing to do anything in my power to avoid it. That's all."

She turned and went out into the hallway, shutting the door behind her. Harry remained in his chair. Memories drifted through his mind like flotsam on the Mersey. Liz had scarred so many lives:

those of Maggie and Derek, of Matt Barley and Angie O'Hare. But then he thought of her commanding Dame's fierce loyalty, and of his own better times with her when it seemed their lives stretched endlessly ahead and that every promise was sure to be fulfilled. He remembered a November night of fireworks and his first sight of a woman with a laughing face. Yes, it was true, he understood the impulse that had corrupted Angie O'Hare.

A cry from upstairs roused him. He heard something crash, then silence.

Oh God, oh God, oh God.

He leapt to his feet and took the stairs three at a time, desperate to save her, to salvage something from disaster. Gasping, he kicked open the bathroom door.

Angie O'Hare lay naked at the bottom of the bath, auburn hair trailing in the water. Harry gazed at her white breasts, the triangle of reddish fuzz between her legs. Her mouth was wide open and the lovely blue eyes were empty of everything. A hair dryer was beside her, its long flex snaking out of the steamy room to a three-pin plug pushed into a socket on the landing. The crimson robe had been folded and put on the towel rail in a last act of futile tidiness.

Harry stared at the body. Impossible to look away. Death after death after death after death - how could he have guessed it would end like this?

He should be exulting. But now he'd lost his taste for blood.

A sentence from Liz on that last Wednesday night floated unbidden into his mind: I ought to feel sorry for her. And as he stood there, he became overwhelmed by pity for the woman who had paid for his wife to be killed.

Chapter Thirty

"The last enemy that shall be destroyed," said the priest, "is death." A young man, bespectacled and earnest, he gazed upwards as if in search of divine approval. His Welsh lilt made the old words seem freshly minted and right. Yet in the front row of the congregation, Harry heard without listening, unable to absorb the sense of the text being preached.

In his new dark suit he was stiff and uncomfortable. Every limb of his body seemed to be hurting, as though for the past fortnight he had been numbed by an anaesthetic whose effect was now starting to fade, leaving him exposed to recurrent waves of physical pain.

Brick-built and drab, the crematorium had hard seats and no heating. A miserable place in which to say goodbye to Liz. But cremation had been her choice; she always hated the thought of burial. "Imagine," she once murmured as they walked past a graveyard, "the worms eating the bodies in their tombs underground." Rolling her eyes in comic disgust she'd said, "I'd rather be burnt." Then she had laughed at the absurdity of the idea of death.

Harry felt a tingling beneath his eyelids as he glanced around at the people gathered to remember his wife. Maggie was sitting on the same row, an arm's length away. Her black jacket, skirt and coat contrasted with the pallor of her skin, and the rings under her eyes testified to sleepless nights and despair of her crumbling marriage. Harry had last talked to her when discussing the plans for this funeral service and had found her glum and preoccupied. "If it wasn't for the children . . ." she had begun at one point, but without completing the sentence. Next to her now, Derek was watching the white-robed priest with stony-faced concentration.

He might have been attending a seminar about capital gains tax or the annual general meeting of a public coftipany.

Across the aisle, Dame dabbed at her cheeks with a handkerchief, drying one of the few unselfish tears that had been shed for Liz. On the telephone the other day she had told Harry about her latest beau, a Ferrari-driving whizz-kid from the world of advertising. There was a chance that he might get her a part in a TV commercial, she said. Beside her sat Matt Barley, his face smudged with misery, his stubby fingers fidgeting with the printed card which set out the order of service. He hadn't spoken to Harry since confessing his brief affair with Liz. On his way in here, he had nodded grimly and hurried by.

A faint movement by the priest attracted Harry's attention. Slowly, the coffin began to slide out of sight. Within an instant, it seemed to Harry, the deep blue curtains had been pulled together and the box was gone forever. He closed his eyes.

When he opened them again, he realised the service was over and that people were beginning to shuffle about, waiting for him to move. He got up from the seat and stumbled towards the exit. From behind, he felt the pressure of an arm supporting him.

Jim Crusoe's voice whispered "in his ear. "It's done."

Gently, his partner propelled him out into the cold morning air where the priest was waiting. Harry mumbled a few words of thanks in mechanical response to the young Welshman's attempt to offer consolation. He scarcely noticed the pile of wreaths and the tied-on cards which bore messages of sympathy and were flapping in the breeze.

A short distance away stood Skinner, head bowed in contemplation. For the police, the official file had closed following the death of Rourke. Enough evidence had been obtained to tie him to both murders: the knife, the shotgun, a couple of witness sightings of him at Pasture Moss at around the time when Froggy Evison was killed. The tabloid press had talked about the suspected murderer who had died in a freak car crash, but there had been plenty of good stories around lately - riots in a Scottish prison, the resignation of a Cabinet minister - and already the deaths of Liz and Evison were yesterday's news.

The papers didn't have an inkling about Angie O'Hare's involvement and neither Harry nor Skinner planned to enlighten them. As far as the outside world was concerned, it was a simple case of a forgotten star of days gone by finding herself unable to cope with life amongst the second-rate. The local rags had called it a tragedy; in the nationals, it scarcely rated a mention. The inquest was unlikely to disclose too many secrets and the verdict was sure to be suicide while the balance of the mind was disturbed.

When he had listened to Harry's story, had it typed up for the record and signed, Skinner had said, "A bitter thing, is jealousy." It was the first spoken indication that he accepted Angie had hired Rourke to do her dirty work, though later a check on her bank account revealed that she had withdrawn five thousand pounds shortly before the stabbing of Liz. Harry had looked at him and said, "Not so much jealousy, Chief Inspector, as the fear of being on her own again."

He took a few paces down the shingle path which led from the building. Feeble rays of sunlight were beginning to filter through the greyness overhead. In a narrow bed under the shelter of the roadside wall, the year's first greenery had started to emerge: snowdrop and crocus leaves, tokens of the coming spring.

He raised his eyes. The early morning mist had cleared and he could look down from the slopes of the crematorium grounds and see the Liverpool skyline in the distance: the contrasting forms of the two cathedrals, the muscular bulk of the buildings on the waterfront. Beyond, the charcoal ribbon of the Mersey flowed towards the Irish Sea. Pasture Moss, though nearer at hand, was masked from view by rows of redbrick terraced houses. According to a bulletin on the local radio the previous day, the waste heap was to be levelled soon and the land grassed over and reclaimed for recreation. There was talk in the papers of a resurgence in local industry and pride. Whether it was a rebirth or just a period of remission interrupting the decline of a dying city, Harry didn't know. He doubted if anyone did.

Brenda Rixton had caught up with him. She had been sitting quietly at the back throughout the service. Now she extended a hand and they shook formally, like strangers acknowledging mutual respect. Their eyes met for a moment and then they walked towards the crematorium gates, together and yet still alone.

Excerpt from *I Remember You*

Chapter One

Flames licked at the building, greedy as the tongues of teenage lovers. They curled out from the windows above the shopfront and up to the gutters, fierce in their hunger, intent on conquest.

The smell of burning filled Harry Devlin's sinuses. Smoke stung his eyes and the back of his throat.

'Don't even think of going in there.'

'For the love of Jases,' said Finbar Rogan. 'What d'you think I have for brains? I'd not try to force my way inside if the missus herself was trapped the other side of that door.' He threw back his head and laughed. 'Come to think of it, if she was - I'd be chucking in a match or two myself.'

A thunderous splintering of glass made them duck in a reflex of self-defence. Straightening up, Harry saw the first-floor panes disintegrate. He shielded his face as a thousand shards showered the paving all around.

Finbar cried out in pain and stumbled to the ground. Seeing blood trickle from a cut on the Irishman's cheek, Harry didn't hesitate. In a matter of seconds, he dragged Finbar back towards the shelter of a doorway on the other side of the street. There they leaned against each other for support, fighting for breath as the fumes leaked into their lungs.

The narrowness of Williamson Lane intensified the heat and Harry felt the skin of his face tingle. Finbar groaned and wiped the blood away with his sleeve.

'Thanks for that, mate,' he gasped. 'So now we know what we're in for when we go to Hell.'

'Speak for yourself.'

'Listen, you're a solicitor. Even I have a better chance of Heaven.'

Harry couldn't help grinning at his client. Even as his business blazed on this cold October night, Finbar showed no sign of fear or despair. He would always scoff at any unkindness of the Fates.

'Are you all right?'

'I'll live to claim the insurance, don't you fret.'

Never before had Harry witnessed at such close quarters the raging passion of a fire out of control. A dozen viewings of Mrs Danvers perishing in the ruins of Hitchcock's Manderley had not prepared him for this; nor could he have imagined that the city centre could be so claustrophobic. He had a dizzy sense of everything closing in on him.

Disaster had begun to seduce late night Liverpool's passers-by, excited by the sound and fury. 'Better than Blackpool bloody illuminations!' someone bellowed from the safety of the adjoining square.

The wail of a siren pierced the hubbub, growing louder as each second passed. Harry could hear the fire engines' roar and saw people pressing back into the shadows, making way as first one, then another of the vehicles rounded the corner and pulled up with a shriek twenty yards away.

'The cavalry,' said Finbar.

Suddenly the place was teeming with firefighters. In their yellow headgear and drip pants, navy blue tunics with silvery reflective stripes and rubber boots with steel toe-caps, they might have been storm-troopers from a distant planet. They moved to a pre-ordained routine, running the hose along the ground, connecting it to a hydrant, waving the crowd back, roping off the end of the street. Harry and Finbar were the only spectators within fifty feet of the fire. A man whose white helmet marked his seniority hurried towards them.

'Anyone left inside?' His urgent tone held no hint of panic.

'No one,' Finbar called back. 'Though I might have been in there doing my books if this feller hadn't been due to buy the next round.'

The officer spoke into a walkie-talkie, ordering help from an appliance with a turntable ladder, keeping watch all the time on the spread of the fire.

'You own the shop which sells leathers? Or the travel agents next door?'

'No, I'm up above.'

The words on the blackened signboard at first-floor level were hard to decipher. The officer peered at them. 'Tattooist's studio, is that? You're the feller I heard on Radio Liverpool this morning?'

'The one and only. Liverpool's Leonardo da Vinci.' With boozy bravado, Finbar shrugged off his jacket and ripped open his shirt. On his chest was an extravagant, multicoloured image of a naked woman astride a horse. Her modesty was not quite saved by long dark tresses, and she seemed unaware of the exophthalmic scrutiny of a caricatured Peeping Tom.

'I'll gladly autograph you as a souvenir,' he offered. 'And if you can salvage the electric needles I keep up there, I'll turn you into the Illustrated Man free of charge.'

The officer tipped his helmet back, a now-I've-seen-everything expression spreading across his face.

'Thanks very much, but I'm pretty as a picture as it is.'

In the distance, a second siren howled its warning.

'Here come the police,' said Harry. Ruefully, he asked himself why, earlier that evening, he hadn't refused Finbar's invitation for a quick one. He knew the folly of becoming too closely involved with his clients and their misfortunes, yet it was a mistake he could never help making. If only he'd been taught at college the knack of remaining aloof, of concentrating on rules in books, instead of becoming fascinated by the people who broke them...

'Anything combustible in there?' demanded the fire officer.

Finbar bowed his head, momentarily abashed. 'I had paint and thinners on the landing. Been planning to decorate. Early resolution for next New Year.' He gazed up at the flame-lit heavens. 'Sod's law, eh? I should have left the dirt to hold the place together.'

'What about the ceiling tiles?'

'Polystyrene.'

'Perfect. A fire trap, waiting for a spark. All right - wait here out of harm's way while I take a gander.'

As the officer rejoined his men, a police car appeared, its lights flashing. One of its occupants raced towards the blaze, the other strode towards Harry and Finbar, waving his arms like a farmer directing sheep.

'Move, will you? Don't - hey, for Chrissake, it's Harry Devlin! What are you doing here, pal? I thought you chased ambulances, not fire engines.'

Harry nodded a greeting. He knew Roy Gilfillan of old.

'Where there's a disaster, there's sure to be a solicitor. Finbar's a client. We were having a pint in the Dock Brief, putting the world to rights, when some bloke burst in and said a building in Williamson Lane had gone up in flames. We dashed over and it turns out to be - '

Another siren interrupted him and he swung round to watch the arrival of the turntable while Roy Gilfillan marched over to his colleague, who was conferring with the fire officer outside the entrance to Finbar's studio. Harry noticed the Irishman's eyes slide away from the fire to a couple of girls in the crowd behind them, blondes *en route* for a nightclub who had paused to goggle at the inferno. Finbar winked at them and was rewarded by smirks of encouragement. Even at a time like this he was incorrigible.

'Do you need to call Melissa?' asked Harry, hoping to lead Finbar away from temptation. 'Tell her what's happened?'

'No problem. She's not neurotic, not like Sinead, doesn't make a fuss when I tell her to expect me when she sees me. I'm not a train, I don't run to timetables.'

'Neither does InterCity, but at least it stays on the rails most of the time.'

Finbar chuckled. 'Truth to tell, I've a lot on my plate already, so far as the fair sex are concerned - even leaving Sinead and her bloody alimony demands aside. I bumped into a girl I used to know only this morning. A lovely lady. I reckon I might be able to persuade her to rekindle the flame - 'scuse the phrase, in present circumstances. And then there's Melissa ... Jases!'

Across the street, the door which led to the tattoo parlour finally disintegrated in an explosion worthy of an Exocet. Awestruck, Harry and Finbar gazed at the wreckage. Above them, men in breathing masks were directing water jets from the top of the ladder down on to the blaze, while at ground level two more firefighters armed with axes moved towards the entrance. Safe behind the cordon, winos cheered as if on the terraces at Anfield. Oblivious to his audience, the fire chief pointed towards the building. The policemen stared obediently at something, then Gilfillan gestured for Harry and Finbar to approach. The two of them edged closer.

'What's up?' asked Finbar. 'Any closer and I'll get scorch marks on Lady Godiva.'

'Smell that!' shouted Gilfillan, pointing towards the doorway.

No mistaking the stink of petrol from close range. Harry exchanged a look with the policeman.

'And see the inside of the passageway?'

The fumes made their eyes water, but squinting through the hole Harry saw charred walls immediately beyond the space where the door had been.

Finbar pushed a hand through his unruly dark hair. He was a stocky man, barely as tall as Harry but broader in the shoulder and a few years older; yet his wonderment was that of a wide-eyed schoolboy.

'Are you telling me this wasn't an accident?'

The policeman shrugged. 'The seat of fire seems to have been the other side of your front door - the burning is worse there than further up the stairs. Add that to the smell and there's only one diagnosis.'

'Arson?' asked Harry. For all the heat, he felt a sudden chill.

'Suspected malicious ignition,' Gilfillan's colleague corrected him primly, before turning to Finbar. 'Is there anyone who might have a grudge against you?'

Finbar looked nonplussed. After a pause for thought, he allowed a guilty grin to lift the corners of his mouth. It was a moment of self-knowledge.

'Only everyone I've ever met.'

The Making of *All the Lonely People*

All the Lonely People was my first published novel, and holds a special place in my affections. So I am delighted to celebrate the 20th anniversary of the first hardback edition by seeing the story enjoy a new incarnation as an e-book – a format undreamed of when Harry Devlin arrived on the scene.

Many authors who are labelled as crime novelists did not intend, when they first started writing, to work within a particular genre, and some are troubled by the desire of publishers, booksellers and readers to categorise their fiction. It seems to be relatively unusual to have had a long-nourished ambition to write not just one detective novel, but a whole series of them. Yet that was always my dream.

The dream came when I fell in love with a remarkable woman , - or rather, with what she did - at the tender age of nine. The woman was Agatha Christie, and her detective stories were the first adult novels that I read. From the beginning, I was fascinated by the way Christie wove her plots, and shifted suspicion between her characters, combining subtle clues with red herrings so as to come up with one surprise solution after another. Her ingenuity took my breath away. Ever since I had learned to read, I had yearned to write the kind of stories I most enjoyed. An only child, I had plenty of time to myself, and to a large extent I lived in my imagination, making up countless stories for my own amusement. Once I discovered Agatha Christie, I became determined to write mysteries that teased and entertained others as her books teased and entertained me.

I devoured every detective novel that my heroine had written, and when I ran out of new Christies, I turned to other crime novelists, including Dorothy L Sayers, and two stalwarts of a later generation, Michael Gilbert and Julian Symons. From them,

I learned that the mystery novel can offer a range of pleasures in addition to a satisfying plot – strong characterisation, evocative settings, and an insightful portrayal of society. And, in a series of detective novels, an author who cares to do so has the scope to chart not only the developing life of the detective – and the supporting cast – but also changes affecting the world in which they live.

I'd started writing mysteries at primary school, producing a series of tales, carefully handwritten in exercise books, featuring a detective duo called Melwyn Hughes and Sir Edward Gladstone; they were an updated version of the Holmes and Watson from a favourite series of films starring Basil Rathbone and Nigel Bruce. At grammar school, I continued to read avidly and fantasise about becoming a published crime writer, but although I wrote a few more detective stories, including one Sherlockian pastiche, I became too self-conscious to repeat the uninhibited melodrama of my pre-teen efforts.

At school, I never came across anyone else who shared my ambition to write, and never met a published author. My parents, understandably dubious about my single-minded focus on such an elusive goal, encouraged me to train for a "proper job" to fund my living costs while I tried to produce something worthy of publication. So I decided to study law at university, and when I went to Oxford, at last I found myself surrounded by would-be novelists, and with the chance to attend talks given by leading authors. I never plucked up the courage to introduce myself to them and seek practical tips, but I've never forgotten, when nowadays I meet people with an ambition to write, how much constructive encouragement can help.

As a student, I dabbled in different types of writing, publishing a little poetry, and having a radio play – a comedy about a bigamist called "The Marrying Kind" – broadcast locally. But when I moved from full-time education to a working life, as an impoverished (no minimum wage in those days) articled clerk in a firm of Leeds solicitors, I returned to crime. But only in the fictional sense. The bleak reality of life as a criminal lawyer never appealed to me.

In long hand, I wrote a breezy thriller about the disappearance of the football star, rejoicing in the title of Dead Shot. I paid someone to type it up, but ran out of cash after a few chapters. I decided I must teach myself to touch-type, and duly did so, but by that time I had come to the conclusion that Dead Shot simply wasn't good enough to deserve publication. So the book as a whole was never typed, and never sent anywhere. A good thing, too, I think....

By this time, I had qualified as a solicitor, and moved to Liverpool. My choice of firm was dictated by my judgment of where I would have the best chance of pursuing a career as a crime novelist. This ruled out the big firms, which demanded that young lawyers devote themselves body and soul to fee-earning, especially after one partner in a leading practice saw mention on my CV of my ambition to write fiction (I was an honest but naive job-seeker) and asked, with a disbelieving sneer, if I saw myself as a budding Graham Greene. The firm I joined paid much lower wages, but its two senior partners had published legal books, and one of them was a frustrated novelist. He and I later tried to collaborate on a "It Shouldn't Happen to a Solicitor" sort of story in the James Herriott mould, but the contrasting styles arising from our different perspectives meant the generation gap proved unbridgeable.

I was encouraged to write for the legal press, and after I'd ghost-written a book review for my boss, the first article under my own name appeared when I was 25. After that, there was no stopping me. I lost count long ago of the number of legal articles I've published, but it is well over one thousand. At the age of 26 I approached a publisher of legal books, and persuaded them to commission me to write a textbook on the subject of buying business computers. At the time, I'd advised on just one such transaction, but I brimmed with the confidence of youth. And I told myself that, even if my legal experience was sketchy, I could write readably on the driest topic. When Understanding Computer Contracts was published, I was intensely proud. At last I had published a book! What is more, it earned excellent reviews and gained me a reputation, however undeserved, as an expert in an emerging field of law. A year later, it was succeeded by Understanding Dismissal Law, a subject I knew a bit more about, and a string of other legal books followed.

The experience of seeing my books on the shelves was gratifying, but I remained as desperate as ever to write a crime novel of quality. The experience of Dead Shot had at least shown that I possessed the stamina and drive to produce a full-length mystery, and that in itself made writing the book which never saw the light of day an invaluable apprenticeship. Stamina and drive matter, because so many would-be writers give up too soon – there are always countless good reasons to devote the long hours spent writing to some other, more immediately fruitful, occupation.

I decided that if I were to write a book suitable as the first entry in a long-running series, I needed to have three strong components. First, a detective character who could credibly become involved in a number of mysteries. Second, a strong setting that had not been over-used. Third, a hook that would entice people to read on.

I wondered about the old adage "write what you know". As advice, it has limitations – I wanted to write about murder, but thankfully I had never been involved in a murder case. At that time, I'd never met anyone who had committed murder, or anyone who later became a murder victim. I was strongly attracted by the escapism of fiction. But I was also keen to write a novel which conveyed an impression of realism. I didn't know any police officers or private eyes, but I did know something about the lives that lawyers lead. And this resulted in my inventing the character of a likeable but unlucky, and rather down--at-heel, solicitor whose work brought him into uncomfortably close contact with crime and criminals. Thus was Harry Devlin born.

I've lived in Cheshire or Wirral, neither of them far from Liverpool, almost all of my life, though I have never had a home in the city itself. But I have worked a stone's throw from the Liver Building and the River Mersey for more than 30 years, and the city still enthrals me. In my experience, the overwhelming majority of its people are marvellously kind and good-humoured, while its history is extraordinary. Once Liverpool was the second city of the British Empire, but it fell on hard times in the 20th century, and decline accelerated after the Second World War. Many people who are unfamiliar with the city associate it as much with crime and deprivation as with the Beatles, but stereotyping Liverpool and Liverpudlians is a huge mistake. Not long after I arrived in Merseyside, the area convulsed with riots, and one week-end, as I took a visiting friend from London on a bus trip through a riot-scarred housing estate near where I lived, I asked myself whether I'd made a mistake in re-locating. When I'd contemplated a move from Leeds, people had warned me against Liverpool; it's a city that arouses strong feelings among both supporters and detractors, and the detractors tend to be in the majority. But I think the detractors are profoundly mistaken, even though Liverpool occasionally seems to be its own worst enemy. After the riots, a senior politician, Michael Heseltine, guided the city along the long and winding road of regeneration. A spectacular garden festival was held, the Albert Dock and its environs were redeveloped, and, despite many mis-steps along the way, Liverpool began to fulfil its potential.

Where better to set a series of mystery novels? Liverpool's critics constantly associate the city with crime, even though statistics do not really support the prejudice. But Liverpool has plenty of mean streets, and you would think it is a more credible location for a long-running series of murder mysteries than Oxford, or Midsomer. And there is so much about the place that is intriguing and deserves to be better known. I thought that if someone like me, from leafy, Cheshire, could fall for gritty Liverpool and witty

272

Liverpudlians, it would be an appealing challenge to write books that portrayed the place affectionately, as well as with warts and all, so as to help people unfamiliar with Liverpool to see it differently. This was always in my mind – to write the books mainly for those who, like me, were not born and bred Scousers, though I'm always glad (and relieved) when people who have lived there all their lives tell me how much they enjoy the books.

I was determined that my detective would be a local man with a dogged love for his native city. I toyed with calling him Harry Dowd, after a goalkeeper of the Sixties, but settled on the surname of Devlin, which had an Irish touch that seemed suitable. Oddly enough, there is a long list of fictional detectives called Devlin, some pre-dating Harry, some more recent, but somehow Harry's name seems absolutely right for him.

So the detective and the locale were sorted; I just needed a strong story-line. I worried too much about plotting to begin with, but eventually I came up with the right starting point. Harry's gorgeous, but estranged, wife comes back into his life; he thinks they can start again, but his hopes are destroyed when she is found murdered. Worse, Harry is prime suspect. So he has a double motivation to solve the mystery. He needs to clear his name, as well as to do justice to his beloved Liz.

The key elements of the novel, and of the series, were signposted on the very first page, in the context of a film by Woody Allen – Love and Death. But the central theme of this particular book was the fear of loneliness, and what better way to reference that than with a Beatles song? 'Eleanor Rigby' provided the phrase that gave the book its title.

I decided on a straightforward linear narrative. Everything would be seen from Harry's perspective. In later books, I have enjoyed experimenting with viewpoint, but for a fast-moving thriller, a single viewpoint helps drive the narrative forward. I felt that a powerful motive for murder was essential, and once I came up with my killer's psychological motivation, I was on a roll.

As far as I can remember, I started work on the story in 1987. The opening chapter went through countless re-writes. I submitted an early version to a competition for first chapters of proposed novels that was run by Southport Writers' Circle. The judge was Hugh C. Rae, a prolific and accomplished writer. He didn't award my effort a prize, but years later I had the pleasure of talking crime fiction with him one evening at a Crime Writers' Association conference in Scotland.

I didn't do much research for the book, although I did look round a flat rented by a fellow lawyer in the Albert Dock which became the model for Harry's home on the fictitious Empire Dock development. This occupied a site which was a car park when I wrote the book, but is nowadays home to a gleaming conference centre. Oddly enough, I needed to consult professional colleagues about the Liverpool Bridewell and Magistrates' Court that feature in the early scenes. Harry and I might both be Liverpool lawyers, but we inhabit different professional worlds – thank goodness. And I talked to a nightclub singer who happened to be a member of Southport Writers' Circle, for background that helped me to depict the Ferry Club. But I didn't, for instance, know anyone remotely like Matt, Ruby, Peanuts, Trisha, Froggy, Coghlan or Dame, let alone Skinner or Macbeth. I simply made them up. Nor, at that time, did I have much experience of bereavement, so I had to work hard to think myself into Harry's mind after the death of Liz. The model for Pasture Moss came from a comparable scavenger-haunted waste heap in Wirral which featured in a depressing article written for The Sunday Times Magazine. That scrap heap had a potent symbolic value, especially as a crime scene, and the mood of the story was inescapably bleak, although lightened with humour. However, I was intent on ending the book on a note of hope about the future for both Harry and his home town.

I continued to work on the manuscript, and joined the CWA on the strength of a publishing a string of non-fiction articles about the genre. After I finished the first draft, one agent looked at a few sample chapters, only to reject them, but a my first CWA conference, in Scarborough, a Wirral-based writer, Eileen Dewhurst, who became a good friend, recommended me to her agency. Mandy Little saw something in the manuscript, and took me on; she has been my agent ever since, and her belief in me as a writer has been a source of strength, as well as a huge motivation to justify her faith.

Mandy proposed various revisions to the book, which I duly made. After she had sent it to a number of publishers, both Piatkus and Hodder & Stoughton expressed interest. Both wanted me to make some changes, which naturally differed from each other. A new author cannot afford to be a prima donna (nor can any author apart from a select few, come to that) and I re-wrote the book so as to address all the editorial comments.

By now it was late 1990: a busy time, but an exciting time. I'd become a partner in my firm and subsequently the head of its employment department, I'd married, and my wife was expecting our first child. I'd entered the Southport Writers' Circle competition again, with a short and rather macabre crime story, and this time I'd won – the story, "Are You Sitting Comfortably?", became my first published fiction when it appeared in Bella, and then in Ellery Queen's Mystery Magazine. A few weeks after the competition success, I received the news that Piatkus had made an offer for my book. I could scarcely believe it.

Everything seemed to happen at once. Piatkus did not publish paperback editions in those days, but the rights were sold to Transworld, and there were audio and book club deals (later there would be TV deals, and scripts written by others for both radio and television based on the book, but frustratingly, none of them ever made it to the recording studio.) When All the Lonely People finally appeared in print, that wonderful moment, the reviews were extensive and generous – no online reviewing in those days, but much more coverage in newspapers such as The Times and The Guardian. One of the most generous reviews came from a highly accomplished lawyer-author, whom at that time I'd never met – Frances Fyfield.

My delight was complete when the book was one of seven nominated for the John Creasey Memorial Award, or Dagger, for the best first crime novel of the year. The other contenders included a talented American, Peter Blauner, but the inevitable winner was his countryman Walter Mosley, whose superb Devil in a Blue Dress was later filmed with Denzell Washington. How thrilling to arrive in such company, after a journey that had sometimes felt as though it would never end.

Harry Devlin's career was well and truly launched; his second case, recorded in Suspicious Minds, was already written up by the time the first came out. And, when time permitted, I wrote occasional short stories that fleshed out some details of his life and encounters with crime. After writing seven books about him, I was ready for a change, itching to develop my work in fresh directions, but following a long break, Harry returned in Waterloo Sunset, a book I loved writing.

For me, it's a huge thrill to see Harry's cases enjoy a new life, thanks to the technological miracle of e-book publishing. When I look back at All the Lonely People, twenty years on, I see a good deal that I would change if I were re-writing it today. That's only natural, especially for a writer as keen on revision and improvement as I am. Liverpool has transformed during the past two decades, as has the legal profession, in ways that nobody could have imagined – certainly not me.

Yet my overwhelming feeling about the book, whatever flaws I might detect if I want to be pernickety, is one of happiness, tinged with pride and an awareness that I've been exceptonally fortunate.

It's good to have a dream, but it's a rare privilege to see that dream come true.

Martin Edwards: an Appreciation

by Michael Jecks

Both as a crime writer and as a keen exponent of the genre, Martin Edwards has long been sought out by his peers, and is now becoming recognised as a contemporary crime author at the top of his form.

Born in Knutsford, Cheshire, Martin went to school in Northwich before taking a first class honours degree in law at Balliol College, Oxford. From there he went on to join a law firm and is now a highly respected lawyer specializing in employment law. He is the author of Tottel's *Equal Opportunities Handbook*, 4th edition, 2007.

Early in his career, he began writing professional articles and completed his first book at 27, covering the purchase of business computers. His non-fiction work continues with over 1000 articles in newspapers and magazines, and seven books dedicated to the law (two of which were co-authored).

His life of crime began a little later with the Harry Devlin series, set in Liverpool. The first of his series, *All The Lonely People* (1991), was shortlisted for the CWA John Creasey Memorial Dagger for the first work of crime fiction by a new writer. With the advent of his second novel, Martin Edwards was becoming recognised as a writer of imagination and flair. This and subsequent books also referenced song titles from his youth.

The Harry Devlin books demonstrate a great sympathy for Liverpool, past and present, with gritty, realistic stories. 'Liverpool is a city with a tremendous resilience of spirit and character,' he says in *Scene of the Crime,* (2002). Although his protagonist is a self-effacing Scousers with a dry wit, Edwards is not a writer for the faint-hearted. 'His gifts are of the more classical variety - there are points in his novels when I think I'm reading Graham Greene,' wrote Ed Gorman, while *Crime Time* magazine said 'The novels successfully combine the style of the traditional English detective story with a darker noir sensibility.'

More recently Martin Edwards has moved into the Lake District with mystery stories featuring an historian, Daniel Kind, and DCI Hannah Scarlett. The first of these, *The Coffin Trail*, was short listed for the Theakston's Old Peculier Crime Novel of the year 2006.

In this book Martin Edwards made good use of his legal knowledge. DCI Hannah Scarlett is in charge of a cold case review unit, attempting to solve old crimes, and when Daniel Kind moves into a new house, seeking a fresh start in the idyllic setting of the Lake District, he and she are drawn together by the murder of a young woman. The killer, who died before he could be convicted, used to live in Kind's new cottage.

Not only does Edwards manage to demonstrate a detailed knowledge of the law (which he is careful never to force upon the reader), with the Lake District mysteries he has managed to bring the locations to vivid life. He has a skill for acute description which is rare - especially amongst those who are more commonly used to writing about city life.

More recently Edwards has published *Take My Breath Away*, a stand-alone psychological suspense novel, which offers a satiric portrait of an upmarket London law firm eerily reminiscent of Tony Blair's New Labour government.

Utilising his legal experience, he has written articles about actual crimes. *Catching Killers* was an illustrated book describing how police officers work on a homicide case all the way from the crime scene itself to presenting evidence in court.

When the writer Bill Knox died, Edwards was asked by his publisher to help complete his final manuscript, on which Knox had been working until days before his death. Bill Knox's method of writing was to hone each separate section of his books before moving on to the next, so Martin was left with the main thrust of the story, together with some jotted notes and newspaper clippings. From these he managed to complete *The Lazarus Widow* in an unusal departure for him.

More conventionally, Martin Edwards is a prolific writer of short stories. He has published the anthology *Where Do You Find Your Ideas?* which offers a mix of Harry Devlin tales mingled with historical and psychological short stories. His *Test Drive* was short listed for the CWA Short Story Dagger.

Edwards edits the regular CWA anthologies of short stories. These works have included *Green for Danger*, and *I.D. Crimes of Identity*, which included his own unusual and notable story *InDex*. In 2003 he also edited the CWA's *Mysterious Pleasures* anthology, which was a collection of the Golden Dagger winners' short stories to celebrate the CWA's Golden Jubilee.

A founder member of the performance and writing group, Murder Squad, Martin Edwards has found the time to edit their two anthologies.

When not writing and editing, Edwards is an enthusiastic reader and collector of crime fiction. He reviews for magazines, books and websites, and his essays have appeared in many collections.

He is the chairman of the CWA's nominations sub-committee for the Cartier Diamond Dagger Award, the world's most prestigious award for crime writing.

Martin Edwards is one of those rare creatures, a crime-writer's crime-writer. His plotting is as subtle as any, his writing deft and fluid, his characterisation precise, and his descriptions of the locations give the reader the impression that they could almost walk along the land blindfolded. He brings them all to life.

(An earlier version of this article appeared in *British Crime Writing: An Encyclopaedia,* edited by Barry Forshaw)

Meet Martin Edwards

Martin Edwards is an award-winning crime writer whose fifth and most recent Lake District Mystery, featuring DCI Hannah Scarlett and Daniel Kind, is *The Hanging Wood*, published in 2011. Earlier books in the series are *The Coffin Trail* (short-listed for the Theakston's prize for best British crime novel of 2006), *The Cipher Garden*, *The Arsenic Labyrinth* (short-listed for the Lakeland Book of the Year award in 2008) and *The Serpent Pool*.

Martin has written eight novels about lawyer Harry Devlin, the first of which, *All the Lonely People*, was short-listed for the CWA John Creasey Memorial Dagger for the best first crime novel of the year. In addition he has published a stand-alone novel of psychological suspense, *Take My Breath Away*, and a much acclaimed novel featuring Dr Crippen, *Dancing for the Hangman*. The latest Devlin novel, *Waterloo Sunset*, appeared in 2008.

Martin completed Bill Knox's last book, *The Lazarus Widow*, and has published a collection of short stories, *Where Do You Find Your Ideas? and other stories*; 'Test Drive' was short-listed for the CWA Short Story Dagger in 2006, while 'The Bookbinder's Apprentice' won the same Dagger in 2008.

A well-known commentator on crime fiction, he has edited 20 anthologies and published eight non-fiction books, including a study of homicide investigation, *Urge to Kill* .In 2008 he was elected to membership of the prestigious Detection Club. He was subsequently appointed Archivist to the Detection Club, and is also Archivist to the Crime Writers' Association. He received the Red Herring Award for services to the CWA in 2011.

In his spare time Martin is a partner in a national law firm, Weightmans LLP. His website is www.martinedwardsbooks.com and his blog www.doyouwriteunderyourownname.blogspot.com

Also Available from Martin Edwards

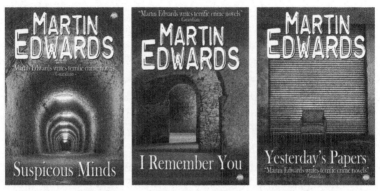

Suspicious Minds   **I Remember You**   **Yesterday's Papers**

The Devil in Disguise   First Cut is the Deepest

CPSIA information can be obtained at www.ICGtesting.com
Printed in the USA
LVOW04s2322061015

457253LV00024B/366/P